Cinema Blue

With thanks to Drew Campbell, to Helen Miles at Solidus and to Ali Nimmo for their invaluable advice and support at different stages of this book.

Cinema Blue

Sue Rullière

Published by Solidus
www.soliduspress.com

For Michel

PART ONE

Le séducteur/ The Seducer

frankie, i've just heard—jp's had an accident. he drove off the road near st-étienne, wrapped the car round a tree. he's been taken to the local hospital—don't know how bad he is. i'll let you know as soon as i hear anything.
    xavier

Frankie closes the laptop and pulls herself up off the bed. In the shower room she stares at the hairnet of cracks in the basin and then raises her eyes to the mirror. As she curls on mascara, her hand trembles and the wand hits her eyelid, smudging it black. She licks a finger and rubs the eyelid clean. Brushes away wisps of hair that have strayed onto her face. Tries out a smile.

The room is crowded. There's soft lighting, bright cushions on pale sofas and original artwork on the walls. Frankie stands in the corner furthest from the door. In black jeans and t-shirt she's underdressed for the occasion, but she's not going to let that bother her.

'*Alors...* What are you doing in Paris?' It's conversation, not a question. He says it with his eyes fixed on the other side of the room.

'Waiting to be discovered,' she says.

'*Ah bon.*' He nods, his eyes still fixed. There's a scratch of blood on his neck where he must have cut himself shaving.

'It's always been a fantasy of mine—starring in one of those moody French films.' She knows he's not listening. She can't remember his name and he certainly doesn't know hers—his eyes did that sideways thing when she told him. 'A tale of unrequited love on the banks of the Seine, or...'

'*Vous m'excusez.*' He's reeled in by his eyeballs before she can finish.

Frankie gulps down some wine and reaches for a crisp. Through the guests she sees the man home in on a young, well-dressed guy by the door. Smiling to herself, she grabs some nuts.

Simon appears: open face, crinkly eyes, a bottle in each hand.

'You okay, Frankie?'

'I feel like a mouse the cat won't eat,' she says, glad to revert to English.

'Sorry?'

'Doesn't matter. I didn't want to be eaten anyway.'

Simon grins and refills her glass.

'So have you settled in all right? Must be pretty cramped up there.'

'It's fine for a mouse.'

'Well I hope the mouse can cope with summer in the rooftops. The worst of the heat's still to come, you know.'

'Who's on the fourth floor?' says Frankie, glancing upwards.

'That flat's... It's not really lived in as such.' He scans the room. 'Most of this lot are arty friends of Monique's. I'll introduce you to some of them when I've got rid of this vino.'

He makes his way through the guests, filling glasses and curving an arm around Monique's slim waist as he passes. They complement each other perfectly: the blond, suntanned Englishman and his mahogany-eyed French wife.

Bits of shell fly everywhere as Frankie eats the pistachios one-handed. She wipes her hand on her jeans and stares into the room. The bodies all seem to connect with each other, but they have nothing to do with her. She can be who she wants with these people, let them think what they like. After all, singles are more mysterious than couples: they leave more to the imagination.

Monique comes over with some chap. He's tall and everything about him is dark and lean; his hair spills over his face.

'Frankie, this is Antoine. He wants to practise his English. Just don't get him started on Surrealism!' A knowing look passes between them, leaving her out. Frankie swirls the wine in her glass. Removes a crumb of pistachio shell with her finger and flicks it onto the floor. When she looks up Monique is eyeing her intently.

'*Bon*. Time to check on the twins.' Monique withdraws her gaze and leaves the room.

'So you're a friend of Monique's?' Frankie says to the tall man in English.

'In a way.'

She expects him to say more, but he doesn't. He just stands there.

'What do you do?'

'This and that.'

'I've only just met them. Last week, when I got here. I'm renting a room upstairs, on the top floor. It's good to have neighbours, though I don't really know them yet obviously, I only got here...' What on earth's going on with her mouth? She swigs back more wine and glances around. Switches her glass from one hand to the other.

'Can't stand parties,' says Antoine flatly. 'Talking to strangers— not worth the bloody effort.' He strokes a thumb down his beer bottle, drawing a line in the condensation.

'Well, I don't know, it depends.'

'Scottish?' He peers at her through his hair.

'Well spotted.'

'Monique told me.'

'Ah.'

He takes a slug of beer. 'I spent time in London once.'

'Doing what?'

'Bugger all.'

Frankie smiles, though she knows she shouldn't: he can't help his accent.

'Why Paris then?' he says.

'Um… fresh start. I needed to get away, do something different. And I'm doing some artwork while I'm here—a portfolio for Art College. That's the plan anyway.'

'Art College? Okay. Let's sit down.'

The sofas are inaccessible so they sit down where they are, on the floor, with their backs against the wall. The buzz of conversation reverberates up through Frankie's buttocks. She watches people's legs, the shuffling feet. And she sees Antoine's knees on the edge of her vision. She's very aware of his knees.

'Bored?' he says.

'Not really.'

'But you'd prefer not to be here.'

'I don't know.' It's true: she really doesn't know.

He takes the empty glass from her hand, gets up and crosses the room: an easy gait, his slim dark legs weaving through. She feels the lack of him beside her and finds herself guarding the space. But it's an old trick, going for more booze, not coming back.

Monique drifts back into the room, followed by a woman in a bright pink sari.

Bright colours are vulgar; stick to black.

It's striking, the sari. Monique is striking too: those intense, deep-set eyes and the way she moves, the fluidity of her gestures. The air hardly knows she's there as she glides her way through it. Behind her a vast canvas dominates the wall: one of her own creations, no doubt, with abstract blocks of colour cut through by a single black line. The sort of art people always claim they could do themselves if they could be bothered, only they never can and they never do. And anyway, it isn't that simple: there's nothing random there, no spontaneity. Frankie has an urge to scribble on the canvas with a marker pen, slash through it with a knife. She squeezes her fingers into the crook of her knees.

Monique's head is poised against a sheen of mauve, her dark hair as sleek as the paint. She's chatting to the woman in the sari. When Antoine joins them Frankie tries not to look, doesn't want him to see her looking. They glance across and she can't help but feel they're talking about her. Antoine is smiling, almost laughing. He has a glass of wine in one hand, a bottle of beer in the other. That's my glass, you bugger, bring it here—I need something to do with my hands.

Monique touches Antoine on the arm. He laughs for real and Frankie looks away.

The bookcase beside her holds bulky art and travel books, collections of photographs, a *Collins-Robert*, an atlas, a thesaurus. Higher up is a jumble of French and English paperbacks. Frankie twists her head in both directions to read the spines: Flaubert, McEwan, Sagan, Keats... The names blur out of focus and she sighs. The last time she sat on the floor beside a bookcase with a man she'd just met, he seduced her. Or forced himself on her, depending on how you look at it. He was twice her age and she made the mistake of marrying him.

Antoine hands her the glass and reclaims the space beside her. The room is interesting again. Interesting enough for her not to leave just yet.

'So you're an artist?' she says.

'Not really.'

'I thought maybe you worked with Monique, or in the same field, though I suppose anyone can be interested in art, can't they?' The wine's still talking crap. She throws back some more.

'I don't know much about Surrealism,' she goes on. 'I mean, I know it's Dalí and Matisse and that, but...'

'Magritte.'

'Magritte, yes, I always get them muddled—the names that is, not the paintings. Magritte did that one of the pipe, didn't he?' Antoine nods wearily, but that doesn't stop her. 'The one that says, 'This is not a pipe', because it isn't, I suppose, it's just a picture of one, isn't it?'

If it's not worth saying, don't say it.

'Actually, I'm more into music than art,' she says. 'I sing in a rock group—retro punk. I've got a sackful of safety pins upstairs.'

'And I wrote the Marseillaise.' His face barely cracks at the edges.

He drinks from his bottle and settles back into the wall, his elbow pressing into her arm. She pretends not to notice, but she's paralysed. She doesn't dare move, she hardly dares breathe. What's happening here? She doesn't know the guy, he's impossible to talk to, his hair is a mess—and his elbow is electrically charged.

They sit like this for ages. They don't even talk. Simon refills her glass a few times and her wine-drinking arm—the one not being touched by Antoine—is the only bit of her she moves. With the party droning on around her, she leans into his shoulder and doesn't care what anyone thinks. A punk rocker can do what she likes.

Monique crouches in front of them with a tray of nibbles: small savoury biscuits, green and black olives, more pistachios, foiled mini-cubes of *La Vache Qui Rit*. One moment they're in bowls on the tray, the next they're all over the place—down Frankie's front, in her lap, on the floor. Monique is fussing, scooping up biscuits and olives. The pressure on Frankie's arm and shoulder has gone and Antoine is kneeling beside her, retrieving bits from the floor. She sits there, surrounded by nibbles. There's a fish-shaped cheesy biscuit floating in her wine. She should be irritated. She should be worrying about the grease on her clothes and helping to pick stuff up. But there's a fish in her wine.

She giggles. Can't stop giggling.

'Frankie?' says Monique, bemused.

Frankie holds up her glass. 'A fish...' It's not funny, it's really not that funny. '*Un poisson... dans la boisson!*' Her face is doing all the wrong things. She's shaking and the wine is rocking in the glass.

Monique smiles weakly. Finishes cleaning her up, brushing her down, salvaging what she can. Frankie can't speak. Her cheeks are wet with tears and her stomach aches.

You're ugly when you're drunk. Really ugly.

That's it, she's blown it. Antoine will go and sit somewhere else now, find someone else not to talk to. Fighting another onslaught of giggles, she manœuvres the glass in the direction of her mouth: with the wine inside her, there'll be less risk of spillage.

'*Le poisson rouge boit du rouge,*' Antoine says with mock solemnity. Then he gets up and leaves the room. The space beside her is empty again and embarrassment floods over her, hot and dry, killing the laughter dead. She blushes from the inside out. All that's left in the wine glass is a lump of soggy biscuit.

'Thanks for coming, Frankie.' Simon's cheek touches hers, one side then the other—a fleeting contact of skin. Monique hovers next to him. Her eyes grip Frankie's face for a moment, then she links an arm into Simon's and steers him back into the party.

Which just leaves Antoine. He's come out of the toilet and is standing in the hallway.

'I'm going now,' says Frankie, avoiding his gaze.

'Okay.' He bends to kiss her. She panics and leans to the wrong side.

'Sorry,' she says. 'It's ... I'm out of practice.'

They try again. This time she feels his lips on her cheek, smells the beer on his breath. For an instant, she thinks... But he homes in on the other cheek. His hand fizzes on her arm and weight drains from her head. She turns, swaying, directing her feet towards the door.

'*Bonsoir,*' he says as the door closes behind her.

Shit. She's walked away, just walked away and left him standing on the other side of the door. She doesn't know how to do this. She hasn't a clue how it works.

Well at least he knows where she lives.

It's quiet on the landing. Dark. The smell of someone's supper clings to the air. Her arm still tingles where he touched it and her cheeks feel flushed. Despite efforts to control her mouth, a stupid grin keeps springing back. She fumbles for the light switch, the timer ticking lazily as the darkness flips to white: vertical lines, horizontals, a curve here and there. She focuses on the verticals. Two whole flights of stairs to negotiate before the *minuterie* runs out.

It's a long way up. Her footsteps echo round the stairwell, bouncing back at her off the walls. A hiccup escapes and tumbles down, followed by a giggle. Still one more floor to go: the narrow bit, twisting steeply up into the roof.

The floorboards creak on the top landing. Groping blindly, Frankie finds the light switch for the toilet and holds her breath. It could do with bleach, rubber gloves, but she hasn't got round to that yet. Positioning her feet on the ridged footprints, she squats over the hole and concentrates hard on staying balanced.

Antoine. Sounds like a novelist or a designer. A restaurant critic, perhaps. No, too slim for a restaurant critic. Might be a film director, if she's lucky. And older than her—she always assumes people are older. Mind you, younger would be fun for a change.

She stands up shakily and jumps back from the *turque* as water gushes over it. Not so sozzled she'll get her feet wet.

Her room looks dull and uninspiring: bed, table and chair; sink and camping stove in the corner; piles of papers, books and clothes. She needs to get organised, finish unpacking, but there's nowhere to put things.

Everything in its place, including you.

Damn it. Why can't he leave her alone?

10

She throws her keys down on the table and weighs up the options: bed versus chair. A view of the ceiling versus one of the wall. She's too old for this. At twenty-nine she should have a place of her own, a home with more than one room and with framed prints on the walls. But when you're ten years behind. When you've lost those years to a black hole that's swallowed them up, you take what you can get. And what she's got is this *chambre de bonne* on the top floor of an apartment block in the twelfth arrondissement. Still, with the Bois de Vincennes within walking distance and the centre of Paris a mere eight métro stops away, it could be worse.

The room is stuffy. She stumbles across to the window and turns the latch. The panes swing in on their hinges and she presses her face out into the night. Traffic fumes scrape the air but there's no view: only tightly-hunched rooftops with black sky above, a smudge of moon, tiny nicks of starlight. A siren wails in the distance and there's music from somewhere. A muted, rapping beat. The kind her parents would complain about if they were here.

It's too late to phone them. They'll be in bed by now, in their spacious Edinburgh semi. Their door will have been left ajar. Across the landing the door of her old bedroom will be open too, whilst Craig's remains firmly closed. It must be years since anyone went into her brother's room, let in daylight, ran a finger through the dust.

Frankie turns away from the window. Despite the clutter, the room feels empty. She lets the cold tap run for a bit and fills a glass. The water tastes stale, or perhaps it's her mouth. Just as well he didn't kiss her.

You'll never find another man...

The brightness of the laptop makes her squint. She sings along with the modem. Sozzled enough then.

There's no message, no more news. Flopping back onto the bed, she tries to stay focused on the room, on the taste of the water, on the persistent thrumming of the music soaking in through the window. But JP's voice nags in her head. She feels his taut body pressing down onto hers and sees that same body slumped in a car by the side of a road. What will she do if he dies? How will she cope if he doesn't?

The smell is of melons, floor cleaner and bread. There's whistling as the lads wheel in stock on a warehouse trolley that squeaks. Canned music trickles out from hidden speakers and falls thinly through the air like drizzle.

Frankie checks the tomatoes and peppers, rearranges the bananas and tops up a crate of leeks. Delving into a sack of green beans, she comes across a soggy clump. Her fingers recoil and bile rises in her throat: she's in no mood for mould.

Nathalie, in white cap and apron, is wiping down the front of the cheese counter.

'*Ça va?*' she calls over.

Frankie frowns and taps her forehead.

'Too much...?' Nathalie tilts an imaginary glass.

'No. Well yes, maybe.'

Shaking her head, Nathalie starts building a pyramid of goat's cheeses. Frankie watches as each is placed with deft precision. The French girl is smooth and polished, with strands of blond creeping out from under her cap. Far too pretty for a place like this.

Madame Taupe pads by, leaning heavily on the push-bar of a trolley. Her hips are as wide as the trolley, her buttocks like jellies above strong, shapely calves. She has bread, yogurts, chicken and pasta, cheap wine—for lunch in the canteen, the one perk of the job. Wiping sweat off her brow, she swings the trolley in Frankie's direction and helps herself to onions, courgettes, aubergines and tomatoes. To be fried in half a litre of oil, no doubt, with a dozen cloves of garlic.

Behind the glass pane of the cheese counter the display continues to grow: a creamy white landscape of thick-crusted wedges, blue-veined slabs and flat, oozing half-rounds. Frankie wonders how Nathalie keeps track of them all.

'*Une livre de cerises, s'il vous plaît, Mademoiselle.*'

The old man doesn't do self-service. Frankie weighs the cherries, slaps a sticker on the bag.

'*Voilà*, Monsieur.' There are crèmes caramels in his trolley, bars of nougat, tins of soup, sardines and cat food. His white stick is there too.

'You seem tired, Mademoiselle,' he says, his gaze skimming the side of her face.

'I'm fine.' His concern is unexpected. She tries to look cheerful, hoping it shows in her voice. Muttering, the old man shuffles away in his tatty trainers and yellow bobble hat, a hem of trouser trailing on the floor.

She's picking dirt from her nails when Simon appears. He has a bag of sweets in his basket, nothing else.

'Hi Frankie,' he says in his soft, confiding voice. 'How's it going?'

'Not bad. I wish they'd do something about the music, though.'

'Do you know, I hadn't noticed. It must drive you nuts.'

'Good job I only work mornings.'

He casts an eye down her uniform. 'Very chic!'

'Mmm. Stripes to die for.'

Adding peaches and a melon to his basket he turns to go, and then turns back to her. 'Did you meet Antoine at the party?'

He knows she met Antoine. 'Yes. We chatted about art and stuff.'

'Right. He's a friend of Monique's. I meant to introduce you to some other people, but... All those glasses to fill, you know what it's like.'

He makes for the checkouts. Frankie leans back against the counter and stares at a smear of parsley on the floor. Antoine. The dark legs, the feel of his shoulder on hers. You never know, maybe he liked her. Maybe something will happen. He's tall though. It would feel very different sleeping with him, sharing a bed. Would their heads be level or would she sleep with her head on his chest? If their heads were level, their feet wouldn't touch and that would feel odd. The detail is all she can focus on, not the full meaning. Like standing too close to a painting.

You'll never find another man. No other man will want you.

What the hell is she thinking of? She was pissed, he was pissed, she made a fool of herself, a complete idiot. He'll have forgotten her already. Or if he remembers, it will be for all the wrong reasons.

Still three hours ten minutes to go. She plugs the gap Simon has made in the melons and starts tidying the apples, arranging them in rows, all facing the same way. When they're done they'll form a pattern of curves and dimples, like pebbles laid out on a beach. They won't stay neat for long though. Nothing does.

'You'll need a sweater,' he said, 'and smart shoes, and something to wear if it rains.' So I packed as best I could and we set off up the A1. He wouldn't say where we were going.

He kept looking across at me and smiling. 'What?' I said. 'Nothing,' he said. Then he pulled into a lay-by, stopped the car and leaned over to kiss me. Just like that, for no reason. When it started to rain it didn't matter—I felt warm inside and I didn't mind any more, not knowing where we were going. We listened to Classic FM and when I found the extra strong mints in the glove compartment I smiled. 'We'll save these for later,' I said, and JP smiled too. At the next junction he turned off the main road and we ended up on a farm track, with Vivaldi on the radio and rain on the roof and it was like when we first met, less than a year before.

14

The mints tasted stronger than I remembered. By the time we crossed the border into Scotland, there weren't many left in the pack. Rain fell heavily on the windscreen and the winter sun was already setting.

The sign to Edinburgh tugged like a rope in a storm, but we didn't turn off the bypass. There was no time, he said; on the way back perhaps. I imagined arriving at my parents' with JP beside me. Tried to slot what my life was now into what it had been before. It wasn't an easy fit.

Finally we reached the hotel, somewhere in the heart of Perthshire. In our room there was a four-poster bed, a vase of red roses and a box of plain and milk chocolates, individually wrapped. A typed card read: *For Francesca, the most beautiful woman I know. All my love, JP.* I wondered how many women he knew and whether he really thought I was more beautiful than Stella: the ex-lover with long legs and blond hair. I flexed the card in my hand.

JP hung up his clothes, shaking out the creases, and we made a start on the chocolates. I scrunched up the foil; he folded his into neat little squares.

I don't know how he risked buying it without asking me first. The sheets of tissue paper rustled as I unwrapped the smooth cream silk: Monsoon, size ten. The sort of thing I would have chosen myself, although not in that colour. I slipped into the dress and he fastened the zip. Then he folded the jacket round my shoulders and twisted my hair up loosely on top of my head. 'You'll do,' he said, putting his hand in his pocket and bringing out a small black box. I heard pennies drop all around me.

The next day he sheltered me with an umbrella as I stepped out of the car onto a pavement pasted with drowned confetti. The room we were taken to was bland and neutral, with a polished table, a single spray of flowers and half a dozen rows of padded chairs. Cold air whistled in through the bay window and I rather envied the Registrar her long grey cardigan with its twin pockets and shiny buttons. As we stood facing her across the table I clasped my hands tightly in front of me. The ring felt strange on my finger, like a hairstyle I wasn't used to. I wondered when JP would get round to telling Xavier and his parents. And I found myself wishing that Craig was there beside me instead of some stand-in witness from the knitwear shop next door. But perhaps he could see. Perhaps somehow he knew.

The Registrar shook as she read from her script and I wondered if it was her first time too, if she'd spent the last few days trying on different cardigans and practising her lines in the bath. But this was serious. I was barely twenty-one and here I was getting married. Committing the rest of my life to the man standing next to me.

And then it was over. JP turned to kiss me, and it felt so unreal that I wanted to rewind and go through the whole thing again, concentrating properly this time. Being married felt pretty damned good though. The voice in my head that said it might not be was very quiet. So quiet I didn't hear it.

Madame la Concièrge teeters out of her ground floor flat with three Pekinese dogs on leads.

'*Bonjour,* Mademoiselle,' she says, tight-lipped, high-heeled. The dogs yap at her legs and pull her out onto the pavement.

Frankie steps past neat doormats and through a cloying smell of polish. Three floors up she hears the muffled sound of a cartoon on the telly, a child crying and Monique's voice cutting through. She looks at the door that closed behind her and imagines him standing there, tall and dark, his breath full of beer. The moment has passed, but she wishes that it hadn't.

On the next floor she pauses, her legs sore from the climb and from standing all morning. There's not a sound. Only the ticking of the *minuterie* and the canned music still gnawing at her head. A plaque on the door says *M. Sennet,* but there are no other clues. 'Not really lived in as such': she wonders what Simon meant.

She drags herself up the final set of stairs to her room. A picture postcard has been pushed under her door. It shows a ship, its hull and sails the same colour and texture as the blue sea that surrounds it. On the back there's the title: *Le séducteur/ The Seducer, 1953, René Magritte*, and a brief hand-written message: *Café des Sports. Midi. A.*

The arrogance of it, assuming she'll want to see him. Assuming she'll know who 'A' is. He can't expect her to drop everything just like that. And anyway, it's already well past midday. He'll be long gone by now.

The man at the bar raises his head. His companion turns on his stool. Their dull eyes fix Frankie in a stare. There's a carafe of water on the counter and two tumblers of cloudy pastis. The stare follows Frankie as she crosses the room.

Antoine is reading the paper. His black leather jacket lies slumped on the table in front of him, next to an empty coffee cup and a scattering of sugar wrappers. The television on the wall shows some news report or other which no one is watching. Everything in the room is drab. A bland palette of beige and brown.

Folding the paper, Antoine stands and kisses her lightly on both cheeks. She gets it right this time.

'Coffee?'

'Tea.'

'Of course.'

Not of course at all, she thinks. She'd simply prefer tea.

He orders and the men at the bar retract their stare.

'Do you want to eat?' he says. The only sign of food is a basket of croissants on the bar. They're the colour of skin that could do with some sun.

'I'm not hungry. But you have something if you want.'

'No hurry.'

It takes her a moment to work out what he's said: the lack of an 'h' makes it difficult.

The barman brings two cups: one large, one small. Frankie asks for milk and blows on the tea to cool it. Antoine stirs sugar into his espresso.

'Been here before?' he says, holding the cup between thumb and forefinger and tipping it into his mouth.

'I've walked past a few times, that's all.'

The tea is still too hot to drink. She fiddles with a pack of sugar lumps, scoring the groove with her thumbnail.

'Did the concièrge let you in?'

'When?'

'When you left the note.'

'Sure.' He throws back his head and swallows the rest of the coffee.

'You're not working today then?'

No answer. He dips a finger into his cup, scooping up the sugary dregs. Frankie sips her tea, wishing she'd chosen a cold drink. On the wall behind Antoine is a mirror advertising Anisette Ricard. She can see herself in the gaps between the letters. The sight is disconcerting: it's what Antoine can see when he looks at her.

'So do you come here... I mean, do you live near here?' she says, trying not to watch herself saying it.

'Not really my patch.' He licks his finger, watching her.

She shouldn't have come. She's wasting her time. The seduction was no more than a fantasy.

'I want to show you Paris,' he says.

The air from the métro has seeped out onto the steps. It has a smell of its own: festering, acrid, the exhaled breath of an eater of dust and metal. The machine at the barrier clunks as it swallows the tickets and spits them back out.

It's busy. They're drawn down the corridor on an invisible conveyor belt, locked into the momentum of rushing feet. Any sudden braking would cause a pile-up. Frankie sticks closely behind Antoine, following in his wake like a cyclist in a slipstream. Footsteps pound and the voice of a busker echoes round the walls. In the crook of the corridor a woman in shabby coat and dark glasses is hunched against the wall, her hands cupped awkwardly in front of her.

They don't talk on the train. There's only one spare seat so she sits, he stands. He seems taller than ever, towering above her in his black shirt and jeans with his jacket slung over his shoulder. The faces around them are blank: emotionless masks going from A to B. Through the graffiti-scratched glass dark tunnels give way to bright stations with tiled walls, crowded platforms and vast, gaudy adverts for Darty and Galeries Lafayette.

They change at Bastille, take Direction Pont de Neuilly/ La Défense. This time there are two empty seats, but Antoine still prefers to stand. The air on the train is sour and warm. A young couple opposite are sitting close together, communicating through their fingers. The muscles in Frankie's face slacken as her mind sinks deep within itself.

He reversed into a parking space and we sat for a moment. The sky was low and rain streaked through the street lights, clattering on the roof of the car.

'So this is Covent Garden?' he said, peering across at the curtained windows and paint-peeling doors. 'Posh name for a scruffy side street.'

'This *is* Cambridge, not London,' I said. 'Anyway, I like it.'

'It's all muesli-eating lefties round here though, isn't it?'

'Of course. They sit around all day doing yoga and recycling their breath.'

JP frowned. 'How did you find this place, Francesca?'

'In the paper. I did think the house was a bit grotty when I saw it, but I liked Jude and that was that.'

We got out of the car, pulled our coats up over our heads and ran across the road. The front door opened straight from pavement onto sitting room. JP trod with caution as he followed me in, as if he thought he might step on something nasty on the carpet.

Jude appeared from the kitchen, wearing combats and spiky hair.

'You must be JP,' she said, her eyes firmly on him. 'Coffee? Or something stronger?'

It was the ultimate test, gaining Jude's approval. She was sworn to secrecy but hadn't stopped nagging, wanting to meet the man she called my undercover lover.

JP perched on the edge of an armchair.

'Got that at the Sally Army,' I said.

'What?'

'The chair. And the sofa.'

'You could surely do better than that, Francesca.'

'There's nothing wrong with them. They were cheap.'

'That's not the point.'

He stayed perched and Jude brought the coffee and the three of us chatted for a while. He told Jude about his work at the University and showed interest in her job. I'd thought hairdressing would leave him cold, but he oozed his charm and asked all the right questions. Even so, Jude's expression was hard to read.

When she'd finished her coffee she left us, saying she had to get back to her knitting. That made me laugh: Jude and knitting were as likely a combination as JP and muesli.

'Interesting face,' JP said. 'Shame about the rest.'

'What rest?'

'The trousers and that tattoo on her arm. And the unwashed smell. Must be a lesbian.'

'Rubbish! She showers every day. And anyway, what if she was?'

'Boyfriend?'

'She's always got some guy in tow.'

'Doesn't prove a thing.'

I showed him round the house. Not that there was much to show: a slit of a kitchen, a bathroom with no windows and a narrow flight of stairs with two bedrooms at the top. He followed me up.

It was cold in my room. I put on a tape to warm things up a bit—a Jacques Brel compilation I'd found on the market. *Ne me quitte pas* seemed appropriate, the way songs do. Having thrown off my clothes, I waited shivering between the sheets while JP got undressed and found somewhere to put his things. He snapped his glasses away in a case and then slipped in beside me, still in his underpants and vest.

'Lumpy mattress,' he said.

'Sally Army,' I said.

Brel was halfway through *Le plat pays* when JP leaned across and switched him off. He didn't even fade him first. I assumed he didn't want a third party to interfere with our love-making, but it turned out he just wanted to sleep.

We hadn't shared a single bed before and it wasn't easy. I spent all night clinging to the side of the mattress, trying not to roll into the hollow where JP lay snoring. It wasn't until morning that our jagged edges had been smoothed by sleep and we lay as one body, entwined. We made love when we woke, with Brel's soulful voice in the background.

It carried on raining and we stayed in all day. JP shaved in the windowless bathroom. He stood in the poky kitchen, studying a biscuit from all angles before dunking it in his coffee. He resigned himself to the sofa, where he tapped on his laptop and marked a batch of First Year essays. At times he seemed restless, clicking his biro, twisting his ring round his little finger, biting his nails. When he chewed the skin on the side of his thumb and made it bleed, I wanted to know why he did it and he said it was his thumb and he could do what he liked with it. To prove the point, he bent it back further than thumbs are meant to bend. I couldn't argue with that.

That night a rhythm of groans came pumping through the wall from Jude's bedroom. Male groans, most definitely male. I asked him how much more proof he wanted, but JP was annoyed that they couldn't keep the noise down. He never came to Covent Garden again.

Our relationship evolved under cover of darkness. We met in shady corners of parks and down secluded alleys. Sometimes he took me to his house, but only if it was late and the curtain twitchers were in bed. He couldn't risk it often. So we would drive through the night just to be together. Classic FM was preset on the radio and the car smelt of the tree-shaped chemicals that dangled from the rear-view mirror. He would stop in a lay-by or on a track going nowhere and switch off the headlights. The car would be warm from the drive, and there'd be Mozart or Mahler, and I'd sit astride him, facing him, easing down onto him as we made the car warmer with the windows steaming up and the cold air outside.

He kept a supply of extra strong mints in the glove compartment which we sucked on afterwards. Always afterwards, never before. More wholesome than smoking, he said. The mint cleared our heads and worked with the air freshener to mask the smell of the sex.

Later, when the steam had left the windows and there was only a crumple of tissue as evidence, he would drop me off at the end of the road and I'd walk home through the streetlights, with sharp air in my lungs and a tang of spearmint in my mouth.

They get off the train at Louvre Rivoli and climb up into the glare of the street. Frankie's pace feels rushed next to Antoine's: he has a way of walking that seems to require no effort, the top half of his body unaffected by the long easy stride of his legs. He couldn't look hurried if he tried.

Skirting the walls of the Louvre, they wander along the river towards the Pont-Neuf: the oldest bridge in Paris, he tells her. Its arches throw deep shadows onto the water and ornate lamps glisten in the sunlight above. The Seine is cluttered with tourist boats and barges. Frankie looks out across the river to the twin towers of Notre-Dame that dominate the skyline behind, and the spirit of the city grips her: its poise and beauty, its dusty fragility. She thinks of the young couple cavorting along the bridge in *Les Amants du Pont-Neuf*, and of other films set in Paris whose titles she can never remember—films in which daytime turns to dusk and doe-eyed women sit in smoke-filled cafés with husky-voiced men. A veneer of chic underscored by decadence and passion.

The stalls on the Quai Voltaire are crammed with postcards and second-hand books. Antoine stops now and then, picks up a book, puts it back. It isn't clear if he's looking for something in particular, or merely looking. Frankie pretends to be interested, but all she's conscious of is Antoine. She wants him to like her, though she doesn't know why. All they have in common is a penchant for black.

In the end he buys some postcards—old black and white photographs—and tucks them into his jacket pocket.

The gallery is a vast structure of iron and glass, an impressive conversion of the former Gare d'Orsay with vaulted roof and large, circular clock face. Visitors pack the floor space, some clearly there for the artwork, others aimlessly killing time. Frankie wonders which category she and Antoine fall into.

They stop in front of a Monet: his famous snowscape with a magpie on a gate.

'What do you think?'

'I like it.'

'Why?'

She hesitates. 'Because of the light. The way there's so little colour, but it's full of sunshine, weak winter sunshine, and your eye's drawn towards the gate as if you could walk into the picture with the snow crunching under your feet and your breath in the air.' She's talking crap again, but it's too late now. 'And there's all different shades of white. Like white is really a colour.'

'I like the light too.' Thank God. They move on.

'What about that one?'

Antoine casts an eye over the Renoir, the blues and pinks of couples dancing in dappled sunlight. 'Too bourgeois,' he says.

On the way out he leaves her holding his jacket while he pops back to the gallery shop. It feels strange to be carrying that part of him, the outer skin that he always has with him but never wears. The leather is heavy and has his smell on it. Keys rattle in the pocket. If she knew where he lived, she would take the keys and leave the jacket. He'd go home to find her naked in his bed, surrounded by shades of white. Or perhaps his sheets are black.

He climbs the steps with ease, two at a time, while she struggles to hide her shortness of breath. Finally they reach the top, where the bulbous bulk of the Sacré-Cœur glints white in the sunshine. Far below, the city is laid out in an intricate design of windows and balconies, rooftops and chimney pots, stretching back to a horizon stubbled with tower blocks. A confusion of tiny parts, as immaculately put together as the inside of a computer. In the middle distance a blue and green structure stands out from the colourless landscape.

'The Centre Pompidou,' says Antoine. 'A symbol of seventies' design ethos. A kind of inverted modernism of its time, with the internal workings externalised and the concept of space redefined.'

Frankie nods slowly. 'Meaning?'

'Meaning escalators, air conditioning, all that stuff on the outside. Intestines spilling out and freeing up space in the body.'

'Right… It's got art galleries too, hasn't it?'

'That sort of thing. We'll go there sometime.'

She's surprised he says that: it smacks of forward planning.

He drinks from a bottle of Evian and passes it to her. Normally she would wipe the top, but this time she doesn't. A coachload of Italian school kids swarms around them in a cloud of chatter, clipboards and rucksacks.

'Let's eat now,' he says.

The bistro is hidden away down a side street. Noisy and crowded, it seems to have drawn custom from nowhere like an amusement arcade on a deserted promenade. Subdued lighting replaces the sting of the sun. The waiter who greets them is squat and paunchy with bloodshot, bulging eyes. He knows Antoine by name. They shake hands and the waiter eyes Frankie with interest, but Antoine doesn't introduce her. She wonders why he's brought her here if she isn't worth introducing. How many other women he has brought here.

The waiter shows them to a table by the bar and props appear: a basket of bread, a carafe of wine, two glasses, two menus. All delivered with a flick of the wrist and a ruffle of starched white apron. Antoine lightly punches the waiter's paunch, saying something about his wife, or women in general—Frankie isn't sure which. It's the first time she's heard him speak more than a few words of French and she's struck by the strangeness of it, by how different he sounds.

She scans the menu. There are four set meals at different prices and three pages of à la carte. She can't expect Antoine to pay, and if she pays for herself she can't afford much.

'So?'

'I'm still not that hungry.'

'You'll be hungry once you start eating.' The look in his eyes is almost a smile and makes what he says seem flirtatious. Frankie flicks back through the menu.

All too soon the bulgy-eyed waiter reappears, a tear of sweat trickling out from his hairline.

'*Pour Madame?*'

'Um… *La soupe de poisson et… la crêpe.*' As soon as she says it, she wishes she'd chosen the steak. The waiter scribbles on a corner of the white paper tablecloth. Scribbles some more as Antoine orders.

'*Tchin-tchin,*' says Antoine, raising his glass.

'Cheers.'

Steaming plates glide by, infusing the air with an aroma of fatty juices and garlic. Frankie's mouth fills with saliva.

'So what do you do?' she says, breaking into a piece of bread.

'This and that. I get by.'

'You don't have a regular job then?'

'Not exactly, no, but I keep busy.'

'Doing what?'

'Technical stuff, mostly.'

What is he—a hit man? A fraudster? A part-time gangster?

'I used to work in advertising,' he adds, his tone implying that that's her lot.

Bowls of mussels arrive at the next table amidst more wafts of garlic, their dark shells gaping like beaks. Frankie still wishes she'd chosen the steak.

The waiter is back with their starters.

'*Anglaise?*' he says, putting the soup down in front of her.

'*Écossaise.*'

'*Ah! Les kilts et le monstre du Loch Ness!*'

She looks to Antoine for sympathy, but he's preoccupied with his *frisée aux lardons*: a mound of green curls housing cubes of pink flesh.

'You didn't have to choose the cheapest menu,' he says when the waiter has gone.

'It's fine. I wanted the pancake anyway.' She makes a start on the soup: real fish this time. Her insides flush with residual embarrassment.

'You can't earn much at that supermarket of yours.'

'It's better than nothing.'

'Money helps though, in Paris.'

'Money always helps!' She laughs. Then stops. She doesn't remember telling him where she works.

'You could find another job, you know,' he says, pushing a strand of lettuce into his mouth. 'There's work that pays far better than vegetables.'

Monique must have told him. That must be it.

The main course arrives on large white plates. The bread basket is refilled and more wine is poured. Frankie has no regrets now about the pancake, plump with mushrooms, bacon and creamy sauce. Tucking into his *cassoulet*, Antoine tells her about a favourite haunt of his on the *rive gauche*—a quirky seafood restaurant with giant fish sculptures hanging from the ceiling. And she finds herself looking into his eyes, searching for clues, trying to see beyond the flecks of brown and green. They're beautiful eyes, with no trace of gangster.

They have *îles flottantes* for dessert—sweet, whisked egg whites floating in custard. Then coffee and slivers of dark chocolate. The numbers on the tablecloth begin to look like mathematical formulae. She still doesn't know who's paying.

Their shadows stretch down the steps in the evening light. The school kids have gone and a stillness has settled. Below them a wash of pink is seeping across the city.

'Are you happy?'

The question surprises her. 'I'm happy right now.' He can read into that what he likes.

'And in general?'

She has to think: Is she happy? Has she ever been happy? No one's asked her that before.

'I'm happier than I've been for a while.'

'It doesn't work if you think too hard. You just have to be.'

She looks at him and realises he's got that sussed: he just is. On one level at least. As she takes a slug of wine from the bottle they've brought with them from the bistro, her thoughts wander back to JP and to how it wasn't her fault, it was his. If only she could believe that.

'I should go,' Antoine says then, standing up and retrieving his jacket from the steps. As he turns, an arm flails across Frankie's face. There's no pain—the stiff leather barely touches her—but she cowers nonetheless.

'Sorry. Did I hurt you?' The question stays on his face as he holds out a hand.

'It's okay,' she says, rising shakily. 'I'm just... It's the wine.' Their hands remain clasped for a moment, then he lets her go.

They make their way down the steps and back through the narrow streets. The light is fading, draining everything to grey, but in her mind are the bright lights of a hospital. The hospital where she lay for days, pain wrapped around her head and a bunch of heavily-scented lilies by her side. How did it happen? How did any of it happen?

'I lived up there once.' Antoine indicates a shuttered window. 'Quite a Des Res. Landlord was a bent copper though.' She meets his eyes and returns their smile: he knows how good his English is.

On the steps of the métro he bends down to kiss her on both cheeks.

'Change at Nation.'

She nods. 'Thanks for the meal.'

Sensing there's more to be said but not knowing what it is, she pulls away from him and sets off down the steps.

*

He didn't like me living in Covent Garden. 'You're going back to that hovel of yours, are you?' he'd say at the end of an evening. 'Back to your lesbian friend?' The lesbian thing annoyed me. He wouldn't let go, even though there was no truth in it. It was as if he resented the fact that I had company and he didn't.

One Sunday Jude was sprawled on the sofa with a copy of *Cosmopolitan*.

'My period's late,' I said.

Her eyes stayed on the page. 'How late?'

'Five days.'

'That's nothing. It'll probably start tomorrow.'

'But what if it doesn't?'

'You are on the Pill, aren't you?'

'No.'

'What then?'

'Condoms. Usually.'

She looked up. 'What do you mean, usually?'

'Well, sometimes... He doesn't always use them straight away, if you see what I mean.'

'No, I don't see.'

'Look, he's forty-three, he must know what he's doing.'

'Are you mad?'

'I can't be pregnant. Not now. I've only known him a few weeks.'

'You should have thought of that before!' Jude shook her head in disbelief.

I kept going to the loo, praying for a red smear on my knickers. I even stuck a finger up and wiggled it around a bit, but it came out sticky and clear. In my head I practised what I'd say, how I'd tell him. Sometimes he laid a hand on my stomach and said how much he loved me. And sometimes he turned away, saying nothing.

The next morning there was a streak of blood on the toilet paper and when I looked away and looked back again, it was still there. Thank you God, thank you, I whispered as I sat on the loo, staring at the blood, marvelling at its redness, its cheerful, confident, full-blooded redness. It was years since I'd talked to God.

Later that week I went to the Clinic and got three months' supply of small white pills in three-weekly strips. Best not to mention it to JP, he didn't need to know. I kept the pills hidden in the zipped pocket of my shoulder bag, in case we ever ended up at his place. From then on my periods came on Mondays, regular as clockwork, and life seemed well-nigh perfect.

Some time after I moved in with JP, I applied for a job in Heffers— nothing grand, just a sales assistant in the main bookstore. He went quiet when I told him I'd got it. Asked me later why I felt the need to work when he was there to look after me. I told him it wasn't about the money, it was about getting out of the house, doing something constructive with my time. He didn't seem to understand that.

It was in Heffers, a couple of years later, that I finally saw Jude again—we'd lost touch soon after the wedding. She asked if I was all right, said I looked tired and had I put on weight? Must be JP's cooking, I said, and we laughed. She hadn't changed—apart from the orange stripes in her hair—and I realised then how much I'd missed her.

In my lunch break we met in a café round the corner. I had a latte and Jude had tea and chocolate cake.

'Did you see that thing on the telly last night?' she said. 'About some guy in the States who thinks he's a tiger? He's had all this surgery done on his face—whisker implants and stripes and pointy ears. And he's adopted tiger habits, they said. Whatever that means!'

'The mind boggles.'

'It makes you think though, eh? I mean, what's normal? If there are people like that, then anything's possible.'

'That's not normal though, is it? He only gets on TV 'cos he's weird.'

'Mmm, try some of this.' Jude pushed her plate towards me.

'No thanks.' I could easily have demolished the lot, but eating in public was banned—it was one of my rules.

'Obsessions, that's another weird thing,' Jude went on, filling her mouth with cake. 'People who can't touch anything in case it's infected, or hoard stuff 'cos they're too scared to throw it away and end up with a house they can't even sit down in. Can you imagine?'

'JP's the opposite. He doesn't keep anything unless it has a use.'

'You'd better watch out then!'

'What?'

'Only joking.'

I forced a smile. Jude stabbed at cake crumbs on her plate and licked them off her finger, one by one.

'Who's your obsession of the moment?' I said then.

'Chance would be a fine thing. Steve buggered off when I made a stand about the motor parts in bed, and Tony was way too boring when it came to it. I mean, there has to be some spark, doesn't there?'

'Not spark plugs, though.'

'Correct! There's this guy called Jason who works at the salon. He's a compulsive flirt, but gay as a pansy, worst luck. The cute ones always are.'

'I don't know how you do it, Jude.'

'Do what?'

'Always have a posse of men after you.'

She shrugged, as if she simply couldn't help it.

'So what about you and JP?'

'What about us?' I lowered my eyes and swallowed the dregs of my coffee. She leaned forwards, forcing me to look at her.

'You would say, wouldn't you, if…?'
'If what?'
This time it was Jude who looked away.

Her brain unsticks itself from sleep. It's dark and she's not sure where she is. She gradually becomes aware of a wall next to the bed and of a piano playing somewhere. And she remembers the shutters that block out the light and play tricks with time. She could sleep all day in this blackened space.

She gets up and throws open the shutters. Sunday stretches out in front of her: an empty road, going nowhere. She's always hated Sundays.

The laptop flickers into action: *You have 0 unread messages.* The bold letters rub the point home and the road looks even emptier. Not knowing what else to do, she makes tea in a bowl and sits beside it on the floor. It feels less lonely somehow than sitting on her own at the table. As she waits for the tea to cool, the feeling strikes without warning. The flash of self-awareness. The sense of falling out of alignment with herself, of being inside her body and out of it. It's unnerving to find yourself alone, suddenly, with the stranger that's inside your own head. The room starts to melt away from her and she breathes in deeply, gathering herself back together.

The piano music is more distinct now. It's a piece she recognises—it could be Bach, she's not sure. Something neat and perfectly balanced, that her mother would call contrapuntal. Nothing like the studies banged out by her mother's pupils— kids not much older than herself who came to the house after school with their brown leather music cases and expressionless faces. They wrestled with the same tunes week after week and faltered through scales and arpeggios. Her mother covered their music with pencil, tapped out rhythms on the lid of the piano, straightened their backs and curved their fingers. But nothing seemed to help much.

Frankie drinks her tea. Sunlight from the window warms her back. In her sketchbook there are pastel drawings of kitchen utensils in Covent Garden, shampoo bottles on a shelf, coats slung on the back of a door. A pen and ink study of the street below her window. A watercolour of Jude lounging on the Sally Army sofa—not a brilliant likeness, but the mood is right. There's a vase of brightly-coloured flowers in JP's house—their house. The actual flowers were white, she remembers, but she added colour. It's the last trace of colour in the book. After that there's a boat on a river. A cyclist on a bridge. A page left blank, not deliberately, but it could have been. Then quick sketches of her parents in different poses. A tree in a garden and a doll on a windowsill. All done in pencil or black ink.

From my window I used to see trees. The shadows of their leaves danced on my bedspread and I heard birdsong in them, and a sound like seawater on shingle when the wind blew through. At night the birds would fall quiet and sometimes, in fog, ships' horns would sound across the Firth of Forth, moaning like stranded whales. After Craig died I thought that maybe he'd joined them. That he was lost in the gloom, calling out, and that I was the only one who could hear him. I didn't say anything to my parents: they never mentioned my brother, so I didn't know which words to use. Even in my head there weren't the words. I just felt things without giving them names.

I was eight when Craig died; he was not quite fifteen.

Before that, holidays had been spent in Gairloch on the north-west coast. From the window of the cottage I'd watched ships passing by, the changing colours of the sea, the slim arrows of cormorants flying close to the water—fighter planes on a mission,

Craig said. My father took cine films in black and white Super-8, not bothering with colour that he couldn't see. He let Craig use the camera too sometimes—an old wind-up Bell and Howell with an electric eye. Back home in Edinburgh, in our blacked-out sitting room, the projector hummed and rattled, its fan blowing cold air as the images jigged across the screen. 'Your lips is movin' but there's nought comin' out,' my father joked when anyone spoke directly to the camera; it was part of the ritual. As was the request for 'The Boy Peeing Backwards'. With feigned reluctance my father would load the relevant reel and fast-forward to the shot of a small boy relieving himself in the dunes. Then, to squeals of laughter, he would run the film in reverse.

When Craig wasn't there any more, we stopped going to Gairloch and my father stopped filming and the little boy stopped peeing backwards.

She turns to a fresh page and starts to draw: the squashed pillow on the bed, the trailing sheet, the window with the diamond-shaped latch. She sketches the shadow that the window frame throws onto the wall and the tear that scars the wallpaper. Her first snapshot of Paris.

The two men are at the bar with their pastis and water: a still life in muted colours. Their stare is the same and lasts as long. This time there's racing on the telly and it's being watched by the barman. Frankie sits where she sat when Antoine was there and orders a hot chocolate. It doesn't matter how hot it is, she's got all day to drink it.

When it comes she's impatient and scalds her tongue.

The Anisette Ricard mirror traps images from the street outside: segments of passers-by glimpsed through the lettering with glints of sunlight sparking from cars. Part of her own face is there too, between the 'e' and the 'R'. Seeing it unsettles her less now that Antoine isn't with her and the collage effect has a certain appeal, reminding her of the montages she used to make from old magazines using scissors and glue.

She takes *Le Journal du Dimanche* from a rack on the wall and lays it out on the table. A puddle of spilt chocolate seeps into the newsprint, buckling it like waves that leave ridges in sand. She scans the headlines, but before long her eyes are drawn back to the mirror. And there, from the vertical strip of her face, a likeness of her brother jumps out. A sliver of features that belongs to him.

As she stares, she has in her head an image captured on film she thinks, though she can't be sure: the memory might be a real one. Craig is peering out from behind two bed sheets that are drying on the line, on a day when the wind is still and the sheets are stiff with moisture. All that's visible between the squares of white cotton is a thin band of forehead, nose and mouth.

Frankie shifts her gaze back to the newspaper, smoothing the pages flat with the palm of her hand. She doesn't look in the mirror again, afraid that if she does the likeness will have gone. As the chocolate cools she sips it and finds it comforting. Like the chocolate her mum used to make for Craig and her on holiday when they'd been for a swim: damp hair, cold hands, sandy feet, hot chocolate.

She was happy then.

Midday comes and then it's after midday and Antoine isn't there. He doesn't wander in, order a coffee, take the emptiness out of the day. He never said he would.

The Entrée Libre sign is faded. Wind-chimes clink when the door is pushed open and the air inside is musty. The young man at the till mutters a 'Madame', hardly raising his eyes from his book.

Shelves go from floor to ceiling, classified with hand-written labels stuck on with tape. The tape has the yellowed curl of sickly toenails. A whole wall is devoted to novels and there are boxes of hard-backed cartoon books: *Spirou, Astérix, Lucky Luke, Tintin.*

Smaller boxes hold bundles of old postcards: views of post-War Paris, buxom women in lacy underwear, vintage cars and mopeds, scenes of summer on the Côte d'Azur. Magazines, sheet music and maps are piled up on the floor, all browning, dusty and decaying.

There was no dust and decay in Heffers. That shop smelt of fresh ink on new paper and the books were silent, their words trapped on the pages. Here is different. Here there's movement beneath the surface, the muffled echoes of unlocked voices. Frankie moves round the shelves, running her finger down the spines. Books left behind by the dead. Books loved and treasured. Books traded in, unfinished or unread: temptation on their covers, disappointment inside. A vast torrent of words, the effect of which is overwhelming. You need to take one book at a time, let it breathe.

She pulls out a copy of *Regain* by Giono: a paperback dated 1960 with a well-thumbed cover and ragged pages that have been torn, not cut. Light has seeped in round the edges and framed each page with a pale brown border. Touching the pages to her lips, she smells the age in the paper. As if inhaling a fragment of the past, the imprint of someone else's breath.

The book falls open at page forty-seven: '*Le dernier doigt du soleil lâche le pin, là-haut. Le soleil tombe derrière les collines. Quelques gouttes de sang éclaboussent le ciel...*' She murmurs the words out loud, releasing them like that from the page. '*Panturle mâche sa chique: une boule de tabac râclé au fond de sa poche...*' The words roll and flow like liquid gold. They hang the setting sun on her fingertips and paint in her mouth the bitter taste of tobacco.

Books are your passport to the world, my father used to say; you'll find all you need in books. He brought home tomes from the library: biographies, travel memoirs, political histories. Never fiction. Real life was more than enough, he said. And in the evenings, when he had finished work, he immersed himself in the lives of others, glass of whisky at his elbow. Trapped as always in his colour-blind, black and white world.

Meanwhile my mother played sonatas on the piano. After Craig died there was a slowing of the tempo and a new depth of emotion in the music that I was aware of even then, with each note suspended for the briefest moment before it sounded. As for my father, he doubled up on the whisky and did without the books. Craig's name was never mentioned. No one asked me how I felt. It was as if the grief in the house had been folded up and put away. The only witnesses to my tears were two old dolls of my mother's who sat on either side of my pillow. Sophie was the listener, the non-complainer, whilst Clementine had a tendency to frown. I held them by the legs once and banged them, face down, on the bed. When I stopped, Sophie was still smiling, Clementine still frowning.

'How much?' she asks the man at the till. He glances at the book and quotes a price. Splitting the difference, no doubt, between what the book is worth and what he thinks she might pay.

Simon is leaving the flats.

'Been out, Frankie?' She likes that—the way he always uses her name.

'Just getting some fresh air.'

'Good idea. You don't want to stay cooped up inside.'

'I found this.'

'*Regain?* I've always meant to read that.'

'Me too. Is Monique in?'

'I don't think so, no.'

'She said I could use your washing machine.'

'Of course. Pop down whenever you like.'

Frankie carries on up the stairs. When she reaches the third floor she glimpses Monique going into the flat. It's definitely her, flitting silently across the landing. Simon must have known she was there.

In her room Frankie sits for a while with the book, but she doesn't open it. The postcard—*The Seducer*— is on the floor by the bed. She picks it up and blows gently on the picture. A light breeze is all it would take for the watery ship to break up and dissolve back into the sea. All it would take for Antoine to sweep her off her feet.

An old piece of Blu-tack clings like chewing gum to the wall. She prises it off and softens it in her palm, fixes the card to the back of the door. It hides a crack in the wood.

Supper is a slice of Gruyère and a hunk of stale bread. Frankie eats at the open window, throwing crumbs to the sparrows. She feels cut off up here in her own little box, isolated in this partitioned cube of air that she happens to inhabit. The window opposite is screened by shutters and she can't see the others without straining her neck. She could die here and no one would know.

Distant church bells mark out the time. Day creeping into evening, families re-grouping, lovers meeting in the cooling air. A girl standing at a window eating bread.

She needs to find a way to stop the bread from drying out. This stuff tastes lousy. A glass of wine would help wash it down, but she doesn't want to drink on her own and all she has for company is a portable radio with poor reception. She tunes to a station that's not too crackly. It's playing a pop song she knows well, though she can't remember who sings it. She turns the little radio up as loud as it will go and she's back in Cambridge, walking home in the rain. The song is blaring out from an open window and she's there in the street, singing along and not caring how wet she gets. For once in her life she wants to be completely drenched from head to toe. She won't catch a chill, she won't catch her death, she'll just be very wet and have to dry out. But then there she is, in his hallway, with her clothes clinging to her body and water dripping from her hair. It's only rain, she's saying, it won't do me any harm…

Inbox (1) *Click*

sorry i didn't get back to you sooner frankie, i was waiting to hear from my parents. it seems jp's still unconscious. the doctors are hopeful he'll recover, though there's some risk of brain damage. and what about you? is the room ok? let me know if there's anything else you need.
xavier

The ablutions of previous lodgers are recorded in the grime of the shower tray. She scrubs with a brush, trying to shift the dark stains and the mottled rash of mould. It would be easier simply to close her eyes and not notice, but that's hard when it's other people's dirt.

He's going to pull through then. There was a time when that would have disappointed her. A time when she wished something would happen to spirit him away and give her an easy way out.

Her arm aches, but the stains are still there. She keeps scrubbing.

Madame Taupe is serving out *rôti de porc*. At one end of the table, the checkout ladies are cooing over an album of baby photos. At the other, the lads who work in the storeroom are throwing back glasses of *rouge* and shouting out jokes. Frankie doesn't even try to follow what they're saying. She picks at a slice of baguette, ignoring the pesticides engrained in her fingers.

39

'For our Scottish friend,' Madame Taupe announces, passing down a plateful of food. '*Bon appétit!*'

Frankie eats the pork in small mouthfuls, chewing slowly. There's a large bowl of salad on the table, but it has to be eaten separately. Meanwhile the raucous exchanges and *bras d'honneur* suggest the jokes are getting cruder. Nathalie, sitting next to Frankie, looks on with mild bemusement.

'Have you worked here for a while?' Frankie asks, doing her best to sound interested.

'Five years.' Nathalie brushes a crumb from her bottom lip. Her nails are perfect: white-tipped and beautifully shaped. Frankie can't tell if they're real or stuck on. A bit like Nathalie herself: the pretty exterior is all there is, an ornate façade with nothing happening behind it. She's a doll that moves and talks and eats. You can brush its hair and dress it in nice clothes. If it cries, you can turn off the tears.

Frankie can't imagine being her. She has no idea how she thinks.

'So how long are you here for?' says the doll.

'I'm not sure. It depends.'

'On what?'

'Lots of things.' Frankie wipes her plate and helps herself to salad. 'Do you live nearby?'

'A few streets away, with my father. I'm hoping to move out soon though.'

'Where to?'

'Don't know. I'm looking.'

'There's a *chambre de bonne* down the road—the room opposite mine.'

Nathalie half smiles, half frowns. 'That might be a bit close for comfort.'

The banter continues around them. Glasses are refilled. A plate of cheese appears and more bread is cut, crumbs shooting everywhere. Frankie wonders how much bread is lost in crumbs each year in France.

Nathalie passes her the cheese.

'*Sers-toi,*' says Frankie.

Nathalie shakes her head, gives a French click of the tongue. 'I don't eat cheese.'

'You're kidding?'

The doll doesn't eat cheese. That comes close to being an opinion and Frankie catches herself smiling. As she cuts a sliver of Cantal, she finds a blond hair on the plate. Her smile fades.

We'd been together for only a few months when JP first mentioned Stella. He rang and asked me to meet him for lunch. We would go out of town, he said, to one of the village pubs; no one was likely to see us there. I wanted to go, but exams were looming and I was behind with my revision.

'I'll ask Stella instead then,' he joked down the phone.

'Oh yeah? Who's Stella?'

'Girl in Accommodation. Young, pretty, unattached.'

'Just like me then!'

No more was said. I went to the library and spent the day writing notes on Proust.

But that wasn't the last of Stella. He would drop her name into the conversation: asides which on their own were meaningless but which began to build up. I should try dyeing my hair blond— it suited Stella. There were more foreign students this year— according to Stella. Had I ever tried yoga?—Stella swore by it. I even found a blond hair on his coat once. He couldn't explain how it had got there.

'How come you spend so much time in Accommodation?' I said when he mentioned the air-cleansing powers of the cactus on Stella's desk.

'I look in when I'm passing, that's all.'

'She's pretty then, is she, this Stella?'

'Mmm, not bad. Nice legs.'

It was the legs that did it.

'Shit, JP! Why do you have to go on about her all the time? Stella this, Stella that. Anyone would think you fancied her!'

'You're not jealous are you, Francesca?'

'Of course not. But just shut up about Stella, will you.'

'There's no need to be jealous. It's you I love. You know that.'

The next day he turned up on the doorstep with a single red rose. As usual he refused to come in. We got into his car and drove out into the countryside. His love-making was passionate and I wondered how I could ever have doubted him.

A couple of weeks had passed. I don't remember what the weather was like. It can't have rained, because we walked by the river and there was distance between us. If it had rained, we would have shared an umbrella and been close. But we weren't close, I remember that.

I felt the dread deep in my stomach. There had been a flatness in his voice on the phone, and there was something not right about meeting by the river in broad daylight. So I made it hard for him by talking about Jude's new boyfriend, and the work I was doing for my exams, and a French film I wanted to see. He listened, but he couldn't bring himself to look.

To fill a silence I asked if he'd seen the concert on TV the night before.

'You know I can't stand that modern nonsense,' he said. 'And anyway, I was out.'

I was meant to say 'Out where?', but the words stayed inside my head. I was clinging to what was left of normality, terrified of the truth that buzzed around us, waiting to sting.

We reached the point on the path where it split into two.

'I saw Stella last night,' he said then, still not looking.

There followed a blur of tears, with my asking if he'd slept with her and not believing him when he said he hadn't. I made angry patterns in the gravel with my foot and did all the talking, which didn't seem right. It let him off the hook somehow.

I don't remember the moment we said goodbye. But he crossed the footbridge and I walked home across the Common. It's weird, the things you remember, the things you don't. Like remembering the gravel but not the goodbye.

That evening I stayed in my room, avoiding Jude, hiding away when I needed her most. Shunning the comfort of the bed, I sat on the floor with my knees hugged to my chest and a ball of soggy tissue in my hand. Brel's rich voice flooded into me. JP was there in the music—I could smell him, feel him, hear him. Everything but see him. Even with my eyes closed I couldn't hold on to his face. But the essence of him filled me. The essence of us.

There was no us any more.

I yanked the tape out of the player, grabbed the ribbon, pulled and kept pulling, hoicking it out until the whole lot lay in a tangled heap on the floor. The empty case cracked as it hit the wall.

King's Parade. The ornate white stonework of the Colleges etched against a vivid blue sky. Cyclists weaving their way through throngs of tourists and language school students.

The clock struck twelve. No one takes their lunch break before twelve. From the steps where I sat I had a clear view of the Accommodation Office further down the street. Young, nice legs, blond hair: I would know her when I saw her.

An hour later I was still waiting. The steps were hard on my buttocks and my stomach was hollow with hunger, but I couldn't leave. I had to see the face. I needed something concrete to hate, not just an invented image in my mind.

And then there she was, crossing the road. Strutting along the pavement towards me. Her hair was long and blond, her lips a blast of red. More striking than beautiful. Definitely striking, damn it. I lowered my head, heart pumping and armpits damp.

I smelt Stella's perfume as Stella walked past. I heard Stella's footsteps. I glimpsed Stella's shoes and saw Stella's heels that were higher than any I would wear. And I wanted to scream, chase after her, dig my nails into her peachy skin, leave bruises on her perfect legs. Instead I stayed where I was on the steps, not daring to move, as the legs disappeared up the street.

I heard nothing from him for a week. And nothing for another week. I felt like shit and sat my exams and couldn't think straight and almost didn't care any more. All I cared about was JP, and I couldn't understand how it had happened, how you can be so in love and think you're loved back and then it all goes wrong and crumbles and you crumble with it. The letters I wrote got screwed up and thrown in the bin. I was haunted by the face. By the legs, the shoes, the smell. Strands of another person trapped under my skin.

'There you go love,' said the man who delivered the flowers. 'Somebody loves you.'

The card said *Sorry*. Nothing else. I didn't know whether to laugh or cry. Whether to throw the whole lot in the bin with the screwed up letters and the food I hadn't eaten, or see if I could find a vase big enough to hold them.

Days went by, I don't know how many. There was knock at the door. JP was standing there with his hands in his pockets. I wanted to slam the door on him. I knew I should, but I couldn't.

'How are you?' he said.

'I've been better.' My face was bare of make-up; he hadn't seen me like that before.

To my surprise he came inside and sank into an armchair. I made coffee. My hands trembled as I carried it through.

'That business with Stella,' he said, his gaze resting on the flowers beside the fireplace. 'It was nothing. I only saw her a couple of times, and it was stupid and I regret it and it won't happen again, I promise.' His voice was calm and controlled; he looked across at me. 'So I want to know if you can forgive me. I know it's a lot to ask, Francesca, but I'll never love anyone as much as I love you. I don't want to lose you.'

'You could have thought of that before,' I said, my anger rising. 'Have you any idea what I've been through? I've felt sick, I've hardly been able to eat, I've flunked my exams because of you. It's all a mess, a bloody mess.'

'I'm sorry, Francesca. If I could turn back the clock…'

'But you can't, can you?'

'No, I can't.'

He put down his coffee and came over to where I was sitting. Crouching in front of me, he rested his hands on my knees. His energy shot through me. My head was saying one thing, my body another.

'I'm going to France next week,' he said. 'Come with me.'

The flat is quiet and uncluttered without the party in it. Monique is busy with the twins. She doesn't see the dirty washing being crammed into the machine, which is just as well—Frankie doesn't want anyone eyeing up her greying underwear and faded black t-shirts. Especially not Monique. Her underwear is bound to be pristine silk and satin, designer label. Not M&S cotton and Lycra.

Water hisses through the pipes. Sitting cross-legged on the floor Frankie watches through the porthole as the sea level rises. How far will it go? How long until she drowns?

'*Mais*… What on earth are you doing?' Monique peers into the bathroom. 'Haven't you seen a washing machine before?'

In the kitchen she fills the kettle and offers Frankie a choice of teabags. There are squeals of excitement from the hallway, then one twin charges in, chased by the other. They spin round the table and out again.

'How old are they?'

'Four and a bit. I can't believe how quickly they've grown. They're still my babies though. Sugar?'

'Just milk thanks.'

Monique is studying her face, as she did at the party. Frankie wonders if she's said the wrong thing. If milk is the wrong thing to have. She crosses her arms, uncrosses them again and puts her hands in her pockets. Withdrawing her gaze, Monique pours milk into a mug, a set of thin gold bangles chinking round her wrist.

'We were glad you could join us the other evening. You seemed to get on well with Antoine.'

'He was nice, yes.' Frankie tries to keep her voice neutral.

'That's good. Why don't you sit down?'

Sitting feels better, elbows leaning on the table.

'Simon said there's no one living in Flat Four.'

'No, the flat above us…'

There's a scream. Monique stops and listens. On the next scream she pushes a cake tin towards Frankie and leaves the room.

Frankie prises the lid off the tin. The warm scent of ginger reminds her of home: her mother's gingernut biscuits dunked in tea. This kitchen could feel like home too, she thinks, given time. It's a life in progress, with jars of pasta, flour and rice, a brown pot of *fines herbes,* cookery books, junk mail and assorted parts of a model castle. Last night's leftovers are congealed in a dish on the stove and fridge magnets like giant Smarties hold postcards of holiday places and pictures the kids have done: drawings of people with fruit bowl smiles and long fingers poking out from line-thin arms. There's one labelled '*maman papa*': two stick figures with their heads hovering above their bodies, almost touching, and small circles for mouths. '*Bisous*' has been written beside the mouths. It makes Frankie smile, the way the kiss is somehow separate from the bodies. The way a child sees its parents.

Her eyes rest on a picture on the wall: evening sunlight spilling down the side of a house with blue-framed windows, in front of which a blue-clothed table and a wooden chair sit poised on a shady patio. It's a painting that says space and stillness and calm. Frankie wonders whether it's a pre-abstract work of Monique's or by another artist altogether. She eats a slice of gingerbread and drinks her tea.

The toilet is separate from the bathroom and has no washhand basin, but at least it's a real toilet, one you can sit on. Frankie stays there for longer than she needs to, for as long as she dares. She imagines Antoine aiming into the bowl, but the thought embarrasses her and she shuts it out. The drone of the Xpelair is interrupted by the occasional squeak, as if some small creature is trapped in the blades. On the back of the door is a framed photograph of the twins when they were younger, sitting in a pile of fallen leaves with light and shade on their faces and shining eyes.

As she stands to pull the flush, Frankie pictures Antoine's hand on the lever and wonders what he was thinking of then, at that moment, before he knew that she was leaving.

In the bathroom a hint of cologne mingles with the hot smell of washing powder. She washes her hands, scanning the assortment of splayed toothbrushes on the basin. A nest of dark hairs clogs the plughole, and at eye level a dusty shelf holds an array of perfumes and make-up, plus some unboxed tampons and a hefty block of soap marked *lavande*. She picks up a tube of face cream and reads the expensive formula. Pseudo-science, but it seems to work for Monique.

She's surprised the bathroom is such a mess. That there are hairs in the plughole and dust on the shelf. She doesn't know which towel to dry her hands on.

The washing is turning and churning, one way then the other. A soapy womb with her clothes in it. Frankie crouches and stares into the drum. Clothes pushed, shoved, jostled. Clothes drowning. What does it feel like to drown? What does it feel like when the water closes in, forces out all the air, invades your face, your head, your mouth, pours itself inside you and sticks to your lungs like glue? What did that feel like, Craig?

She closes her eyes and breathes in slowly. Breathes in air, not water. Air, not fire. That was one of Craig's favourite questions: Which would you rather, drown or burn in a fire? She always said drown, but she's not so sure any more.

'Hi Frankie, how's it going?'

Simon has the stirred-up look of someone who's been on the move. The top buttons of his shirt are undone, exposing a triangle of tanned skin.

'I should have been back an hour ago,' he says, 'but I had to cover a lesson.'

Frankie has stood up too quickly. She puts a hand on the wall to steady herself, then she follows Simon through to the kitchen. He smells of the city, of over-used air. Slinging his briefcase down on the table, he takes a bottle of water from the fridge.

'What do you think of my gingerbread then?' he says, spotting the tin.

'You made it? Monique didn't say.'

He wipes his mouth on the back of his hand. 'She hasn't been pestering you, has she?' That confiding tone again.

'How do you mean?'

'She gets these ideas—projects. Tries to get people involved.'

'She didn't mention anything.'

'That's good. Best to steer clear!'

Monique reappears. She and Simon kiss and hug briefly, all in one movement, with the hug as part of the kiss. Not like the child's drawing at all. And Frankie imagines leaning into Antoine, the front of her body in contact with his, all the way down. But she doesn't know if that's going to happen and she's scared to think about it in case it doesn't.

'How have the kids been, love?' Simon asks.

'*Pas mal.* Bruno hit his head on the fireplace, but the brave little soldier will live.'

The boys charge back into the kitchen and fling themselves at Simon's legs, giggling. Simon scoops them up, one in each arm, and carries the laughter out. He threatens to throw them both in the bathtub and the laughter turns to squeals.

'He always over-excites them,' says Monique, her expression wavering between amusement and irritation.

The floor judders as the washing spins in the bathroom. When it's finished Frankie will go back upstairs to her room. It's quiet in her room. There's no noise unless she makes it and nothing happens unless she makes it happen. Sometimes she likes that. Sometimes she doesn't.

A cobweb twitches in the breeze from the window, though there's no sense of one. A fly hops along the wall. There's a crack in the ceiling that goes all the way across, a fault line which may one day split the roof open and leave it gaping like parched earth or wounded skin. All this seen from the bed, lying down, because the chair gets to your back after a while.

The brave little soldier will live. And so will JP. He'll live just to spite her, to prove that he's still in control. But what if he does have some brain damage, some residual amnesia far worse than her own? What if he comes to Paris and Xavier, in a rash moment, sets up a meeting, hoping to jog his memory?

With her eyes fixed on the crack in the ceiling, Frankie plays through the scenario in her head. Imagines turning off the boulevard St-Michel into one of the side streets of the Quartier Latin, walking through wafts of roasting lamb and past shop windows laden with honeyed pastries. It isn't Xavier who's sitting in the café, as she expects, but JP. She stiffens in the doorway.

His gaze rests on her for a moment and she wants to run, but something stops her. A need to know. When she asks if she can sit at his table her voice trembles. His nod is indifferent. Smudges of purple and yellow stain the hollows beneath his eyes, his wrist is in plaster and he may have lost weight—yes, his body is gaunt, wrung dry. She orders a tea. He glances across, scanning her features as if trying to make out something far away. She fumbles in her bag and takes out a book. He asks what she's reading in that voice that's so familiar, that still has its claws in her brain, and she answers him in French, holds her breath. His look remains dispassionate, a mirror reflecting the wrong image. She grips the book and closes her eyes for an instant, like a child who thinks no one can see her like that. When she opens them his gaze is back on the door and he's tapping his fingers on the table. She thinks of how he used to click his biro and chew his nails, of how quietly he used to turn the pages of a book, and then he looks at her again, frowning this time. 'You're Frankie, I suppose.' The first time he's ever called her that. 'Xavier said you'd be here. He says we were married once—were we?' She stares back at him. He's a blank page in front of her. She has the pen and she can write what she likes. Whatever she likes…

The phone rings. Frankie jumps. She doesn't get many calls.
  '*Allô?*'
  'Hi. There's a film I want you to see.'
  She changes her top, rolls on deodorant, designs a face on the bare canvas of her skin: eyes, cheeks, lips. Spraying cologne into the air, she walks through it—perfume should be an accompaniment, not a solo, so her mother used to say. There's no time to wash her hair. All she can do is brush it, flatten it, try to make it look a little longer. She should never have done it. Never have paid to have the reddish-brown locks lying dead on the hairdresser's floor, swept away by a sixteen-year-old in heels

who didn't have a clue and didn't give a damn. Just a job. A bit of money. Some woman's hair.

She wonders whether Antoine will kiss her. Next time she's in this room, she'll know. Taking a final check in the mirror, she wipes off the cheeks and the lips, leaves the eyes. The door of the shower room snaps shut behind her.

His tall dark frame is recognisable from some way off. As she makes her way down the road Frankie feels his eyes on her, the gloss of his gaze, and she wonders how they do it in films—how extras walking past in the background find expressions that say nothing. It's hard to look natural when that's what you're trying to do.

As she draws closer she realises he isn't watching her at all. He's leaning into the wall, mobile phone to his ear. Talking too quietly for her to hear.

He finishes the call and looks up. Their cheeks touch as they kiss.

'Sorry I'm late.'

'No matter.'

'How did you know my number?'

'Ah! A little bird.'

'Monique?'

'What sort of bird do you think she is?'

'The early one that catches the worm, no doubt.'

Antoine guides her into the cinema, his hand on the small of her back.

'You don't have a mobile?' he says, paying for the tickets.

'It died. I haven't got round to replacing it.'

'A free spirit, *hein?*'

She smiles. She can still feel the imprint of his hand on her back.

The film has already started. They follow a blob of torchlight to seats on the end of a row and Antoine presses a coin into the usherette's hand.

The camera pans across a city, taking in a sweep of buildings, warmly toned and gently lit by sunshine. The music is a piano piece she vaguely recognises. It may be one her mother used to play, she's not sure.

'Where is it?' she says into Antoine's ear.

'Marseille.'

A large industrial port in the south, that's all she knows of Marseille. The camera lends it an urban beauty though.

The first part of the film is all to do with Antoine sitting next to her. But then the story takes over. A tale of drug addiction, poverty and despair, but most of all a tale of love. Love breaking through the harshness of lives with little hope. A deep, empowering love.

It's dark when they leave the cinema. Antoine suggests Les Deux Magots, a café on the boulevard St-Germain once frequented by Prévert, Breton, Picasso—names he drops like scraps of paper.

They sip cold lager. Despite being late it's still warm enough to sit outside, and the drinks are expensive, all the more so because they're outside. They've discussed the film and somehow they've ended up talking about depression and what it can do, and he seems to know too much, but she doesn't ask and he doesn't say. 'Depression screws you up,' he says, and they leave it at that.

A man sits down at the table next to them: white shirt, dark skin and gold-rimmed glasses. Packet of Gauloises in his hand. He orders Irish coffee.

'So what films do you like?' says Frankie.

'The old silent movies. Chaplin, Keaton, Laurel and Hardy. You?'

'All those arty French films where nothing much happens. You know, a beautiful woman walks down a seedy backstreet—immaculately dressed, alluring but vulnerable. And some guy draws up on his moped and whisks her away to a building with an echoing staircase and waxed wooden floors. The camera watches from above as they wind their way up.' She pauses as the picture forms in her head. 'He's a sculptor, or maybe a musician, and his flat is sombre but creatively lit, with tall mirrors and heavy furniture. They sit at an open window with a wrought iron balcony, and the camera takes in the view—a street lined with plane trees and the shadows of the trees crawling up the building opposite. Then the lens homes in on his hands, her face, and a fleeting expression that passes between them...' She glances at Antoine and feels herself blush. 'Well that's what seems to happen in French films. The ones I've seen, anyway.'

The man next to them lights a cigarette with a flashy gold lighter. Smoke drifts out past the folded parasols. As Frankie sips her beer, her knees brush Antoine's under the table and she pulls her legs away; he leaves his where they are.

'You don't smoke?' she says. He clicks his tongue, raises his glass to his lips. 'You look the type that would.'

'What type is that then?'

'You know—the dark, mysterious type.'

He catches the glint in her eye and almost smiles. 'Gave up the weed years ago.'

'Dope?'

'Nope. Not any more. Got other drugs now.'

'What, strong stuff you mean?'

'Christ no. Other passions.'

His eyes rest on her, gathering her in. She feels his knees again, almost touching.

'Like what?'

'Like waiting for the sun to rise.'

Frankie leans back in her chair and watches the trail of smoke dispersing into the streetlights. For all she knows he has another woman tucked away somewhere. A string of other women.

'The sun rises, the sun sets,' Antoine goes on, sweeping the hair out of his eyes, 'and there's nothing anyone can do about it. Thank heavens for the sun. It keeps mankind in its place.' The Surrealist vibes in the café have gone to his head. That or the beer. 'It's all predestined, you know. Even the fact we're sitting here now.'

Frankie stares into her glass. Perhaps, after all, what happened with JP was simply meant to be. As was coming to Paris and meeting Antoine. Fate doesn't distinguish between good and bad, they say. That's if you believe in fate.

But thoughts are little more than words, and it isn't always words that matter. She's aware of Antoine's gaze wandering over her body, settling for a moment on her breasts, and she wants to rip off her top and show him, let him see, let him touch.

His hair has fallen back over his eyes.

'Who cuts your hair?'

'Marie-Claude. Big woman, huge tits. I go for the tits, not the hair.'

Wrong question. Stupid question. What size tits has he got her down as?

'Hey,' he says, catching her scowl. 'I cut it myself. Can't you tell?'

She relaxes. 'You missed a bit,' she says, reaching over and taking a curl in her fingers. He doesn't move. She releases the curl and tries to hold his gaze, but her eyes lose their nerve and end up back on the smoke.

'Time to go,' he says.

'You could come back to mine if you like.'

He stands up, slinging his jacket over his shoulder. 'Some other time, perhaps.'

Shit. She wishes she hadn't said that. Wishes he'd said yes, he'd love to.

On the steps of the métro he reaches out and touches her arm.

His eyes meet hers and she glances at his mouth, slightly open, slightly moist.

'*Bonsoir*,' he says, and he leaves.

The white house on the corner, opposite the métro station. Tall grey metal gates and an intercom answering system. You'll find it, said Nathalie; the name is on the letterbox. Monsieur Claude Villet. The old man in the trainers and yellow bobble hat. The blind intellectual who once taught at the Sorbonne and who sees more with his ears than most of us see with our eyes. Nathalie should know: she comes here every week, reads to him, keeps him company.

But she can't make it today. A hospital appointment, she didn't say what for. He's expecting Frankie instead.

'*Oui?*' The voice on the intercom is full of crackle.

'It's Frankie, Monsieur.'

'*Entrez*, Mademoiselle.'

The courtyard is pale and dusty: an oasis of peace cut off from the noise of the street. There's uneven crazy paving, broken Greek-style columns and a shallow birdbath with parched leaves tumbling over the sun-bleached stone. A cat lies stretched in the shade. Sunlight cutting through railings scores stark black lines across the random patterns of the paving.

Frankie doesn't know this place. She hasn't been here before and yet there's something familiar, an atmosphere she has already met, in a dream, perhaps, or another life. A deep calm swells within her, gliding up from her feet to her head: a fleeting sense that everything is perfect, the light and the stone and her being here, somehow meant to be here, fitting in for once with no ragged edges, no rough surfaces. Like the feeling she used to get from the sound of rain, the shape of a wave, dew on grass. And once watching Craig fix the wings on his balsawood plane, she had the feeling then.

The front door is open. Grey paint is peeling off the wood. There are worn-down steps you could trip on if you didn't pay attention and a pair of grubby trainers on the mat.

'Through here, Mademoiselle.'

It's dingy inside and a smell of onion masks something more permanent, like resin or leather. Frankie crosses the hall. In the main room a baby grand sits with its lid propped open and a well-stocked bookcase runs the length of one wall. The sofa is littered with cats.

Monsieur Villet is slouched in a high-backed armchair. He holds out a hand and Frankie shakes it, surprised at the strength of the grip. He's wearing slippers and without the hat his head looks strangely vulnerable.

'*Alors*, Mademoiselle, you are going to give me the pleasure of your pretty little English accent?'

Not English, she thinks, but she doesn't bother to correct him.

The old man hands her a book, stabbed with a thin silver bookmark. Gently pushing a cat to one side, she sits down on the sofa and holds the book up at an angle to catch the light from the window. The only sounds are the sluggish ticking of a clock and the intermittent purring of the cats.

Her heart is thudding as she rushes from the house, down the path and out into the street. Keeps thudding as the gate clangs shut behind her.

It was fine at first, a page or two describing the kitchen, the woman with a passion for expensive jewellery, the man who'd come to check something—the boiler, she thinks. She was coping with the language, even managing to put some expression into her voice. And Monsieur Villet was sitting with his eyes closed and a look of contentment on his face. Poor man, loving literature but unable to read for himself. She wondered how long he'd been blind and if he could read Braille—that would be the answer, surely. Funny how the brain can cope with thoughts at the same time as reading. And then the tone of the story changed, the language changed. The boiler man was sucking the woman's expensive ring, and sucking other things, parts of her body. There were descriptions of naked flesh, then the woman's husband appeared and Frankie thinks he joined in, she's not sure, she was finding it hard to follow, her eyes were flitting down the page to see what came next, and her voice was faltering, trapped in the flow of the story with no alternative but to keep reading. At the end of the paragraph she glanced across at Monsieur Villet and saw the smile on his face and his hand… For a moment she thought she wasn't seeing properly, but that's what he was doing. She stopped reading. Her heart hammered on the back of her throat. 'Keep going, Mademoiselle,' he said, his voice breathy. '*Il regarda son cul…*'' She felt sick. She put down the book and stood up shakily, holding her breath. 'Are you leaving already, Mademoiselle? Won't you stay for a cup of herbal tea?' He seemed to be looking straight at her and she was scared, he was there between her and the door but when she left he didn't try to stop her, he merely laughed. She could still hear him laughing as she made for the gate, and now she's out in the street and all she can hear is the noise of the traffic but his laughter is still in her head.

It's busier than usual in the café. She orders a *coupe maison*, just for the hell of it, and senses all eyes on her as the giant sundae is brought to her table. She licks cream off the end of the cigar-shaped wafer and a smile creeps up on her. Biting into the wafer only makes it worse. She covers her mouth with her hand and imagines herself laughing out loud. It works: it defuses the giggle. Sinking the long-handled spoon into the glass, she looks up. No one is watching.

She can't believe that's what Nathalie does. She could have warned her. Or perhaps he isn't like that with the French girl: no carnality with the smooth white doll.

Madame la Concièrge struts past the window, cut off at the waist, her nose and chin pointed forwards and her firm little breasts sitting cone-shaped beneath her blouse. Frankie can't see the dogs but she knows they're there. Madame is in a hurry as usual, goodness knows what for. Once she has sorted the mail, washed the front step and swept the stairs, the day is her own. She has only the dogs to look after, no one else. As Frankie probes the next flavour of ice cream, she has a vision of the Pekinese vying with the cats for space on the sofa, with Madame sitting primly amongst them, book in hand, and Monsieur Villet asking her to skip to page forty-two. Her stomach tightens as she fights off another giggle.

Her clothes feel grubby. She changes her top and hangs the old one on the window latch to air. Standing on the table, she brushes cobwebs off the ceiling with a rolled up newspaper. She eats a few black olives to counteract the sweetness of the ice cream. Then she sits on the bed and checks her e-mail:

jp didn't make it, frankie. there were complications and he died earlier today. now they're saying he'd been drinking—was way over the limit, *putain d'imbécile*. i'll let you know about the funeral.
    xavier

Sign out. Sign out completely. Disconnect.

She stares at the screen. Stares at the clouds in the summer-blue sky. Stares as the red bricks career into action, twisting, spinning, turning, the ceiling replacing the floor, the floor the ceiling, passages trapping, tricking, dead-ending...

She doesn't know how long she sits there. Doesn't know how many dead ends she veers into, swerves out of...

*

58

I was late. It was cold. My breath misted the air as I cycled across the Common. He stared at me as I crept in at the back. Kept looking as I took off my hat and peeled off layers of fleece and wool. I was flushed from the heat of the theatre and from the strength of his gaze. My pen clattered to the floor and I wished I'd stayed in bed.

I headed a page *2ⁿᵈ Yr: French Hist—Prof Mart*. Everyone called him that: Professor Martindale was too much of a mouthful. By the end of the lecture there was an elaborate doodle in the margin of flowers and interlocking triangles. There weren't any notes.

Later, in Sainsbury's, I was looking at yogurts.

'The raspberry ones are good,' said a voice over my shoulder. Prof Mart was standing there with a loaf of bread. I blushed like a school kid who sees her teacher in the street and can't cope with the normality of it. I put two raspberry yogurts in my basket. 'What are you doing now?' he said.

It was one of those old-fashioned teashops that smell of scones and boiled milk. We went to the back, away from the window. The table was round with a lacy white cloth. The sugar bowl had off-white sugar crusted round the edge, but the carnation in the vase was fresh. We ordered coffee and fruitcake. I spent a lot of time tracing my finger round a kidney-shaped stain on the tablecloth. I don't remember everything we talked about, but I do remember what he said about my hat: 'I like the hat, Francesca. It suits you. Not everyone looks good in a hat.' And his expression as he said it, his eyes lingering on my face for longer than felt comfortable.

We went to his house. He wanted to lend me a book on de Gaulle, but I never saw the book. Instead I saw his eyes without glasses and felt his hands on my skin, all over, the weight of his body, the stab of pain as he pushed himself into me. It all seemed too soon, too quick, but I was flattered and I couldn't quite believe it and anyway he wanted me and by then I couldn't stop him.

It happened in the sitting room, on the floor, next to the bookcase.

'I'm known as JP,' he said as he re-buttoned his trousers. 'Short for Jean-Pierre.' It seemed to be his lot in life, being cut down to size.

Later he said that seducing me was out of character. That he wasn't really like that. That he didn't know what came over him.

'I did,' I said, and he laughed.

The following week I was on time for the lecture and I didn't doodle. I sat near the front and watched the way he straightened his notes and smoothed down his thinning hair. Listened to the lilt of his voice. I tried to catch his eye, but he didn't look at me once. To the others in the theatre I was just another student and this was just another lecture. But I knew how Prof Mart smelt close up. I knew the taste of his skin and his mouth. Knew the feel of him inside me.

I hung around at the end. Took time putting away my things, fumbling with my coat. Made sure I was the last one there.

We walked by the river, a safe distance apart. Leaves were rotting on the pathway and a light breeze was stroking the water. He gave me a potted history of his life: French mother, English stepfather, half-brother called Xavier, all bilingual and living in France. He'd been a student at Cambridge and had got the lectureship on the strength of a PhD on the Huguenots. He wasn't allowed to date undergraduates—it was strictly against the rules. I knew what was coming next: *Last week was a mistake. I'm sorry.*

His bed was warm. Our clothes lay strewn on the floor. He slept with his arm slung across my waist.

He said we should go for a drink, that he knew a place off King's Parade where students seldom went. It was a cosy bar with photographs of rowing boats on the walls and a low beam in the centre marked *Duck or Grouse*. I studied the photographs while JP got the drinks. 'Orange juice?' I said when he came back to the table. 'I don't drink,' he said. I sipped my cider and we shared a packet of cheese and onion crisps. There were small cracks at the corners of his mouth. His nails were bitten short and he wore a chunky signet ring on his little finger—details I had a thirst for. He wanted to know where I'd been hiding, how he hadn't come across me before. I was different, he said; I had an earnest expression that he found attractive. Our feet touched under the table. Each time the door swung open we pulled them in, just in case. Our guilt must have stood out a mile.

But for me it wasn't guilt, it was excitement. Everything around me was vivid: the sheen on the table, the biting sweetness of the cider, the fug of beer and tobacco. This man made me feel different. He was clever and he was twice my age and he'd picked me out from the crowd. The guy I'd gone out with in First Year— my first real boyfriend— seemed like a schoolboy in comparison.

We stepped out into the street. JP pulled me towards him and wrapped his arm around my shoulders. We hadn't walked like that before and it felt dangerous. Deliciously dangerous.

Sunlight floods her eyelids and prises her eyes open. It's bright, too bright, she must have forgotten to close the shutters. Squinting sideways into the room she sees table legs, chair legs, dust. An empty bottle and a deep red stain on the floor. Her skin feels crumpled, her muscles tight and compressed. She's still in her clothes and her mouth stings with a taste of bad dreams and cheap wine. The laptop is humming by her head. She has no idea what the time is.

Bricks. Dead ends. Spinning. A bad choice of screensaver.

She drags herself through to the shower room with one hand on her stomach and the other on her head. Pain pulses behind her eyes and her insides feel dizzy. Why did she drink so much? Why does she always drink so much? She turns on the shower and peels off her clothes, waiting for the water to run warm. Then she remembers to lock the door. It's not like her to forget.

The mirror steams up. She wipes a squeaky hand across it. What a sight. Her face is slipping, all the bits are dragging downwards, even the blood has packed it in. The eyes are hollow: sunken holes on a sagging background. The hair is raffia stuck on with glue.

You were pretty when I first met you.

She's still pretty. Sometimes.

In the shower she closes her eyes and feels the rush of warm water on her skin. Squeezes gel into her hand and strokes it over her body. Breathes in the sandalwood steam. Her hair falls lank and heavy as she plunges her head into the spray.

He can't have showers any more. He can't feel water on his skin. He can't glide soap down his chest, under his arms, over his buttocks. It's what she used to wish for and now it's happened.

I love you, Francesca. Don't leave me.

She slides her fingers back through her hairline and traces the Y-shaped scar on her scalp: rough to the touch, healed but still defiant. She fell, that's what he told her, and knocked her head. But the day remains a blur. All she remembers are the bright lights of the hospital, the bunch of flowers, the relentless storm of pain in her head.

She grasps her scalp in both hands and rocks it back and forth, loosening the tension from her skull. The story she tells herself, about her life, has changed. All she sees now is a coil of time with no clear beginning or end. A random allocation of days in which she drifts, disconnected, a figment of her own imagination.

She wants to stay in the shower forever. Let the water smooth her flat, strip her down, wash her away until there's nothing left.

Eleven o'clock. An hour to go. She's been working on autopilot, weighing without thinking, saying what has to be said. The canned music has got stuck in the sticky web of her brain. She can't shake it out. But at least it holds her here, in this workplace, where she knows what to do and she does it.

Just as well Monsieur Villet hasn't been in today, that he hasn't run out of cat food.

There's a break in the flow of customers. Frankie wanders across and reads the packets in the nearest aisle: *Galettes St Michel, Cœurs aux Noisettes, Langues de Chats, Sablés d'Or*—a gallery of edible poetry. One packet of *Tuiles aux Amandes* is torn. Slipping a finger into the tear, she slides out a biscuit and pops it in her mouth.

Nathalie is wiping down the cheese counter. Her movements are stiff: she bends from the waist with her legs and back straight. Frankie wonders where the hole is for the key that winds her up. She imagines her at Monsieur Villet's, sitting on his cat-strewn sofa in her white cap and apron, book in hand. Tries to picture it, but can't.

Pushing her hair back under her cap, Nathalie stops wiping for a moment, looks across and smiles. She's even prettier when she smiles.

You should keep your mouth shut when you smile.

Frankie pops a couple more biscuits in her mouth. Well they can't sell them, can they? They'll only go stale.

You'll soon be past your sell-by date.

That happens sometimes. Things go stale and don't work anymore.

A woman appears, two kids in tow, her body taut with tension. One child is in the trolley, screaming her head off, the other is loose on the floor. The loose one charges past the cheese counter and disappears down an aisle, narrowly missing a free-standing display of *biscottes*. Frankie wishes he'd knocked them over. It would have given her something to do.

They're only small, these biscuits, and can't be that fattening. The packet is nearly empty. It must be a sackable offence, stealing food from the shop, but right now she doesn't care. There are worse crimes than this.

She should be feeling something. She should be crying. She should have taken the day off work. Instead of which, here she is eating biscuits to pass the time.

She heard he started drinking, soon after she left. His lectures became crowd-pullers, the theatre packed with students as he struggled to remain upright and make sense of his notes. Rumour had it he'd been cautioned and threatened with redundancy. And now he's dead. If it hadn't been for her. If she hadn't left him…

There's a refreshing coolness in the air. The *tabac*, the grocer's and the bookshop are all closed for lunch. Frankie passes the Café des Sports, tracked by the eyes of the kerbside drinkers. Round the corner is a street like so many others: cars parked bumper to bumper and a solid row of apartment blocks on either side. A dog is sniffing in the gutter, otherwise the place is deserted. People have retreated to their designated spaces and are taking their siestas in chairs, on sofas, on beds.

How do they dare close their eyes? What makes them so confident they'll wake?

As a child sleep troubled me sometimes. I couldn't understand the nothingness that filled the spaces between my dreams. Some nights, when the wind was howling against the window and the sky was emptying itself of all its rain, I lay in bed and was scared to let go of the day. I thought the weather was angry, that it would whisk me away in the night and dump me in some distant place, a place I couldn't get back from. So I would lie there with my eyes open, clinging to Sophie and Clementine and asking God to keep me safe. Not knowing what else to do.

The same thing happened once in Gairloch, the last time we were there. A storm raged all night and I slept fitfully. When I woke the next morning it was the wind that had died, not me, and I ran out into the rain and threw back my head and tried to catch the water on my tongue.

I remember the taste of salt in the air that day, and the bitter smell of the sea. And how I went to my rock, close to the waves, and watched them lapping, heard them crashing, felt the spray on my face, the breeze in my hair, let the sounds fill my head with the cries of the seagulls, felt alive like that.

I spent the rest of the day on the beach, collecting shells and chasing crabs, while you and Dad went fishing with Dougie in his boat. I looked out for you from my rock, Craig, but I didn't see you: you must have gone the other way, north of Gairloch. You did that sometimes.

The wind picked up again and the waves were high. When a helicopter circled overhead I waved and thought of you—you loved anything that flew. They must have had a view of the whole sea from up there, and half the land as well. Then a cloud blocked the sun and the air turned chilly. With my pockets crammed with shells I made my way back up the beach, past the phone box and down the track. I could see that the door was closed and I thought they must be out, but they weren't. They were sitting at the table. Dad had a blanket round his shoulders and Mum's face was limp and grey. The silence in the room was heavy, so heavy I could feel it press into me.

'Your brother went to sea and he won't be coming back,' said our father. His eyes were on the window when he said it.

No one said dead, no one said drowned. All I knew was that you'd gone, taking with you your whistling and all hope of laughter. I was an only child now. And I could tell by the way they didn't look at me that I wasn't meant to be there. A son was more use than a daughter. The wrong one had come home.

Later I heard crying behind their bedroom door. But when I went downstairs Mum was there, in the kitchen, and I didn't understand. So I went to my rock, and I sat there, and I watched the waves rising, curling, tumbling. I saw the sunlight caught as they belly-flopped forwards, the fragments of rainbows trapped in the spray. And I threw stones into the sea, the biggest I could find, huge stones that made the water thrash and shout. I threw the stones so hard they broke the waves in two.

We drove back to Edinburgh with three people in the car and four bags in the boot. The house was cold and empty. Your football boots were lying in the doorway, where you'd left them, covered in mud. We had supper as usual in the kitchen. No one spoke. I ran my finger along the rough patch on the side of the table, digging my nail in, scoring it deeper. The skin on our parents' faces moved like rubber as they ate, mouths stretched across chaotic teeth, eyes like marbles in soft pouches. I couldn't tell what the faces were saying. The more I looked, the less I saw. They could be anyone, these people: witches in disguise, aliens posing as parents. And I was angry. Angry with you for leaving me on my own with them.

I was scared again that night and couldn't sleep. Mum couldn't sleep either: she was downstairs playing the piano, with sighing gaps between the chords. She stopped before the end of the piece— just petered out and stopped. When I looked the next morning, *Clair de Lune* by Debussy was propped open on the piano with *morendo jusqu'à la fin* underlined on the last page. Inside the front door, where your football boots had been, there were rings of dried mud.

The pedestrian light flashes green. Frankie crosses, turns right and right again, expecting to rejoin the main road. Instead she ends up in a cul-de-sac and has to retrace her steps. There's a bin by the side of the pavement, overflowing with empty bottles: wine, whisky, pastis. It smells like a pub. That's what JP must have smelt like when he drove his car off the road. If he left blood on the ground, you could have set it alight with a match. And the blood on her hands must reek of alcohol too. But all she can smell is the earth from the vegetables trapped under her nails. That and a hint of almond.

Back at the flats, she finds Antoine sitting at the top of the stairs with his long dark legs splayed out. She tries to stay calm, hopes her face doesn't look too flushed. Wonders who let him in.

She makes him coffee and offers him biscuits. She doesn't have any sugar. He says he doesn't mind, but she suspects that isn't true. He lies diagonally across the bed with his jacket beside him and his feet hanging over the edge. The fact that he's lying down is seductive, as she's sure he knows. She pushes away clothes and sits on the chair. JP had small feet for a man—that's what she finds herself thinking.

'No space to spin a cat in here,' says Antoine, scanning the room. Frankie smiles at the mistake, but says nothing.

He eats a biscuit and leafs through her sketchbook.

'This one's not bad.' It's the kitchen in Covent Garden: pots and pans stacked in the sink, a bottle of Fairy Liquid, a half-peeled avocado on the draining board. Done in lines of fine black ink filled in with watercolour. The paper is too thin for the paint and has buckled. She takes 'not bad' as a compliment.

'What's it called?'

'I don't do titles.'

'You should.' He holds the picture at arm's length. 'Titles can add an extra dimension, get people thinking. Magritte used them all the time, you know, to create a sense of confrontation—things not being as they seem, logic defied, everyday objects displayed in unexpected contexts. The usual perceptions of the viewer were turned inside out, hidden meanings revealed, and the titles were an intrinsic part of that.'

'So that's what Monique meant, when she said not to get you started on Surrealism!'

'People call it pretentious crap, but it's no more pretentious than modern society. In fact if anything, it's a lot more relevant.' There's no smile. 'Magritte was a thinker, not a painter. People forget that.'

Frankie glances down at the picture. 'How about... *This is not an Avocado?*'

'Been done before.'

'That's the point!'

Still no smile. He takes a pen from his pocket, writes something in the bottom right-hand corner of the page and closes the book.

'Where do you live?' she says.

'A flat. Rented.'

'Wouldn't you prefer somewhere of your own?'

'There's more freedom, renting. You're not trapped between walls made of money. And anyway, a house is only a place to put stuff, somewhere to eat and sleep. I can do that anywhere.'

She's got more than she was expecting, but she still can't picture where he lives. Suspicions of a Stella re-surface.

'You live alone then?'

'Sure.' He pulls himself up off the bed and stands at the window. 'I like my own space, you know. And families—they fuck you up.'

That's been done before too, she thinks.

'As for marriage,' he goes on, 'that's the ultimate trap, *hein*?'

The tears come from nowhere, catching her off her guard. She grabs a tissue and hides her face. He comes over and kneels beside her. Folds his arms around her. Her body is tense, resisting. But his arms stay around her and she tells herself it's Antoine who is holding her, that he's not going to hurt her. She buries her face in his shirt and smells his skin, its spicy scent. With him holding her, not hurting her, she starts to feel safe and protected, and gradually her tears smooth away. And slowly, very slowly, so slowly she hardly notices, he begins to stroke her hair. Just one small area, behind her ear. Then his fingers brush her cheek, her neck. As his hold on her loosens, she turns towards him and feels the warmth of his breath on her face, and... *you'll never find another man...* they move to the bed. He pulls her t-shirt up over her head, unclips her bra, and his hands touch her chest, her breasts, his fingers talking to her skin while she can taste his mouth… *no other man will want you…* his tongue. He rummages in his pocket and pulls something out, and he's fiddling with the packet, tearing it open as she lies there, ready, waiting… *you're not a natural, are you, when it comes to sex?…* and then she's crying again, sitting up, hugging her knees to her chest.

'I'm sorry,' she says.

He's hurt, annoyed, surprised, she doesn't know which. He turns away. She reaches out to touch his back but her hand stops short. There's a twang of rubber, then he fastens his trousers, picks up his jacket and leaves the room.

Frankie slumps back onto the bed. His smell is on the pillow. It's the middle of the afternoon and the room is filled with light, but somehow she falls asleep.

I wake with him beside me. My face nuzzles into his breath, his warm skin. It's nice to wake with you, I say. He kisses me once, twice, again. I melt into him, feel my edges blur, defined not by space but by wanting him. He kisses me more, kisses more of me, wraps himself around me, breathing hard, caressing my body with his eyes.

Shh, I say, don't let my parents hear. A vague awareness of something amiss. My parents? What are we doing in my parents' house? I'm an adult, damn it. I can do what I like, see who I like. But my parents mustn't know, they mustn't hear.

It's all right, JP says. We can make as much noise as we like.

I don't have a double bed like this in my parents' house. The bedroom door is on the other side. What are we doing here? Why do the sheets smell of alcohol? Why is JP lying on top of me now, heavy, cold, not moving?

It's still light and she's alone in the room. Another postcard has appeared under the door. On the back is the printed title: *Le plaisir/Pleasure, 1927, René Magritte*. No message. She turns the card over. A girl in a brown dress trimmed with lace is standing in front of a tree. There are birds in the tree. The girl has a bird in her hands and she's sinking her teeth into it. Her fingers are dripping with its blood.

PART TWO

Les amants/ The Lovers

There's no shade on the motorway, nothing between sun and tarmac. The heat in the car is stifling. Opening the windows doesn't help: it lets in more hot air and the noise makes conversation difficult. Not opening the windows isn't an option however. As usual he's driving too fast, but for once she doesn't mind. She just wants to get there, get out of this heat.

It was a clever move on Xavier's part, turning up unannounced, not giving her time to think.

'Grab a few things,' he said. 'We can leave straight away.'

'When is it?'

'Saturday. But we should go down today, spend a few days with my parents.'

'Won't I be in the way?'

'Of course not. You are—were—his wife, don't forget.' How could she forget? 'You'll need something black.' He caught her eye and she smiled: the black was a fait accompli, after all.

Xavier pulls out, overtaking a red Clio and a Norbert lorry. 'So how are you finding Paris?' he says, raising his voice above the noise of the road.

'It's fine. I've met a few people, got my bearings, more or less.'

'Good. We should have got together before now, but I've had stuff going on, things to deal with.'

'Don't worry.'

'And the job?'

'The job…' She leans forwards to let the air circulate, but to no avail: her t-shirt still sticks to her back.

'You don't have to pretend you're enjoying it. It's only a stop-gap till you find something better.'

'Can't say it's riveting, but a job's a job.'

'Don't I know it! I'd swap my desk for a field any day. Buy a few goats and eke a living out of the land, far from the madding crowd.'

'I can't see you as a lonely goat-herd, somehow.'

'No?' He attempts a quick yodel and pulls a face. 'Ah well, looks like the tax office is stuck with me.'

They speed along in the middle lane, passing air-conditioned cars with their windows firmly closed. Frankie's mind is cluttered with images: a hillside of goats, Antoine's legs, rows of apples, cats on a sofa. Everything except the fact that JP is dead. She can't seem to hold onto that—she knows it's there, but it keeps slipping off the edge of her thoughts.

'Is Béatrice coming down later?'

'Doubt it. She's a bit snowed under with work at the moment.' His tone stops her from asking more and she turns her attention to the scenery: flat farmland stretching out in all directions. France's arable core. A road sign announces the next *Aire*: toilets, picnic benches, and shade if you're lucky.

The funeral hangs like fog between them.

'You okay?'

She nods. This must be hard for him too.

'I think I've met someone,' she says.

'Oh yeah? Tell me more.'

'He was at Simon's the other night—that's my neighbour two floors below. We got chatting.'

'Don't waste much time, do you?'

'It wasn't like that!'

'No? Bet you wished it was, though.'

'Look, he's an interesting guy, okay? He took me into Paris, we did the river, the Musée d'Orsay, Montmartre. All very cultural.'

'Then what? Sex on a bateau mouche?'

'Xavier!'

'Sorry. It's the cultural bit that doesn't ring true. Name?'

'Antoine.' Saying it makes her stomach tremble slightly.

'So what does he do, this Antoine?'

'I'm not sure. Something artistic, I think.'

'That could cover a multitude of sins.'

'I know, but...'

'But you're smitten, so you really don't care what...' A car pulls out in front of them and he slams on the brakes. '*Putain de con!*' Checking his mirror, he drops down a gear and roars out into the outside lane. Frankie grips her seatbelt.

'Slow down, for God's sake!'

'Bloody idiot! Did you see what he did?'

'Slow down, Xavier!'

He eases off the accelerator. She lets go of the seatbelt and decides to trust him. Not that she has much choice.

His hands are hooked over the steering wheel. They're JP's hands, with the same shape of nails. He has the same way of tapping his fingers on tables too, with the double-jointed thumbs sticking out at an angle. And then there's the voice: when the three of them were together and she closed her eyes, she couldn't always tell which of the half-brothers was speaking. The choice of words was all that gave them away.

I was surprised the first time I met Xavier. He was fair, for a start, with blue eyes and thick wavy hair, and he wore his tension on the outside, undisguised, not coiled beneath the surface like JP. But then he was ten years younger than JP and only part-related, so it should have been the similarities that were surprising. The voice I noticed straight away; the hands took longer.

It was late afternoon when we arrived in the built-up area on the outskirts of Paris. JP squeezed the car into a parking space and lifted our bags out of the boot. Tall blocks of flats enclosed a square of anaemic-looking grass, in the centre of which stood a single tree. The August heat rebounded off every surface, as if the concrete had soaked up as much as it could and was spitting out the excess. When JP pressed the buzzer labelled Martindale nerves played in my stomach.

Xavier held his cigarette to one side and smiled when JP introduced us—a wider smile than any JP ever risked. He kissed me on both cheeks as if I was already part of the family and my stomach calmed. Call me Frankie, I said, and he did, despite JP's protests. He produced bowls of olives with herbs and thin slices of *saucisson*— a little *amuse-gueule*, he said in his JP-like voice. We ate with our fingers and for once JP didn't complain. Then Xavier fetched his car from the underground garages and drove us into Paris.

I sat in the front and clung to the seatbelt as we manœuvred through traffic on the *périférique*, weaving erratically in and out of lanes. A silver Mercedes undertook on our right and there was a shaking of fists, a klaxoning of klaxons, and Xavier let rip some vocabulary that I wasn't familiar with. Then he carried on chatting to JP in the back, glancing over his shoulder as if nothing had happened. He's driven this road a thousand times before, I told myself, and he hasn't killed anyone yet. Relax.

We came off the ring road at Porte Maillot and drove into the city past the Arc de Triomphe.

'Look back,' Xavier said to me, taking his eyes off the road again. 'Can you see it? The arch?'

Perfectly framed within the Arc de Triomphe, at the far end of the road, was another arch.

'That's La Grande Arche. It's part of La Défense—a giant chessboard of corporate skyscrapers. Kind of other-worldly, futuristic.'

'Nonsense,' said a voice from the back. 'It's an eyesore.'

We swept down the Champs-Elysées. The shiny façades of car showrooms, nightclubs and cafés were visible through the trees that lined the avenue. Expensive-looking people decorated the ample pavements like unwitting actors on a film set.

Having crossed the Seine at the place de la Concorde, Xavier parked the car illegally in a narrow one-way street.

'Is this wise?' said JP. Xavier shrugged.

We walked by the river and ended up in a Greek restaurant in the Quartier Latin —kind of paradoxical, I said, and Xavier laughed. JP was studying the menu and missed the joke. Despite his concerns about indigestion, he admitted grudgingly that the food was good. Meanwhile Xavier got through two baskets of bread, several cigarettes and a bit too much ouzo for someone who was driving, but I was drinking too and after a bit I stopped worrying.

'The thing about ouzo,' said Xavier, 'is that it tastes of Greece, which means sightseeing and sun and too much alcohol.'

'No need to go to Greece for that,' I said.

'Precisely! Why bother when you can get a package holiday on your doorstep? Mind you, package holidays are a bit down-market for you, aren't they, JP?'

'Depends what's in the package,' I said, answering for him.

'Well, with you as part of the deal...' Xavier blew smoke across the table.

'I don't come that cheap, you know!' It was meant as a throwaway comment, but JP decided to catch it: he glowered at me over his moussaka.

When he'd finished eating, Xavier got up and went to the gents.

'What do you think you're doing?' JP's voice was edged like a knife.

'Sorry?'

'Flirting like that with my brother.'

'I'm not flirting, I'm talking.'

'There are ways of talking.'

'Like what? What ways?'

'Ways that say I like you, I fancy you.'

'Don't be ridiculous, I don't fancy your brother!'

'You're sexually aroused. It's embarrassing to watch.'

'For God's sake, JP—that's absurd!'

'He's been seeing someone, you know. A girl called Béatrice. She's away at the moment.'

'So? What difference does that make? And anyway, you can talk!' I drained my glass.

'That was different, Francesca, and you know it.'

'I don't see why. Except I haven't even done anything.'

'You should stop drinking for a start, that's part of the problem. You're ugly when you're drunk. Really ugly.'

'He won't fancy me then, if I'm ugly. Will he?'

I twisted a corner of tablecloth round my finger. JP's face was set with anger across the eyes. He was biting his lower lip.

'Right then,' said Xavier, back from the gents. 'More ouzo?'

'We should go. Francesca's tired from the journey.'

I sat in the back on the way home and didn't say a word.

Xavier made up a *clic-clac* for us in the sitting room. I'd been looking forward to sleeping with JP in Paris, to making love in the city of lovers. But that night it was sex, not love: he screwed me like an animal, with no words, no caresses. I kept my eyes closed while it was happening and opened them when it was finished. The seconds ticked by on the video timer while he slept beside me. I saw more than an hour's worth of seconds.

The *clic-clac* went *clic* and *clac* all night and collapsed in the morning. Xavier thought it was funny. JP didn't.

We left Paris a day earlier than planned. JP was quiet in the car, only breaking the silence to criticise other motorists and give updates on the mileage covered. I wanted to ask him about his parents, what they were like, but his mood wasn't right. So I stayed silent too.

By the time we drew into Beau Soleil my body had stiffened into the shape of the car seat. There were potholes in the driveway, a snarling dog on a chain, red geraniums in earthenware pots. The farmhouse itself gave the impression of having always been there, with flaking stone walls and weathered blue shutters moulded snugly to the windows. JP's stepfather came out to meet us. His handshake was firm and his gaze was steady on my face, but if he was surprised at how young I was, he didn't show it. My own gaze darted from place to place, not knowing where to settle. In the kitchen his mother held my shoulders as she kissed me and I remember being struck by her eyes, by how blue they were. And by the fact that JP seemed no more at ease with his parents than I was with mine.

They stop for petrol. There's still no escape from the heat, with the few patches of shade already taken. Frankie pulls herself out of the car. Her top is drenched in sweat and she's soaked through around the crotch. While Xavier fills the tank, she rummages in her bag and locates a fresh pair of knickers. Scrunching them up tightly, she makes for the toilets. A line of sweat trickles down the back of one leg as she walks.

It's cool in the toilets and the dry knickers feel like heaven. She throws the damp pair in the bin, then she stands at a basin and splashes cold water on her face, runs her wet hands down her arms, dabs the back of her neck and the backs of her knees. The water kills the heat in her skin but evaporates all too quickly.

A plump, pale-faced woman at the basin next to her is doing the same. 'Say show,' she says, fanning the air.

'Ah oui, très chaud.'

Xavier has moved the car away from the pumps and is parked in the full glare of the sun. He's drawing on a cigarette, inhaling deeply as if taking in air before diving under water.

'Thought you'd given up,' she says.

'I had.' He passes her a bottle of Volvic from the icebox in the boot. Heat rises off the tarmac and the front of the car is smeared with dead insects and tiny splatterings of blood. One morning's carnage.

The pale-faced woman from the toilets rejoins her partner: a beer belly on legs sporting short brown socks and sandals. Their car has a GB sticker on the back and a chunky British number plate. And suddenly Frankie wants rain and *EastEnders* and apple crumble. Hogmanay and Milk of Magnesia.

It feels hotter than ever in the car and Xavier smells sharply of tobacco. He puts on a CD, but the noise from the road drowns out the music. The journey seems endless, a relentless surfeit of tarmac and traffic. There's still nothing but blue in the sky.

Their sandwiches are long sections of baguette with more emphasis on the bread than the filling. Xavier eats his one-handed, with his other hand resting casually on the steering wheel—at least they're in the inside lane. Frankie needs both hands for hers.

'Sorry about the crumbs,' she says, brushing her lap.

'No problem. The pigeons will eat them.'

She smiles: JP would never have said that.

The landscape becomes more undulating. Vines score the hillside in rows so regular it's as if a huge, multi-pronged fork has been dragged across the soil. A buzzard circles overhead. Watch out pigeons, Frankie thinks to herself.

They pass a display of vast fibreglass squirls lined up on their sides, all kinks and curves like giant roadside doodles. Incongruous as beached whales.

'Now there's something to aspire to,' says Xavier. 'A pool in the garden.'

'I wish.'

'JP always wanted one. He used to pester my parents about it.'

'But he can't even… couldn't swim.'

'Didn't matter. He wanted to fill it with goldfish.'

'Goldfish?'

Xavier shrugs a 'Why not?' and Frankie finds herself wondering how a little boy who wanted to fill a pool with goldfish turned into JP.

'I had a goldfish once,' she says. 'Won it at a fair. It died before the week was out.'

'Must have been very old.'

'Or very sick.' She remembers digging a hole for it in the garden and marking the spot with a cross made from ice lolly sticks. Her first experience of death.

They pass another display of pools and a place selling garden ornaments.

'Tell me more about this Antoine guy then.'

'There's not much to tell. I've only seen him a couple of times.'

'Do you think something will come of it?'

'Probably not. I think I've blown it already.'

'How come?'

'By being too cautious.'

'You mean, he wanted sex on the first date and you didn't?'

'No! Well sort of, yes, I suppose.'

'You have to throw caution to the wind sometimes,' he says. 'Only living once and all that.'

'It's not always that easy though, is it?'

They both fall silent. There are things she'd like to say to Xavier. Things about JP. Things about her. She'd like to voice a thought that's nagged at her for years. But saying it would be like plunging a red hot poker into ice. And anyway, it's too late now.

It was Graham's birthday. His seventieth. We took an early flight to St-Etienne, hired a car and drove cross-country through fields packed hard with frost. It was strange, being in France in the winter. Wearing jumpers and having the heating on in the car.

The car bumped up the driveway, past the dog on its chain. In the garden the plants looked sparse and brittle, and the geraniums had been taken indoors. Even the farmhouse seemed frozen, its stone walls echoing the pallor of the sky. Graham was waiting in the doorway.

'Good of you to come all this way.' His eyes lingered on me for a moment, as if he was reminding himself of what I looked like. He was still wondering, perhaps, how his son had ended up with someone like me. But he never referred to my age. Neither of them did.

The kitchen was warm and smelt of cooking: a rich steam of sautéed onion, boiling vegetables and roasting meat.

'You made it then, *mes enfants*,' said Colette, rushing towards us with a smile wrinkled over her face. 'Offer them a drink, Graham.'

'What's it to be, Francesca? Wine? Shandy? A Kir?'

I glanced at JP.

'Don't mind him,' said Graham. 'What would you like?'

'A Kir would be great.'

I could feel JP's disapproval, but I made sure I didn't see it. Graham got white wine out of the fridge and a bottle of cassis, while JP made up a *sirop à la menthe* with water. It annoyed me that he couldn't break his rules for once.

When they'd finished their drinks JP and Graham went to fetch our bags from the car. I stayed in the kitchen with Colette, hoping the effects of the cassis weren't too obvious.

'So you've got married?' she said, handing me the bread knife.

'Yes, it all happened so quickly. It's a shame you weren't there.'

'And your parents?'

'They weren't there either.'

'That must have been sad for them.'

'Shall I cut both loaves?'

She nodded. 'You aren't pregnant, are you?'

The room felt suddenly too hot; flakes of bread crust shot across the table. 'No, I'm not.'

'And how long have you known each other?'

'Um… Nearly a year now… Not quite. But as JP said, why wait when you know something's right?'

Colette turned back to the stove and I stood there with the bread knife, wishing she'd had the conversation with JP, not me. Wishing he'd invited them to the wedding and that my parents had been there too. Trying to steady my swimming head.

The neighbours arrived sometime before midday, with children who didn't stay still for long enough to be counted. Xavier was expected too, with Béatrice, but he rang to say they would be late. Something to do with an accident on the motorway.

The table had been extended and took up most of the dining room, along with an assortment of chairs retrieved from various corners of the house. It was laid with Colette's best plates—white ones with cockerels in the centre—and an array of glasses, into which Graham poured more Kir while the children drank *sirop* and stuck their hands into bowls of cashew nuts and *petits gâteaux*. The room throbbed with movement and noise: a commotion with nothing much happening. Just a gathering of people who seemed happy to be there.

Finally we sat down and drank to Graham's health. Then Colette carried in a succession of deep bowls and wide platters: leek soup, *pâté en croûte*, roast beef, mashed potato with gravy, green beans fried with shallots, a selection of cheeses, *tarte aux pommes* and plums from the garden preserved in syrup. Cutlery was kept and plates wiped, not being changed until it came to dessert. A system JP would never have sanctioned at home.

The meal lasted most of the afternoon, with the kids racing back and forth from the table, eating bits here and there and sipping watered-down wine from tumblers. Meanwhile the adults talked, shouting across to no one in particular, tossing in opinions. I felt superfluous. I had nothing to say to these people, no point of contact.

With the meal cleared away and the washing up done, we sank into armchairs and the room fell quiet. Graham closed his eyes and snoozed. Even the dog outside was silent. JP and I sat saying little. There wasn't much to say.

Wheels crackled across the gravel and the dog barked wildly, rattling its chain. Then Xavier came into the room with Béatrice: small and neat, with glasses. I hadn't expected the glasses. Xavier introduced us and we air-kissed politely, cheeks barely touching. Platefuls of leftovers were produced which Xavier attacked with enthusiasm and Béatrice picked at. Refreshed from his snooze, Graham launched into a political debate with one of the neighbours. Surprisingly, JP didn't join in.

The room felt different with Xavier in it.

'Long journey?' I said, opting for English.

'Bloody nightmare. All those idiots going too fast.' He winked, aware of the irony, then filled his mouth with cold potato and green beans. 'You didn't meet Béatrice last summer, did you?'

Hearing her name, Béatrice looked up.

'*T'inquiète pas,*' said Xavier. '*Je révèle tous tes secrets.*'

Béatrice raised an eyebrow and carried on picking at her food.

'She was away on a course,' I said.

'That's right.' Xavier tore into a heel of bread. 'Still haven't mended that *clic-clac*, you know. Can't imagine what the two of you got up to on it!'

I feigned a smile and dropped my gaze, conscious that JP was watching.

Colette pulled up a chair. 'Has JP made you his *soupe à l'oignon* yet, Francesca?'

'I don't think so, no.'

'If he had, you would remember. It's legendary.'

I looked at JP, but he failed to react.

'It always used to give you dreadful indigestion though, didn't it, Graham?' Colette added, interrupting the politics.

'Like father, like son!' said Xavier, laughing.

I laughed too. But my laughter was suddenly loud. It hit a jagged silence with faces set and eyes darting. JP glared at Xavier who looked away, while Graham made some comment about the weather and how it was affecting the garden. Conversation resumed, voices filtering in one by one. But I'd seen. I'd felt. I knew there was something.

That night JP's snoring was clumsy and uneven. I pulled a jumper on over my pyjamas, felt around in the dark for my book and crept downstairs.

The light was on in the kitchen. Xavier was at the table, fully dressed, with a bottle of wine and a cigarette.

'Can't sleep?'

'No.'

He poured me a glass. The rest of the house was silent and I felt like a naughty schoolgirl.

'What are you reading?'

'A Sébastien Japrisot.' I passed him the book. He read the back cover and flicked through the pages.

'They made a film of this, didn't they?'

'I think so, yes.'

'You haven't seen it?'

'JP isn't that keen on the cinema.'

'That doesn't stop you from going, does it?'

'Suppose not. There's a French film club in Cambridge, but…'

Xavier pushed the book back towards me and I thumbed through the pages myself, catching words in isolation: *couloir, soudain, amoureuse.*

'The onion soup,' I said. 'What was that all about?'

'My mother's recipe, but JP used to make it on Sundays. It became a tradition: *la soupe du dimanche.* He spent ages slicing the onions, wouldn't let anyone help.'

'And the indigestion?'

Xavier exhaled slowly and tapped ash into an ashtray that was already full. 'Yeah, me and my big mouth. I should have known better.'

'How come?'

'Well, 'like father, like son'—it's not really appropriate, is it?'

'Because Graham is JP's stepfather? So what?'

'There's a lot of tension between them. Always has been. You must have noticed?'

'I thought Graham was a bit distant, that's all.'

'It goes deeper than that. Some kind of resentment, I suppose. From what I can make out, things were pretty bad between them when JP was little.' He tapped more ash. 'They aren't much better now.'

'Who was JP's real father?'

'Don't know. It's something my mother refuses to talk about.'

'JP's the same. I tried asking him once, but…'

We both sat with our thoughts. I replayed scenes in my head, conversations between JP and Graham. There weren't that many, I realised; the men seemed to have a co-existence that didn't involve much interaction.

Xavier brushed ash off the table with his sleeve. 'We're very different, you know, me and JP. He's a bit of an oddball—not that you need me to tell you that.'

He drained the wine bottle into his glass. The word 'oddball' bounced between us. I'd never thought of JP quite like that.

'I hit him with a rake once,' he went on, grinning. 'I can only have been five or six, but I resented the way he towered over me and could do everything better than me. So one day when he was lying on the grass I tried to sweep him up with the rake. Just to show him. I didn't mean to hurt him—not really—but the rake caught his head and there was so much blood, it scared the shit out of me. Scared him too, I think, looking back. He's never quite forgiven me for that.'

'So *that's* where the missing brain cells went!' I was pulling at a cuticle without realising I was doing it. Xavier reached across and put his hand on mine.

'You'll make it bleed,' he said. And he left his hand there, warm and heavy. 'He doesn't know how lucky he is, you know. Having you.'

I looked up and looked away again. Looked back. His gaze on me was steady. I let my eyes stay there this time, but he took his hand away and the gaze went with it, and whatever might have happened faded back into the night.

They have the road to themselves. The sun is lower in the sky and parts of the road are shaded by trees. It's a relief to be off the motorway.

They haven't spoken for over an hour. Xavier has seemed preoccupied, and Frankie has had thoughts of her own that she wanted to hear. It's hard now to break the silence.

He draws in to the side of the road. 'Won't be a moment.'

The wing mirror shows a distorted image of him relieving himself against a tree. Frankie gulps down more water. The insistent metallic chatter of the cicadas reminds her of a holiday with JP in the Cévennes: sitting on the terrace of the gîte eating goat's cheese and *salade niçoise*, with the unseen cicadas singing loudly all around them. As a child, JP told her, he'd thought the noise came from the sunflowers rattling their seeds, and he'd longed to be tall enough to stretch up and hear the rattle in his ear. It had moved her to hear him talk like that—he seldom mentioned his childhood.

Xavier gets back into the car and tries the CD again. It sounds all right now: a gentle rhythm of guitar laced with the voice of a female singer. He whistles through his teeth as they drive along, tapping out rhythms on the steering wheel. The road ahead shimmers with a mirage of water that fades as they approach.

'I can't believe he's dead,' says Frankie.

'Me neither.'

'Burial or cremation?'

'Burial.'

'And will we see him? You know, the body?'

'He'll be laid out, yes. That's the norm here.'

An image of Craig's body lying face down in the sand flits into her mind. Wrong body though. Not the one this journey is about.

'Have you been to many funerals?' says Xavier.

'Not many, no.'

'It'll be bells and smells, the full works. JP was dead cynical about all that, of course—excuse the pun. Don't suppose he'd been to church for years, had he? He'll be sneering down from above, cursing us for dragging him along against his will!'

She shudders and looks out through the side window. Did he think of her before he died? Did he say her name in his comatose head? Can he see her now?

Wooden signs point up rough tracks: Chantallouette, Le Grand Cerisier, Les Petites Maisons. Names that paint pictures. Further on they pass Le Moulin Rouge and Le Vieux Moulin. The landscape is parched and sun-baked. Houses stand in isolation, square and dusty, with satellite dishes attached to their crumbling walls.

'I probably shouldn't say this,' says Xavier, 'but I wasn't entirely surprised when things didn't work out between you.'

'How come?'

'Well, I could tell things were a bit… strained, perhaps.'

A flush of heat scalds Frankie's face. She looks out at the field of sweetcorn that borders the road: a dense green forest of plants standing straight, taller than a man, with feathery spikes on top and leaves bending like yuccas below. The field opposite is ablaze with sunflowers.

'He had an affair,' she says then, without thinking. 'Some woman called Stella. I never knew for sure if he'd stopped seeing her.'

Xavier says nothing. He should be shocked, ask questions, but he says nothing.

'He didn't tell you, did he?'

Still no response. She chews her lip. It's not like Xavier to go quiet on her.

The storm arrives from nowhere. Dark clouds prowl overhead, blotting out the sun, and then the edgy white light is switched on, flickering and sparking across the sky. The ground trembles and groans. Huge drops of water clatter onto the windscreen like pebbles, dissolving on contact, spreading flat before the wipers can get to them. Xavier slows down the car and speeds up the wipers. 'At least it'll cool the air,' he says. 'Dampen down the dust a bit.' He fumbles in his pocket for a cigarette.

Frankie gazes at the mottled windscreen as smoke fills the car. She opens her window, but rain spikes in and she has to close it again.

It's early evening when they reach the village. The streets are deserted, bar a couple of lads on *mobylettes* who roar restlessly up and down. Sunlight glints in the water left behind by the storm and damp-petalled geraniums, pink and red, spill out of tubs by the roadside. There are the usual shops: *tabac, boulangerie-pâtisserie, pharmacie, assurances, salon de coiffure*. All the French need to compromise their health, remedy the damage, insure against disaster and keep up appearances.

A young woman appears from an alleyway with shopping basket and child. Her dress hugs her slim body; her legs are long and tanned. A shiver of cool air slips over Frankie's skin.

'She won't be there, will she?' Her voice sounds raw; it's a while since she has spoken.

'Who?'

'Stella. At the funeral?'

He almost laughs. 'No, she won't be there.'

'Are you sure?'

'Quite sure.'

'How do you know? I mean, what if she turns up? I couldn't stand that, Xavier.'

'Look…' He drums his thumbs on the steering wheel.

'What?'

'The thing is…' He eases off the accelerator. 'The thing is, Frankie… There is no Stella.'

'How do you mean, no Stella? She wasn't with him in the car, was she? You're not saying…?'

'No. No, she wasn't.'

'What then?'

Xavier looks at her, then draws his eyes away. He's stopped drumming and has slowed the car right down.

'Stella never existed, Frankie. He invented her to make you jealous and then bragged about it to me. There, I've said it, and I swore I'd never tell you.' He's angry—it isn't clear who with.

She can't think straight. She's going back over everything, scoring bits out, writing bits in, and the whole thing is a mess, an illegible scrawl that doesn't make any sense.

'I'm sorry,' says Xavier. 'But you know what JP was like.'

Yes I do, Frankie thinks; I know exactly what he was like. She stares ahead at the road, at the grey asphalt flicking steadily beneath the car.

They turn the final bend that leads to Beau Soleil. The garden will be in flower, the shutters open to the evening light. When the dog barks on its chain Graham will appear at the front door. The father alive and the son dead. The son lying in bits in a wooden box while the father stands there, looking out. The brother and the wife about to haul themselves out of the car and crunch across the gravel to the house. The house where JP is lying in the box, unable to move or make any sound. Unable to explain why he lied, why he made up all that stuff, why he treated her as he did…

'I can't do this, Xavier.'

'Can't do what?'

'Go to Beau Soleil. The funeral. I can't do it.'

'Don't be daft.' A look of panic crosses his face. 'My parents are expecting you.'

He's stopped the car. The cicadas are rattling and there are creaks from the engine as it cools.

In the carriage the air smells tired and used. Sitting opposite is a woman with a child asleep on her knee. The child's mouth is open and there's a hiss in her breath. On the table is a colouring book, a cardigan and the latest *Marie-Claire*. That's all Frankie knows of these people. Only this fragment of their present, which without a past is two-dimensional. They'll sit like this for the rest of the journey, not intruding, and that will be as close as they get. A mere overlapping.

Fields rush past the window in a blur of green and ochre as the train slices its way northwards. For the second time in the space of a year she is leaving JP.

I was taking mugs out of the cupboard when I heard his keys in the door. My skin shrank on my bones: he wasn't due back yet. I glanced at Jude.

'You have told him, haven't you?' she said.

I rubbed at a stain in one of the mugs. It wouldn't budge. Footsteps smacked the kitchen floor.

'What's she doing here? What's going on?'

'I'll wait for you in the car,' said Jude, leaving the room.

'What's going on, Francesca?'

'What does it look like?'

He scanned the shelves and the cardboard box. 'What the hell are you doing?'

I scrunched newspaper round the mugs and jammed them into the box. I was trembling. I felt sick. But it would be all right with Jude waiting outside. Surely it would be all right.

'You can't do this, Francesca.'

I ran upstairs and grabbed a few more things. When I came down he was slumped at the table with his head in his hands. His bald patch looked shiny—an odd thing to notice, but I noticed.

'Why now?' he said, eyes lowered.

'Because if I don't go now...' I took a final mug out of the cupboard.

'But you need me, Francesca. You can't survive without me—you're mentally unstable.'

'So you say.'

He raised his head, looked straight at me. 'I love you, Francesca. Don't leave me.' His voice was thin and there were tears in it.

I pulled a Van Gogh poster off the wall, took recipe books off a shelf, opened a drawer: the tin opener with the white handles was mine, the wooden salad spoons, the knife he called *le couteau qui coupe*—the sharp one he used for potatoes. For the past eight years he'd treated it as if it was his. It wasn't his anymore.

'You'll never find another man,' he said. 'No other man will want you.' There was an edge now to his voice and my hands shook as I folded down the lid of the box. It wasn't only him I didn't trust, it was me.

Jude dragged my suitcase down the path and lifted it into the boot of her car. I followed with the box and came back for a couple of bags. JP appeared in the hallway. Turning my back to him, I left my keys on the hook and pulled the door closed behind me. My guts were knotted but I made damned sure he didn't see me cry.

I went to Jude's and slept on the sofa. He wouldn't have approved of me sleeping like that, on a sofa from the Sally Army, but it wasn't his business any more. I could sleep where I liked. I packed in my job and spent a lot of time on that sofa. Staying in was easier than going out.

He came to the house more than once and knocked on the door. I knew it was him and I was scared. Scared to let him in and scared not to. I locked myself in the bathroom until he gave up, or if Jude was there she opened the door and told him to bloody well fuck off and leave us alone, and no she hadn't seen his goddamn laptop. She didn't seem scared, just angry, which made me feel worse in a way. I told her I'd left him because we'd got bored with each other, that was all. She didn't believe me of course.

Time passed. Days joined up into weeks. I stayed stuck on the sofa, unable to motivate myself. All my energy had been used up on leaving him. On trying to remember what had happened that evening a couple of months earlier when I'd found myself in hospital, on stiffly starched sheets, with pain splintering my head.

One night I couldn't sleep. My back ached and my mind wouldn't rest. There were footsteps outside, on the pavement, and I was convinced they were his. He was peering in through a crack in the curtains, breathing hard on the window. When the wind banged on the door it was his fists I heard. I switched on the radio: '*Viking, Forties, Cromarty...*' The Shipping Forecast reached every dead space in my head, sparking an awareness of others awake, of days started while I lay snugly in bed, waiting for my day to begin. It made me long to be a child again.

When my mother answered the phone I found it hard to speak. I knew my voice would churn up calm waters. Mum managed not to cry and by the end of the call I had agreed to go home.

Nothing had changed. The years had left no mark on the house. Time had simply etched itself in more deeply with the lines more thickly drawn and each ornament, each item of furniture so firmly embedded in its space that it could never be moved. The smell was engrained too: a mixture of dusty upholstery and something faintly medicinal.

Upstairs in my bedroom I found traces of the child I used to be: Sophie and Clementine with their heads on the pillow, plastic expressions intact; an old-style library card, a hair band and a pair of knitted gloves in a drawer; in another drawer, a tin of Caran d'Ache crayons. I opened the tin: a rainbow of thirty colours, all different lengths and with that smell, like sweets in a bag. The row of Swiss chalets was still there too, on the lid, with the snow-covered mountains behind. A place where the sky came in three shades of blue and the grass was four shades of green.

It was my parents whom the years had touched. They shuffled back and forth, their bodies shrunk and shrivelled as if they'd been left out in the rain. An initial fraying of old age that shocked me.

Life carried on as usual; I was expected merely to refill the gap left some ten years earlier when I'd stopped coming home. The first evening, as we sat round the table in the kitchen, the tears in Mum's eyes were the only indication that my being there meant anything at all. They didn't comment on my sullenness or on the fact I'd put on weight. They asked about Cambridge and my job, but not about JP. His name hung unspoken in the air as the conversation turned to the weather and the cost of petrol. I was thankful that they couldn't see the scar on my head.

The following morning it was early when the gusting wind woke me and I heard the murmur of the radio drifting up from below. I went downstairs. My mother was standing in the half-light of the kitchen, in dressing gown and slippers, waiting for the kettle to boil. 'Tea?' she said. 'Bacon?' I sat and watched as she drowned two teabags in the familiar brown pot. 'Your father won't be down for a while yet. He likes to sleep these days.' She got out cups and saucers and put them down in front of me.

'*Forth, Tyne, Dogger, northerly seven to severe gale nine...*' After Craig died, the radio was my refuge in the mornings, a link with the world that was out there. At other times the house was quiet. Only Mum's sighs broke the silence, along with the scraps of conversation over tea. I used to stare at the silent radio on its shelf, imagining all the voices trapped inside and thinking how the box might burst if we didn't let them out. And I spent hours at the table, head bowed, my hand gripping sheets of paper on which intricate designs appeared of boats and shells and fish. Sometimes there were forests of trees packed densely side by side with each leaf shown and the eyes of unknown creatures peering out. The pictures seemed to draw themselves and I liked to think that Craig was watching, that he was guiding me somehow.

I poured the tea. White light spilled out from the fridge. My mother put butter and milk on the table. At the stove she peeled strips of bacon from their plastic and dropped them into sizzling fat. 'He's taken to making bread bins in the garage,' she said. 'I've told him we don't need more than one, but that doesn't stop him.' She flipped the bacon over in the pan. It spat out juices, staining the air with a fiery smell. 'He misses his work, you know, though he won't admit it.'

She brought the bacon to me on a pale green plate that used to be Craig's. I cut slowly through the flesh, felt the grease coat my tongue.

'Kirsty's mum was asking after you,' my mother said then, dropping slices of flabby bread into the toaster. 'She always likes to know how you're doing. And Kirsty's expecting her third in July. I'm sure she'd love to see you.' She added more water to the teapot, stirring in colour with a teaspoon. Behind her, through the window, the sky was a sheet of slate scratched by branches stripped of leaves.

'I'm sorry things didn't work out for you, dear, in Cambridge.' She kept stirring. 'There are some things your father doesn't like to talk about. He just switches them off somehow.'

We sat for a while, with the tea and the toast and the storm that was coming. I dug my nail into the rough patch on the side of the table. For a moment I thought I heard whistling, but it was only the wind in the trees.

*

The street is dark. A van is parked outside the flats, with two wheels on the pavement and its sidelights on. Two men are dragging something out of the back and a third is standing by the door to the flats, holding it open. Frankie puts down her bag and hangs back on the other side of the road. The men heave whatever it is out of the van. As they reach the door, light from a streetlamp falls onto what they're carrying: a long wooden box, tapered at both ends. Her heart lurches. They're bringing his body back to her, dumping it on her doorstep, punishing her for running away...

The door closes on the men and she crosses the road. They don't look right—they're dressed more like workmen than undertakers. What are they doing here at this time of night? Has Madame la Concièrge fallen off her stilettos and suffered a coronary? Has the man on the first floor choked on an olive?

Inside, the men are laughing and joking, saying something about the size of the thing and how many bodies it can take. Frankie creeps up the stairs behind them. They're struggling now, laughing less. When they start heading towards the third floor she feels a stab of panic. Not Simon or Monique, surely? But all is well: they continue climbing. We're running out of options here. For a moment she imagines she might be following her own coffin and she's tempted to call out, tell them to save their efforts for someone more needy. But that might startle them and they'll drop the coffin, which will come crashing down the stairs and send her flying, and she'll fall all the way down and end up dead on the landing below. What a way to go. Snuffed out by the descent of her own coffin. She wonders if it's ever happened.

On the fourth floor the footsteps stop. Round the bend in the stairwell Frankie sees the coffin being manœuvred into Flat

Four. Not lived in as such, just died in. She shrinks back into the shadow. Once the men are inside, she slips past the door and a few moments later, from the top landing, she hears them leave. Their footsteps are light. They've left the coffin in the flat and she's none the wiser.

A corner of postcard is visible under her door.

The picture shows a man and a woman. The man is wearing a jacket and tie, the woman an open-necked top. Their faces are hidden by lengths of plain white material that's draped over their heads and gathered in at the neck, like large headscarves worn back to front, with the shapes of their noses showing through the cloth. *Les amants/ The Lovers*. No message. Smiling to herself, Frankie sticks the card on the back of the door with the others.

There's a stillness in the room. An emptiness. She's been gone for less than twenty-four hours, but already it feels as if the air has gone blank. She'll have to start again, sketch herself back into the space.

She's tired. She needs a shower but can't be bothered. All she wants to do is sleep.

The piano is playing again somewhere. The air is thick and heavy. The bedclothes are heaped on the floor next to the bed. She tosses and turns with her arms up over her head and her legs apart, trying to let the heat escape. In the end she gets up and leans out of the window. It's as humid outside as it is in the room. She switches on the lamp. With cupped hands she drinks lukewarm water from the tap. To think she actually forgave JP for sleeping with someone who didn't exist. How the hell does that work? It's like being jealous of a cartoon character or falling in love with a ghost.

The shoebox is tied with string and it takes a while to undo the knot. She doesn't know why she's doing this, why she's doing it now—she's always kept the box with her, but she hasn't looked in it for years. She removes the lid and takes out a necklace of cold green beads. A troll dressed in silver foil clothes. Some shells and a stone. A small plastic box of face paints. A bundle of letters. A colour photograph.

Why do people keep old letters? They're only words on paper. And photos are only dots of light and shade. Moments from the past, ironed flat and frozen.

The photograph was taken on one of those disposable cameras made of cardboard, with twelve exposures and a flash. When Kirsty lent it to me, the day after my fifteenth birthday, there was only one shot left. I held it to my eye, trying to choose which framed segment of the present to capture. And it felt strange, because at fifteen I was older than you would ever be. The photo would be a record of a place you'd never been, which is why I chose carefully, my eye pressed up against the viewfinder and my finger tense on the shutter release, hardly daring to squeeze it in case the moment wasn't right. A single chance to show you what you were missing.

In the picture our parents are sitting together at the kitchen table, but they don't look together, they look separate. There's something of Sophie and Clementine about them: Mum is smiling, her gaze off to one side; Dad is looking straight into the camera, with red dots in his eyes from the flash and an expression that hints at disapproval. He resents the fact that his daughter has passed a point his son never reached. That's how it felt at the time.

If he'd known I was taking the picture for you, Craig, Dad would have smiled.

She's doodling on a scrap of paper: a doll-like face with round cheeks, exaggerated eyelashes and bulging forehead. Three freckles on each cheek and wavy hair. A smile. Next to it, the outline of a second head, more compact than the first, with scant hair and sunken cheeks. As she starts on the features, her grip on the pencil tightens and the lead presses into the paper, making dents. She draws deep-set eyes, frown lines on the forehead and a mouth that turns down at the corners. *You should be at Beau Soleil,* her father is saying. *You shouldn't have come back to Paris when you did.*

Why didn't he let her go to Craig's funeral then? Where was she that day? What was she doing while the rest of them put on their sombre clothes and sang their hymns and watched the coffin disappearing into the ground?

You were swept away like broken glass. I didn't see your body. I didn't see the coffin with the lid nailed down. I didn't see the hole in the ground that the coffin was lowered into, with you inside it. All I could imagine was blackness. Blackness in the coffin and in the hole. No light. No sound. Nothing.

What if you woke up and no one knew? What if you banged on the wood and no one heard?

I still wake sometimes with screams trapped in my throat, my head crammed with images of what I didn't see: limbs thrashing in the water, eyes mad with panic, the sea spitting out the body and slapping it down on the shore. The body lies face down in the sand, waves licking at the sodden clothes, the grey-blue skin. Then it stands and comes towards me, wet but not drowned, a mask of seaweed clinging to its face. I wait for the mask to fall away, but it never does. The body holds out a hand and I take it, slippery, fish-like, cold. I hate the feel of it but I cling on in case it's you. With my other hand I reach up and tear at the mask, hungry for the face. I dig my nails in, but all that comes away are thin strips, tiny slivers, and underneath there's more, always more, endless strips of dark green slimy rubber. And I'm scared in case the face has been eaten by the sea, the way maggots gorge on rotting flesh. That's when I try to scream, and when I wake and put a hand to my own face to make sure it's still there, that the flesh is still on it.

She places the photograph back in the box with the letters, the shells and the stone, the necklace and the face paints and the troll. A childhood reduced to seven items.

Dear Mum and Dad... It has to be easier than phoning. *Dear Mum and Dad, Just to let you know that JP was in a car accident. He died a few days ago. The funeral's on Saturday, but I'm not planning on going as it's a long way south from here and would be tricky to get to. Hope you're both well. Love, Frankie.*

She'll write the letter in the morning.

She's in bed again, trying to sleep. There's a noise in her ear. A high-pitched whine. She swipes at the air and listens: nothing. It's landed somewhere and is planning its next move, its next foray into the darkness which will just happen to take it straight past her ear. Despite the heat, she pulls the sheet over her legs and covers her head with her arms. As she's about to doze off, the mosquito whines again. Ignore it, she says to herself, just ignore it.

She can't. She gets up and switches on the lamp, straining her ears, searching for a fleck on the wall, book at the ready. She can't see it, can't hear it. If she goes back to bed, it will gleefully remind her of its presence. And if she dares to sleep, it will sink its sting into her, suck her blood, leave behind red spots that will swell and itch for days. Bloody thing.

She puts on the main light and rummages in the cupboard under the sink. The stuff must have been there for years: a rusty tin of paint, old brushes and masking tape, bits of rag, dregs of *eau de Javel* that she supposes she could pour down the toilet. No insect repellent and none of that sticky brown tape you see hanging from ceilings with dead flies on it.

All she can do is leave the lamp on and hope the beast is more interested in light than in her. Pulling the sheet up over her head, she lies sweating in a hot cocoon. She gathers the sheet in around her neck, stretches out a hand and feels the contours of her face through the folds in the fabric. Love is blind and incredibly stuffy—that should be the message on the latest postcard.

She loosens her grip of the sheet and turns away from the light. Her skin tingles. To think it's down there, in the flat below. Only a floor and a ceiling and a few feet of air between her and a coffin. Her and a corpse...

He's lying on the kitchen table at Beau Soleil, his body as pale and naked as a plucked chicken. A cloth covers his face: a square of crisp white linen. And Stella is there too—or is it Nathalie?—leaning over, long blond hair stroking his chest, white-tipped nails scratching lines on his skin. 'Where am I going to cut the bread?' Colette is saying; 'When will I get my table back?' No one seems to notice the blood seeping through the cloth and falling in large, fat drops onto the floor.

She doesn't feel as if she's slept at all. Her head is fuzzy, hung over by tiredness. She checks her arms and legs: no bites.

Cool water flows over her body, washing away the stickiness of the journey and the night. Gel lathers in her hair and strips it of grease. She closes her eyes and feels the water trickle down over her face. She wants to cleanse her thoughts, unclog her brain, get rid of the sludge and see things clearly.

Antoine. Think of Antoine. Think of the card and his voice and the way his leather jacket rubs on his shoulder as he walks. Think of his eyes peering out from beneath the mop of his hair.

Just one moment more, and one more, trying to grasp the feel of the water, nothing but its feel, soothing, caressing...

She steps out of the shower. Moisture sets stiffly on her skin as it meets the dry air. She shivers.

The mirror is clouded with steam and the glass squeaks as she runs a finger over it, drawing a five-pointed star. Neat segments of her face are reflected in the lines. A stained glass image in reverse.

There's a bar of pink soap on the basin. She doesn't have pink soap, hers is white. Nathalie must have moved in opposite after all. She wishes she'd kept her mouth shut now, about the room. Hopes Antoine never meets the pretty, blond-haired doll.

Milk floats in blobs on the surface of her tea. Frankie sniffs the carton and pours what's left down the sink. Pours the tea down after it. Her stomach feels hollow but there's nothing to eat. If she finds another broken packet of biscuits at work, she'll get by. At least yesterday was her day off—there'll be no explaining to do.

She stands at the window with a glass of water. *Les amants/ The Lovers*. Her heart squeezes. She can do this, she tells herself; she can do it.

Days pass. There's no sign of Antoine and no chance meeting with Monsieur Villet. She doesn't talk to Nathalie at work or bump into her on the landing. It's as if the things that happened before she travelled south have vaporised, leaving no trace. Just a residual taste in the mouth.

The shoes appear before the legs: red leather, pointed toes, high heels. The legs that follow are long and muscular, the skirt is short and the t-shirt fits tightly across the ample bust. Pushing her red-haired fringe back off her forehead, the young woman gives Frankie one of those smiles that go no further than the mouth. Her eyebrows are dark and heavy and she's incredibly tall for a woman. If she's a friend of Monique's, they must make an odd-looking couple.

Frankie waits for the girl to pass, then she continues up the stairs. The air gets closer the higher she goes and the steps become steeper, wood replacing the concrete and marble. There's no postcard under her door.

The room is stuffy. She opens the window, but no air comes in.

Her shoes lie abandoned in a corner: it's been too hot recently for anything but sandals. There are creases in the leather where walking has bent them and scuff marks on the toes, the shape of her feet implied by the way the shoes have set like moulded clay. She remembers what her art teacher used to say, about the spaces between objects being as important as the objects themselves, and she tries to see those spaces, learn their shape.

She starts with a rough outline, her pencil trying out different routes and making small adjustments until the shoes slot into place. Then she presses more heavily, committing, letting the picture emerge from the page like a Polaroid photograph. She really should be out there sketching monuments and cafés, balconies and railings. Drawing in public scares her though.

There's knocking from below, sounds of hammering and scraping. Frankie holds her breath and listens. When the noise stops, she opens her door and leans out onto the landing. Nothing. Then a door snaps shut and there are footsteps on the stairs, running down. Someone has just come out of Flat Four. Someone who doesn't live there as such and had a coffin delivered in the middle of the night.

She goes back to the drawing and adds detail: the stitching where the leather joins the sole, the frayed end of a lace. There's still the shading to do, the illusion of three dimensions. It will take time, but she has plenty of that. As she works on the eyelets, she wonders what the point is of trying to recreate the shoes on paper when she has the real thing there in front of her. She's not sure, but she does the drawing anyway.

Later the banging starts again. When she puts her ear to the wall, the noise seems further away but she can hear it more clearly. Hammering of nails into wood, perhaps, a spot of DIY—there's no law against that.

This time she edges down a few steps, growing bolder, leaning round until she can see the landing and part of the door. The light from the landing window doesn't reach far up the stairs and she feels safe there. She steadies her breathing and swallows hard, knowing the step will creak if she shifts her weight.

The banging stops. A moment later the door lock clicks sharply. She holds herself back in the shadow, frozen, not breathing, as Antoine leaves the flat and disappears down the stairs.

There's a knock on the door. Frankie combs her hair hastily with her fingers and smooths down her t-shirt.

Simon is on the landing. A mixture of relief and disappointment slips through her.

'Hi. Come in.' She assumes he won't.

He comes in. 'You're not busy, are you?'

'Not really.'

'I wanted to give you this book the other day, but there was no answer.'

'I was at a funeral. Or on my way to one, anyway.'

He's standing there, with the book.

'Do you want a coffee?'

'Thanks.' He moves further into the room, as if a second door has been opened.

She throws her clothes onto the bed and offers him the chair. 'Sorry it's so hot in here.'

'Not your fault. That's the problem with these *chambres de bonne*: stifling in the summer and freezing in winter.'

While she's making the coffee, he tells her about the book: a Giono he found in the bookcase. 'It must be Monique's. Have you read it?'

'*Les Grands Chemins*? I don't think so.'

'Borrow it then. Keep it, if you like.'

'But if it's Monique's?'

'She won't miss it.' He sounds certain. As if he'll make quite sure of it.

Frankie sits on the edge of the bed with her coffee and it's like being back at University, in First Year, when people came to her room and sat on the bed or the floor. In those days there was free-wheeling conversation, with grand theorising and careless revelations. There's unlikely to be any of that today.

'I'll lend you *Regain* when I've finished.'

'Thanks. I ought to read more, feed my mind. But what with the job and the kids…' He leans on the table and runs his fingers over the keys of her laptop. 'Do you use this much?'

'Yes and no. It depends.'

Taking it was a risk. At the time though, it seemed a fair exchange: the laptop for the jewellery. If he sold the jewellery, he could replace the laptop. But that wasn't the point. The laptop had all his lectures typed into it, all his contacts, all his research. Knowing him he had backups, but still. I took what really mattered to him, what I knew would hurt.

When I got to my parents' I found Xavier's e-mail address and sent him a message. Something bland about the Scottish weather and how I hoped he was enjoying his new job in Paris. I reckoned he'd tell JP that he'd heard from me and that I sounded fine, and I hoped that would hurt as well. Xavier wrote back and that's how it started. Messages exchanged every few days, nothing deep, simply what we'd been doing, little jokes. They kept me going, those e-mails. As time passed, Xavier must have noticed a change in my tone. You sound fed up, he wrote one day. Why don't you come to Paris?

I didn't want to at first. I was scared of being on my own and even more scared of being tracked down by JP. But being at my parents' wasn't working. Each day I felt myself slipping further into a vacuum where I hardly knew who I was any more. So in the end I agreed, on condition that Xavier didn't mention it to his family, and especially not to JP. I want a clean break, I said. No problem, he said.

'May I?' Simon picks up her sketchbook and turns the pages, studying each drawing: Jude on the sofa, the flowers, the cyclist, her mother at the piano. The avocado on the draining board that's labelled *The Pregnant Pause* now in thick black ink. It feels as if he's reading her diary.

'Didn't know you were an artist,' he says. 'You've got talent. You should do something with it.' He thumbs through again from the beginning. 'A colour period and a monochrome. Is that significant?'

She shrugs, shaking off the question.

'So what's the plan then, Frankie? You won't stick the supermarket for long, will you?'

'Didn't I tell you? I'm hoping to go to Art College, if I can get somewhere with my portfolio and sort out my finances. Failing that, I wouldn't mind working in a bookshop, like I did in Cambridge. I loved it, but then… other things got in the way.'

There's a pause when she fears he might ask about the other things, but he doesn't.

'There's that place down the road,' he says. 'You could always try there. As for the art, you should… Well you should talk to Monique about that.' He looks at her, then looks away, fidgeting with his mug. She feels bad that she can't put him at his ease. Usually he's so relaxed. Perhaps he's merely being polite, having the coffee because he knows she doesn't get many visitors.

'So what was this funeral you went to?' he says.

'Just someone I used to know. Only I didn't go in the end—it was all a bit silly.'

'What happened?'

'Road accident.'

'You had an accident?'

'No, he did.'

There's still coffee in her mug, but she gets up anyway and puts more water on to boil. Wipes round the sink with a cloth. She has her back to Simon when she says: 'I saw Antoine coming out of the flat below. He doesn't live there, does he?'

'No one lives there.'

She turns round. 'Who's 'M. Sennet' then? And what was Antoine doing there?'

'There are things about Antoine... Just keep out of his way, Frankie, that's my advice.' He glances at his watch. 'Got to go. I've got classes in an hour.' He leaves the Giono on the table, with the sketchbook and the lukewarm dregs of his coffee.

hi frankie, how's things? hope you got back to paris all right. the last few days have been a bit fraught here at beau soleil. some cousins were meant to be flying in from canada, but their flight was cancelled. my parents have decided to postpone the funeral and the church can't do it for another week, so the body's had to go back to the mortuary. what a fiasco. let me know if you change your mind about coming. mind you, i told my parents you'd broken a leg, so we'd have to find a way round that one...
    xavier

JP will be smirking, damn him, revelling in the fact that everyone's being kept waiting. But the broken leg is a stroke of genius.

She pops down to the *alimentation* round the corner for orange juice, bread and peaches. Comes back with apple juice, bread, peaches, yogurts and dark Poulain chocolate. Antoine is on the pavement outside the flats with a brown leather suitcase. He's unlocking the door. Frankie holds back for a moment, then she walks up to him with the shopping clutched to her chest.

'How come you've got keys, Antoine? What's going on?'

She follows him up the stairs and through the door marked *M. Sennet*. It's cool in the flat, and dark—the shutters must be closed. Antoine puts a hand on her elbow and guides her through.

'Wait here,' he says. His footsteps pad across the wooden floor. As her eyes adjust to the darkness, shapes emerge: bulky objects with no detail. There's a smell that's vaguely chemical, with an edge of spice that reminds her of Antoine.

A light comes on, then another, and another. Spotlights aimed at different parts of the room, stripping the objects bare. In the centre is an old-fashioned gramophone on a table, a hat and coat on a chair and a chaise longue-style couch upholstered in deep red velvet. To the side a vase of flowers sits on a small round table draped with a stiff white cloth. There's a polystyrene boulder framed by red satin curtains and a sleeveless white nightdress on a hanger. Two coffins.

Antoine leaves the suitcase beside the couch and wanders back to where Frankie is standing.

'This is where I work.' There's no hint of apology in his voice.

'I didn't realise. What do you do?'

'Photography. Technical stuff.' His tone suggests that she wouldn't understand. She goes along with that for now.

'But you don't live here?'

'No.'

She puts down her shopping and walks round the room. Large canvases are propped against the walls: a painting of mountains with three heads peering over an intricate railing below; two views of the sea, one with sand and waves and a glow of light on the horizon, the other with ripples and a clear sky above; an unfinished tableau done mainly in black. Along the length of one wall hangs a frieze: a string of disconnected images like a set of giant postcards placed side by side. Looked at more closely the white nightdress has breasts and pubic hair, which makes her vaguely uncomfortable.

'Magritte,' he says. She nods.

The coffins are lying on their sides, the wood thickly varnished and bordered with large metal studs.

'More Magritte?'

'It will be, when it's finished. Cost us a leg and an arm, those things did.'

'An arm and a leg, you mean!'

'Whatever.'

There's a table just within the light, a working table, not posed like the others. More like a props table for a play. On it are lengths of material, rough sketches, paint brushes soaking in turps, a couple of hats, some candles, a pink silk rose, a box of postcards. Frankie sifts through the cards: images of heads and limbs, segments of women's bodies reflected in mirrors, a tuba on fire, the pipe that isn't a pipe. All bizarre and surreal, as if she's stepped into someone else's dream, full of symbols she can't interpret but which somehow she's a part of.

'Stand over here for a moment.' Antoine leads her across to the boulder with the plush red curtains behind it. He manœuvres her gently into position to the side of the boulder and turns her round. The spotlight shines into her eyes. 'Lean on the rock. Like this.' He curls the fingers of her right hand over the edge of the boulder. 'Put your right leg slightly in front of your left.'

She does as he tells her, and as she faces the light with her hand on the boulder she experiences the sensation again, the trance-like state as a wave of calm washes over her and holds her in place, rooting her feet deep into the ground.

Something is being dragged along the floor behind her. One of the backdrops perhaps. When the dragging stops, Antoine reappears and places the pink silk rose in her other hand. He smooths her hair away from her face. Then he retreats into the shadow.

'Perfect,' he says. 'Almost.'

'What's wrong?'

'A few alterations are needed, that's all.' He steps back into the light and stands in front of her, his shirt and chest filling her vision. She closes her eyes. His energy tingles across her face and down her body; his smell is like nutmeg or cinnamon. 'Don't move. Stay exactly as you are.' He takes the rose from her hand and she feels his fingers on her lips, feels them gliding over her chin, down her neck, skimming the surface with a touch so light it's barely there. And when his fingers reach her blouse they press into her chest, coaxing the top button through its hole before moving on, inching down between her breasts, loosening, undoing. She doesn't move. She hardly breathes. Her eyes remain closed as he frees the final button, slips his hands around her back, inside the blouse, and feels for the fastening. When the bra goes slack he slides the straps and the blouse off her shoulders and she straightens her arms to let the garments fall to the floor, and as they fall his hands move down to her waist. He undoes the zip of her skirt and eases the fabric over her hips and down her legs. Then he tucks his fingers into the elastic of her knickers and, stretching them away from her skin, he peels them off too. She lifts one foot at a time as he pulls them free.

He puts the rose back in her hand and curves her fingers back over the edge of the boulder. She hears his breathing. Feels his gaze on her body, caressing each curve, each shadow of the sculpture he has just completed.

'Stay like that,' he says, his voice slipping out of reach. 'Keep your eyes closed.' She stands quite still. For the first time in years she feels no shame in her nakedness.

The intensity of the lighting changes and there's a humming sound in the background. She doesn't know what he's doing, but it feels right to be standing here. He's in control and she trusts him. She stares into the darkness of her eyelids, alert and yet close to sleep. Her skin is singing and her muscles are warm. She's in a shower without water.

The lights dim further. Movement ruffles the air. She senses him near her, sliding in behind her, his spicy scent, and he's kissing the back of her neck, exploring, moving slowly round until he's in front of her again, so close he's almost touching. And when he inches forwards she feels his shirt against her breasts and she quivers. She opens her eyes, and he takes her hand and leads her out of the light and across the room which is dark now, veiled in shadow. He lays her down on the deep red velvet of the couch and his body presses onto hers, his breathing loud and fast and hot, his trousers scraping her thighs as he loosens his belt. She slides her hands under his shirt and clings to him, wanting all of him, every last bit of him as he sinks himself inside her.

The letter consists of local news and a Births and Deaths column. Her eyes skim down the page as she hurries along the road, late for work again. *Do take care love,* her mother has written before signing off. *Paris is an awfully big city.* No mention of JP, but then Frankie never did write to tell them.

She slips the letter back into its envelope and tucks it in her pocket. She doesn't care about the break-in at the newsagent's or the neighbour's heart attack or the weight of Kirsty's latest baby, but it's still a little bit of her mother. A slice of home.

Not so long ago home was Cambridge—a word that had once been no more than a dream in my head. Somewhere very still, very quiet, where the air had no taste and the houses were filled with books and the people were tall and slim. My French teacher insisted that a degree in Modern Languages would enrich my mind. Art wasn't a proper subject, after all, it was more of a hobby—so I was told. 'Cambridge?' said my father when I mentioned it. 'Are you sure?' He poured himself a whisky and sat staring into it. 'Cambridge is a long way away,' said my mother. I knew what they were thinking: it was Craig who had always been the clever one, not me. I simply worked hard.

Months later the three of us sat at the kitchen table with the letter from Clare College in front of us. Mum's excitement was tinged with anxiety; Dad said nothing. He sat drawing cubes on the back of the envelope. For him the success was inappropriate. More a source of bafflement than a cause for celebration.

Nathalie is in the changing room, pinning her hair up. Frankie watches her via the mirror. She has one of those faces you want to study and get a grasp of before conversation gets in the way. A fragile face, with the eyebrows plucked to a thread and a tiny gold stud in one neat, shell-like nostril. Her prettiness is constant—not like Frankie, who is only pretty sometimes.

'Did the stud hurt?'

'*Pas trop.*' Nathalie carries on pinning.

'So you've moved into the room?'

'Which room?'

'The one opposite mine.'

'I haven't moved anywhere yet. I haven't had time.'

Frankie sees her own face relax in the mirror: no live-in rival then for Antoine's attentions. Unless the mystery owner of the pink soap is a stunning blonde as well.

Nathalie adjusts the white cap on her head. A pin falls on the floor and she bends down for it with her straight legs and back. Graceful, but stiff.

'You must have had a lot of practice at that. The cap, I mean.'

Nathalie nods, her lips pursed around the pin. A fine gold chain circles her neck. Frankie puts a hand to her own neck and feels only skin.

'I will get my own place eventually,' Nathalie says out of the side of her mouth.

'Your father won't mind?'

'I'm not so sure about that. He's disabled, which is why I don't get out much.' She slides the pin into her hair, securing the cap.

'I went to Monsieur Villet's,' Frankie says, starting without knowing how she'll finish. 'He's a bit weird, don't you think? It was pretty risqué, the stuff he asked me to read.'

Nathalie has another pin in her mouth and her expression gives nothing away. One of the checkout ladies bustles in. Annoyed at the bad timing, Frankie leaves the mirror to Nathalie. She puts her bag in her locker, along with the half-drunk bottle of Evian she bought on the way here. Thirst hits her like that sometimes and she has to drink. It's as bad as when she craves chocolate. Or sex. She can't remember the last time she craved sex as much as she does now. One bite and she wants more. The whole damned bar.

She zips up her apron, sealing the vertical stripes, and pushes through the doors that lead out into the shop. The canned music sounds inoffensive. In fact she hardly notices it. A buttery smell wafts across from the bakery. She smiles at Madame Taupe as she passes with her trolley. Restocks the trays with Argentine lemons, Thai ginger, mangoes from Senegal and pineapples from the Ivory Coast—a carnival of colour and texture produced by foreign soil.

It's all Antoine's fault. He's stripped her raw, sharpened her, left her aching to be touched. She only has to think of him and lust pumps through her body. If JP could see her now!

The bobble hat moves down the aisle. Frankie cringes, panics. She can't leave the counter unattended. She bends over a tray of shallots. Surely he'll leave her alone, buy his vegetables in tins or at the *alimentation* down the road.

'Mademoiselle?' His voice makes her jump—just as well he can't see. 'A pound of green beans, please.' She can't bring herself to look at him. She weighs the beans and puts them in his trolley, still not looking. *'Et une grosse courgette.'*

Bloody nerve! She has a vision of the hand down the trousers, the smug look of contentment on the face. His laughter echoes in her head and she can hardly bear to touch the courgette. He's doing this on purpose, the pervert. She drops the offending vegetable in a bag and throws it in beside the beans.

'Oh là là, we're not at our best today, are we, Mademoiselle?'

Piss off, she thinks to herself. You can take your courgette and stuff it where the sun doesn't shine, you sad old git. And she looks him in the eye, emboldened suddenly. You should try the real thing, she's thinking. The real thing's much better.

His eyes are fixed on a point just beyond her. As he turns to go, he bumps into a crate of apricots. She has half a mind to put a couple in the bag with the courgette.

Time passes quickly after that. The quiet moments when she has nothing to do are filled by Antoine.

There's a woman who sells flowers on the pavement. Frankie buys a bunch of tulips, an unusual shade of purple, pre-packed in shiny paper with a scalloped edge. She doesn't think much of the paper, but she likes the flowers. No eye contact is offered by the woman as she takes the money, and no words. If you turned her upside down and shook her, numbers would fall out: mental sums of the day's takings with Frankie's euros added on. Frankie wonders what the woman's life is about when she isn't selling tulips.

JP used to buy me flowers: creamy white lilies or pale yellow roses, wrapped in paper. Never the gaudy bouquets in cellophane you get in supermarkets. The flowers were his way of telling me he loved me. I put them on a table in the window and when I needed reminding, I looked at them. Even when the petals were falling or turning brown around the edges, I hated throwing them away.

He gave me jewellery too. Finely-crafted jewellery that must have cost a fortune. Gemstones set in gold and silver to remind me I was precious, that he hadn't meant to hurt his precious girl. He gave them to me nestled in neat little gift bags dressed with ringlets of shiny ribbon. In the eight years we were married I built up quite a collection. When I left him, I left the diamond engagement ring and the other jewellery too, to remind him how precious I had been. Just in case he forgot. A few days later I threw my wedding ring into the Cam. It had suddenly looked ugly on my finger. The river swallowed it whole, like a pill. The only bit of jewellery I have now is the jade necklace my mother gave me when I was little and which used to belong to my grandmother. I keep it in the box with the letters, but I never wear it. I'm not really a jewellery person.

A voice calls across the road. Monique waits for a break in the traffic and then slips between a couple of mopeds and glides towards Frankie. '*Un café?*'

Frankie's heart sags: she'd wanted to go straight home and put the flowers in water. She was hoping Antoine might call.

They sit outside the café, Frankie in the shade of a parasol, Monique in full sunlight. Her clothes have a way of sitting down with her, rearranging themselves naturally, with no effort. Frankie feels curiously misshapen beside her. She lays the tulips on the table, hoping they won't wilt in the heat.

'Nice flowers. From an admirer?'

Before Frankie can answer, the barman flicks his head in their direction. They order lagers. Funny sort of coffee, but still.

Monique closes her eyes and tilts her face towards the sun. Individually her features are nothing special, and yet together they look exactly right—like the colours in her paintings. And her skin is unblemished, the make-up applied in such a way as to enhance without distracting. Frankie wonders where women like her learn the skill.

The beer arrives in goblets with doilies slipped around their stems and condensation clinging to the glass. Monique sips daintily, while Frankie struggles to find a way through the thick head of froth. With the chairs facing out into the street there's no pretence, no sideways glances at passers-by. This is full-on staring and Monique has it down to a fine art.

'Been working?' she says, scrutinizing a pair of passing shoes.

'This morning, yes.'

'And have you seen Antoine?'

'Um…' Frankie falters, caught off her guard. 'I saw him at the weekend. He showed me where he works.'

'The studio? He showed you?' Monique stops pavement-watching and watches Frankie instead.

'I'd been wondering what went on in there.'

'You don't mind, then? We thought you might not approve.'

Frankie isn't sure what she means. Perhaps she's misunderstood. Her French isn't perfect, after all.

'It was a bit unexpected,' she says. 'But I'm not complaining!'

'That's good.' Monique's gaze darts back to the pavement and another pair of shoes.

Frankie wants to know more. She wants to ask about the flat and the lights and the props, what they're for, what Antoine does. But she's wary. Reluctant to admit how little she knows and fearful that Monique may judge her.

'He's had his eye on you since the party,' Monique says, unprompted. 'Your face was perfect, you see, but I told him not to rush things. I didn't want him scaring you off.'

Frankie wonders what her face has got to do with Monique. 'You use the studio too then?'

'*Mais oui*. Didn't he say? I paint the backdrops and help set up the scenes. It's a challenge, getting the detail right. Some of our clients are very particular. They notice any inaccuracies.'

'Right…' She's none the wiser. 'And the coffins?'

'Don't worry, we won't make you do anything you don't want to. Anyway, it's not ready yet. The carpenter's having problems with the third one. Tricky shape to get right.' She drinks her beer, gold bangles slipping up her arm. 'He's an interesting guy, Antoine. I've known him for years. Not that Simon would agree. He thinks he's trouble, which is why he's been so protective of you, didn't want you to get involved. He thought you weren't the type.'

'What type's that?'

'The Flat Four type—that's what we call it!' She laughs, and then her expression changes. 'I'm surprised he didn't tell me.' Annoyance has crept into her voice.

'Simon?'

'Antoine. Usually he keeps me informed.'

She gets out her purse and puts it on the table. 'At least he has good taste,' she says. Frankie doesn't know if she's referring to the flowers or to her.

The tulips are struggling: their heads are bowed and their leaves have gone limp. She put them in a jug as soon as she got back, cutting the stems to make them fit, but it was too late perhaps.

Antoine has her number. He said he'll ring.

She tidies the room. Puffs up the pillow, shakes out the sheets, folds her clothes. Sweeps up crumbs from the floor.

She eats a peach and two squares of chocolate.

She starts a letter to her mother, but can't get past the first sentence.

She doodles on the back of an envelope.

She goes downstairs and listens at the door of Flat Four, leaving her own door open in case the phone rings. She does this several times. She hears nothing.

She eats a few more squares of chocolate.

She draws the jug, with its pattern of noughts and crosses and a tulip hanging over the side.

Three tulips later and she can't bear the waiting. She wants to be with Antoine. That's what JP said: *I don't want to see you, Francesca, I want to be with you. Come and live with me*, he said.

Jude watched as we carried boxes down the stairs and out of the house. She watched as I made a final check of each room, retrieving shower gel from the bathroom and a pair of slippers from under the sofa. She hugged me, then she stood in the doorway as I got into JP's car, but she didn't say anything. She didn't wave as the car drew away.

She thought I was making a mistake, of course, dropping out of university and moving in with JP after only a few months. But she hardly knew him. She didn't know how good we were together. The Stella business had tainted her views, left her with the wrong impression. You could almost have thought she was jealous, if you didn't know her.

I felt awkward going into JP's house with all my possessions, filling up space that was empty before, so I tried to make myself small and not get in the way. JP had cleared a few drawers and pushed his jackets up to one end of the wardrobe, making room for some of my clothes. The rest had to go to Oxfam, he said. So I spent a couple of hours filling a bin liner, then emptying it again. In the end I just had to do it, throw some stuff in—he couldn't believe how long it was taking. I arranged my toiletries on a shelf in the bathroom, where he showed me, and hung my coats in the left-hand side of the coat cupboard. My files and lecture notes took over a table in the spare room, which he said I could use as a desk, although I didn't think I'd need it: no more toiling over essays and translations. There wasn't room in his bookcase for my books, so most of them had to stay packed. I slid my shoebox of old letters and keepsakes under the bed.

The bed. I looked at it and my stomach tightened. Was that where he and Stella had made love? In this room, on that bed? Or perhaps it had happened in his car, or in her office, or at her house? I'd asked him once, but he'd refused to discuss it. He wouldn't even admit that he had slept with her.

It was over. I had to forget. It was me he loved. This was the bed we were going to sleep in together, him on the right, me on the left. 'Everything in its place,' he'd said, 'including you.' I would make love with him, fall asleep with him, wake up with him. See his face before the day had got to it and smell the night on his skin.

When I went downstairs he was in the kitchen, preparing vegetables. I offered to help, but he told me to relax, put on some music. His CDs were nearly all classical: chamber music, opera, Bach, that kind of thing. I chose one at random and sat on the floor, next to the bookcase, which was where it had all started some nine months before. Now this was home and he was making me supper.

I hardly noticed what I was eating. What I did notice was the way JP poured water into my glass—slowly, carefully, as if it was wine. The way he adjusted the position of my plate. The way he watched me as I was eating. 'I'm glad you're here, Francesca,' he said. 'You'll always be here, won't you?'

The e-mail says nothing, or perhaps it says too much. The words both limit what has happened and leave it wide open. With her finger poised over *Send*, she delays the moment, unsure.

Click. The message is snatched away and in that instant she wants it back. Too late. It's gone.

It's been only a few days since she saw Antoine, but it feels a lot longer. She had to make contact with someone and mention his name. The message was originally intended for Jude, but having tried her address with a dot, a hyphen and an underline and still had the message returned, she wrote to Xavier instead. She didn't mention the funeral. He can make of that what he will.

A rich chorus of jazz cuts through the air. She goes across to the window and looks out. The haphazard geometry of the rooftops is thrown into sharp relief by the slanting evening sunlight. Unexpectedly the shutters opposite are open and there's someone sitting in the window with his back to her. A man, head and shoulders only, with the music swirling round him. Music that seems too big for the space it's in. Frankie rests her eyes on the back of the head and everything that happened in the flat below rushes back to her in a surge of memory. Her body flushes, tingles. If the man turned round he'd see a naked woman at the window—that's what it feels like.

The phone remains silent. Friday evening hangs limply in the air, with the blank screen of the weekend behind it. She wants something to happen. She wants shapes and colours and textures. She wants Antoine to call.

Keys jangle as the door opposite opens and closes. Frankie steps out onto the landing and listens. Nothing. Not even a smell. Most people bring their scent to a place, but not this person. This person is a ghost that flits through the air. A ghost with pink soap and noisy keys.

She goes down the stairs to the door that says *M Sennet*: white letters sunk into black. The door is ajar. Nudging it open, she slips inside.

'Antoine?'

No answer.

The room is brightly lit. Props have been taken away and new ones put in their place. There's a tuba, a bowler hat, a full-length mirror, several phallic-shaped balusters, a plastic mannequin and a pile of photographic equipment. The two coffins have been pushed up against the wall and the couch has been moved to the other side of the room, along with the gramophone and the brown leather suitcase. Hanging slightly out from the wall is the frieze, its delicate paper curled over lengths of bamboo. Frankie follows it round. A mixture of media has been used: paint and ink interspersed with photo montage depicting leaf-birds and limb-shaped tree trunks, night-lit buildings against sunlit skies, back-to-front mermaids with white doves on their shoulders. There are clouds, mountain landscapes and flames leaping from rocks. A giant apple on a turquoise sea.

She runs her fingers over the red velvet of the couch—rough one way, smooth the other. Remembers the feel of him, his smell.

The limbs of the mannequin pop easily out of their sockets. She drags the tuba across in front of one of the coffins and lays it on its side, with the brown suitcase next to it. Drapes a scarf over the mannequin's head, covering its face, places the bowler hat on top and props the torso against the coffin. Discards two of the limbs and tries out the others in different positions. When she's finished, a leg is protruding from the tuba, an arm dangling from the suitcase. Switching off the main light, she directs a spotlight onto the tableau, then she sits down on the couch and waits.

Back in her room she wonders what he'll think when he finds it. Hopes he'll get the joke. Wonders why he left the door unlocked if he wasn't planning on being there.

The masking tape is grubby along the edges but it should still do the job. She tears off a strip and sticks it along the wall. Three more strips make a frame. She steps back. What was an unremarkable square of wallpaper is now a space waiting to be filled. Think big, she says to herself. Think of drawing in sand. Holding a 2B pencil, she faces the wall and waits for an image to form. She wonders how Monique does it, how she decides between one shape and another. How other artists find images in their heads if they're not copying what they see. Monet may have stood in the snow to paint the magpie on the gate, but what about Magritte? Did he set fire to a tuba, sew breasts onto a nightdress, make a girl stand in front of a tree and sink her teeth into a bird?

Her picture can't get started. It's hiding deep in the wall.

She puts a pan of water to boil on the stove and gets out pasta, Gruyère and a tin of tomatoes. A proper meal tonight, why not? She opens the tin, shaves the cheese with *le couteau qui coupe* because there isn't a grater and puts a plaster on the finger that gets shaved as well. When the water boils she throws in a few handfuls of pasta and gives it a stir. The packet says '8-10 minutes': not long to wait.

You can't go wrong with pasta.

8-10 minutes can seem a long time.

JP did most of the cooking. There were dishes he liked, he said, and it was best if he did them the way he'd always done them. I could do the shopping and the washing up. I didn't mind, of course. That was fine. I wanted to help. So I bought what he wrote on the list and then watched as he chopped and scraped and peeled, stirred and tossed and poured. Sometimes he let me top and tail beans or prepare raw vegetables for a salad, but only after he'd shown me how. There were ways of doing things, he said. Right ways and wrong ways. It was important to get things right.

I once spent the morning leafing through one of his cookbooks. Having eliminated all recipes containing tofu, coconut milk or shellfish—far too risky—I drew up a shortlist. Then I read through the instructions, visualising the process and wondering how similar to the picture I could make each dish look.

When JP got home the ingredients were laid out in the kitchen. 'You're not allowed in here,' I said. Reluctantly, he retreated to the sitting room with his paper.

An hour later I called him through. The table was laid. I'd lit candles. The food was ready on the plates: seared salmon on a bed of rice, with roasted vegetables and a basil and yogurt sauce. Pretty damned impressive, I thought.

As we ate JP told me about a Scandinavian historian he had met in the library and an anomaly in the filing system. He talked about the research he was doing into the structure of the Vichy government in wartime France, frowning at me over his glasses when I suggested its policies had been driven by a glut of fizzy water. In the silence that followed, I wished I hadn't mentioned the water.

Eventually he asked what I'd done that day.

'I spent most of it planning this meal,' I said.

'All day?'

'Was it all right?'

'Not bad. A bit on the dry side, perhaps, and the vegetables were undercooked—not good for the digestion.' He pushed his plate away unwiped, with lumps of rice congealed around the edges. 'Maybe you should stick to ironing in future, leave the cooking to me.' I looked for a smile but couldn't find one.

The washing up took a long time and I made a lot of noise as I was doing it. At one point JP came out of the sitting room and closed the kitchen door. I made even more noise after that.

That night he took me in his arms and kissed me and held me tightly. 'You're beautiful, Francesca,' he said. 'I'm glad you're here.' And as his love seeped into me, I felt my anger subside and I kissed him back and held him tightly back. 'Next time, try pasta,' he said. 'You can't go wrong with pasta.'

The walls are damp with steam. She doesn't have a colander or a lid that fits the pan, so she uses a plate to drain the pasta and nearly scalds her hand. Half the pasta ends up in the sink. Her eyes rest on the sharp little knife poking out: a blade drowned in scrambled brains. She should have thrown it in the river along with her ring.

She eats slowly. As long as she's eating she has something to do, a reason for being. She's made a meal and now she's eating it—nothing wrong with that. She doesn't look at the phone because looking won't make it ring. It will ring when it's ready. When he's ready.

The pasta doesn't taste of much. The sauce is watery and the cheese has melted away to nothing. She stabs the tubes onto her fork and moves the fork from plate to mouth, feeding fuel into her body. The pasta flops onto her tongue and slips down her throat with minimal chewing. The last few mouthfuls are cold and have even less taste. She forgot to salt the water, that's what it is.

Maybe you should stick to ironing.

Damn that voice. If he'd left photographs or letters, she could have torn them up and thrown them away. She can't tear up the voice in her head.

She washes the plate and the pan, taking her time, spinning it out. The tubes of pasta feel like slugs as she fishes them out of the plughole, allowing the water to drain.

Antoine still hasn't rung.

She opens a book, but her brain won't stay on the page. When she attempts a bit more tidying, all she does is move things around, rearranging the mess. Dusting is better. You can dust and not think at the same time. Not thinking takes up all your energy right now. Not thinking about how you used to like cleaning his house. Vacuuming up the dust that was half your skin and half his. Rubbing out the line of his dirt and yours in the bath. Washing the sheets that smelt of both of you. You used to hold the pillowcases to your face before putting them in the machine, smug that you could tell which was which: your odour lighter, his more pungent. When you ironed his shirts, you caressed the cotton with the iron, gliding down each arm, round the shoulders, across the chest and down the back. You admired them when they were finished, hanging crisply on their hangers, and you imagined his body inside them, filling them out, branding them with the scent of his citrus soap and some other smell that came only from him. If you spotted a crease you couldn't leave it, you had to get the iron out again. He never complained about your ironing. He never complained about that.

There are no more places to dust. Hating herself for doing it, she sits down on the floor and stares at the telephone. To give herself a break now and then, she imagines Antoine taking his mobile out of his pocket, dialling her number and putting the phone to his ear. Then, as if caught on a wave that refuses to break, she waits for the sound of the ring.

It's gone midnight. He won't call now. She falls asleep with a frown tensed across her forehead.

The frown's still there when she wakes the next morning. He didn't phone. Bastard.

After work she sits on the bed and cuts her toenails. The idea is for the clippings to land on a saucer balanced on the bedcovers, but some of them miss and she has to get down on her hands and knees to find them. It's a pitiful sight: a woman scrabbling around on the floor of a drab little room, looking for bits of toenail. She gives up and burrows underneath the covers instead, hiding from the daylight that says she should be doing something more meaningful than this.

The ringing of the phone is an intrusion. She pokes her head out from under the bedclothes and finds herself trembling. She's planned anger and retribution, practised what she's going to say. But the rich, seductive voice acts like a tranquilliser: she takes the injection lying down, without a fight.

There's a stillness in the cemetery, a dense silence. They stroll down the cobbled pathway, close but not touching, shaded by plane trees and horse chestnuts. The miniature temples look like stark, imposing beach huts in need of repair: pointed roofs and dark recesses packed side by side, row upon row, vying for prominence.

'Dead man's village,' says Antoine. 'Ghetto of the bourgeoisie. All those puffed-up egos still competing.' He doesn't even lower his voice.

She doesn't know why he's brought her here. They were fine on the train: he was sitting beside her and she was loving the nearness of him, his warmth, the weight of his arm on hers. She hadn't moaned at him for not ringing sooner, nor had she quizzed him about the things Monique had told her. All that could wait.

They would go back to Montmartre, that's what he said on the phone. And they did. They walked and they ate ice cream and there may have been other people, but if there were she didn't notice. And when he said he'd take the same train as her to go home, her mind started racing. They'd get off at Daumesnil, she thought, and they'd end up at the studio. Or perhaps he'd take her to where he lives, undress her in his spice-scented, black-sheeted bed.

But as they pulled into Père Lachaise he stood up, saying there was somewhere he wanted her to see. They pushed their way to the doors and dropped out onto the platform. She imagined a pretty garden, a courtyard shaped with modern sculpture, the birthplace of a well-known author.

When they left the street and passed through the cemetery gates, the atmosphere changed. It was like going indoors, where the air is tighter. A coolness brushed over her arms and legs. The silence weighed more than the noise they'd just left.

They continue down the tomb-lined alley. Each temple is different, individually designed. On the intricate grilles of the wrought-iron doors geometric grids are interwoven with twisting leaves and trailing roses, many of which are cracked and crusted with rust. Chiselled into the stonework above are dedications: Famille Gaudier, Famille Duchamp, Famille Leduc.

The pathways are named too, like streets in a scaled-down city, with the Avenue de l'Ouest leading into the Avenue Circulaire:

an even more affluent neighbourhood where the temples are one size larger. Sunlight floods over the rooftops, casting solid blocks of shadow across the cobbles.

'Good lesson in perspective,' says Antoine, stopping and gazing down the alley. 'Light and shade, angles. Great place for artists.'

One day she'll have to come and sketch here—if she's brave enough.

'Chopin's here somewhere,' he adds. 'Proust. Jim Morrison. Oscar Wilde.'

The door to one of the little temples has slumped on its hinges and has been left wedged open. Frankie steps inside. It's no bigger than a cupboard. There are cobwebs, dead leaves and a vase of silk roses and lily of the valley, dulled by a thick coating of dust. Above the altar a tiny but perfect stained glass window shines out, throwing its colours onto the stonework where the names of the dead are engraved. She wonders what happened to Aline: died September 1862, aged twenty-two. The young wife of a well-to-do Parisian, perhaps, who succumbed to childbirth or disease. Or stabbed by her jealous husband following a tryst with a penniless musician in the Jardin du Luxembourg...

'What are you up to?'

'Nothing.' She steps back into the sunlight.

At the next crossroads a group of visitors are poring over a plan of the cemetery.

'*A la recherche de Proust perdu*,' Antoine mutters. He steers Frankie off the main alley and into a narrow, unnamed pathway where dry leaves crack underfoot. The temples are replaced by more conventional tombstones: blocks of stone and marble, some overgrown with moss, others adorned with flowers—fresh or silk or china. Behind them a mass of stones and temples rises steeply, forming a hillside shanty town of tombs. A refugee camp for thousands of souls with a skyline of roofs and crosses.

'Sit down over there,' he says.

'Where?'

'On the edge of that tombstone.'

'What for?'

'I want to see what it looks like.'

The speckled marble feels cold through Frankie's skirt. Beside her in a pot stands the withered stem of a geranium. Crows shuffle in the trees overhead and there's the sound of leaves being swept on the main pathway, but otherwise they're alone.

Antoine has pulled an old-fashioned camera out of his bag and is changing the lens.

'What are you doing?'

'Don't move.'

She's heard that before. This time her eyes are open.

'Stay like that,' he says, crouching in front of her. She smiles into the lens. 'Don't smile, stay as you were before.'

He takes a few shots, clicking the shutter, winding on. Moves in closer. 'Uncross your legs.'

She uncrosses them and sits sideways on, knees together.

'Not like that,' he says. 'Face me, and open your legs.'

'What?'

'Let your legs fall open.'

'But…'

'Come on Frankie. Let me in.'

And she does. In a graveyard in the middle of Paris, in the late afternoon, she lets a camera see up between her legs.

The shutter clicks several times. 'Now take off your knickers.'

'Here? You're joking!'

'No one's looking.'

'I can't. Not here.'

'Yes you can, Frankie.' He takes his eye away from the lens and looks at her. That irresistible look that's part scowl, part smile. 'Show me how sexy you are.'

She glances around. There's no one in sight. What the hell. Why the hell not. She stands up and slips off her knickers.

'Now sit down,' he says. 'The same as before, but pull your skirt up a bit.'

Warm air brushes the insides of her thighs as the staring eye of the camera zooms in. She's being fucked by a 75mm lens! She pulses and moistens as the shutter opens and closes.

'Why here?' she says, struggling to keep her voice steady.

'Sex and death. I like the juxtaposition. The erotic throb of life above while the bones of the dead lie festering below.'

She pulls her legs together. 'It's not right. Not here.'

'I've finished now anyway.' He unscrews the lens and flicks hair out of his eyes. 'What's the problem?'

'I can't believe you made me do that!'

He grins. 'That was your creation with the mannequin, I suppose.'

'You saw it?'

'Monique did.'

'Oh.' She pauses. 'It had a title, of course: *The English Lesson*. A leg and an arm—remember?'

He zips the camera away in his bag. 'You'll need to get used to it, Frankie.'

'What—your dreadful English?'

'Letting go. Taking risks. Injecting passion into still life.'

She's not sure if he's being serious or merely playing with words.

It's rush hour. The train is packed. More passengers get on at every station and no one gets off. They're wedged together, his arm round her waist and her back sweating from the heat of his body. She's trying not to touch the woman in front, pulling back from the wild mane of hair that's too close to her face. Her breathing is shallow: she doesn't want to take in the woman's odour or her exhaled breath. When the woman shifts her position a stabbing pain burns Frankie's foot. She stares past the hair, her gaze resting on an embroidered logo on a shirt.

A tunnel closes in around them. Brakes squeal and there's a grinding of metal on metal as the train jolts and slows down. Slows down some more. Stops. The lights flicker and go out. Frankie blinks, trying to open her eyes even though they're already open. There are sighs and mutters and *oh là làs*. It's hot, she can't move, she can't see. She breathes in air that others have breathed out and knows she mustn't panic. She must hold in her fear because there's no room here to let it out, no room for it to howl and kick its legs. Clinging to Antoine's arm, she tries to picture a turquoise sea with seagulls circling in a cloud-streaked sky above.

No light comes on, the train doesn't move. The woman with the hair sighs loudly and her hair wanders into Frankie's face. Frankie twists her head away. She feels Antoine's breath on her neck as he bends over her. His hand presses into her waist, kneading it like dough, then it's fumbling with her skirt, undoing the button, loosening the zip. She giggles silently, squirms tightly, tries to push the hand away without bumping the woman, but the hand keeps coming back and the skirt gives way with the hand sliding in, down over her stomach, under the elastic of her knickers and down into the sticky warmth between her legs. His breath is hot now on her cheek, in her ear, as his fingers probe deeper, reaching, rubbing, slipping, a peak of intensity balanced on their tips until with eyes squeezing purple, head tilted, mouth silent and gaping, back arched…

They climb the steps and emerge into the daylight. Her lungs fill with air that's alive, that has movement in it. The smile on her face won't go away.

'I want to see those photos,' she says, 'as soon as they're developed. And I'll take charge of the negatives too!'

He smiles and kisses her on the mouth. 'I'll call you.'

And with that, he's gone. He's disappeared and she can't see him any more. She doesn't know where he lives, she doesn't even have his number. The day has stopped dead and she's standing there, lost, with no purpose. The only purpose she had for the evening has just walked off down the street.

Simon stands bleary-eyed in the doorway, dressed but barefoot.

'Did I wake you?' she says.

'No such luck.'

'I need some milk. For my tea.'

'Come on in.'

It's unusually quiet in the flat. She follows him into the kitchen, picking her way through the bits of Lego that are scattered across the floor. The table is strewn with dirty dishes.

'It's early for a Sunday. I'm sorry.'

'Don't be. I'm glad you're here.' That's what he says, but she's not sure if he means it. He seems distracted.

The fridge is crammed with leftovers wrapped in clingfilm, pots of jam and pickles and yogurt, bottles of wine. Either Simon can't find the milk or he's forgotten that it's milk he's looking for. He stands with the fridge door open, gazing in, letting cold air out.

'What am I going to do with all this?'

'All what?'

'All this food. What am I going to do with it?'

Frankie frowns. She's walked into a room with jagged edges.

Simon closes the door of the fridge. 'She's left me,' he says.

'What?'

'Last night. Took the kids. Just walked out and left.' He grips the back of a chair and stares at the floor. 'Things have been wrong for ages—months—but we were working at it, it was getting better, she promised she wouldn't leave. Then last night...'

'But I thought... I'm sure everyone thought...'

'Simon and Monique, the perfect couple? Is that what everyone thought?' He looks at her; she doesn't know how to answer. 'Sorry,' he says, 'I shouldn't take it out on you—you weren't to know. No one knew. We worked hard at keeping up appearances. The thing is, part of me knew this had to happen—we couldn't go on as we were. But that doesn't stop it from hurting. Something to do with pride, I suppose.'

'So you just drifted apart then?'

'God, how I'll miss the kids.' His voice wavers. He's staring at the floor again. 'I'd have done anything to keep the kids.'

'There isn't someone else, is there?'

'What am I supposed to do now? What the hell am I supposed to do?' He opens a cupboard and closes it. Picks up a jar of rice and puts it down. 'Would you believe, she wanted me to pay for the latest load of food she'd bought. Fourteen years of marriage and we're squabbling over a few bags of groceries!'

He's at the sink now, looking out of the window, his body a slumped silhouette framed by sunlight. The tap is dripping but he doesn't seem to notice.

'She's been having an affair, Frankie.' The words sound compressed, as if he's forcing them through too small an opening. 'I only found out the other day. Not long before I brought you that book, in fact.'

Frankie pictures him in her room, uneasy, fidgeting. She pictures Monique in the café with her perfect clothes and perfect make-up.

'Who...? I mean, it's none of my business, but...'

Simon turns back into the room. With the light behind him, she can't read his face.

'We met here in Paris, you know, at the Marché aux Puces. There was a lot of rubbish for sale—clothes and books and stuff.

But there was also a painting. That's it there.' He indicates the picture on the wall. 'My eye was drawn to it immediately. I liked the colours, the tranquillity. Anyway, I wasn't going to buy it, poor student that I was in those days, but then a voice behind me said, '*Vous l'achetez?*' And I looked round and there she was, all pretty in an emerald dress and those brown eyes of hers sparkling, and that was it—the point of no return. I said she could have the painting, but she refused. So I bought it, with money I didn't have. We ended up going for a drink, with the painting wrapped in newspaper, and I said if she ever wanted to see it again she'd have to come and visit me in Bristol. Three weeks later she turned up on the doorstep and that was that. We were engaged before the month was out.' He sighs. 'Married for fourteen years, two kids, and now...'

'What a lovely way to meet.'

'Bloody awful way to end.'

'At least you've got the memories. She can't take those away.'

'You can't live on memories, Frankie. Memories are only words in the end. Words and pictures.'

He transfers the dirty dishes from the table to the sink, mechanically, his face disengaged from what he's doing. Frankie wonders if he'll keep the painting. If he'll hold onto the *Vous l'achetez?* and the emerald dress. If that's really all memories are.

'Come for supper this evening,' he says. 'Help me eat all this food.'

hi frankie, the funeral went okay though it was ridiculously hot and my mother felt faint. i've decided to take some leave and go down to the coast for a bit. i'll be in touch as soon as i get back.

xavier

The funeral. Yesterday. When she was baring all in the cemetery. The irony makes her smile, though there's guilt there as well.

She sips her black tea, which doesn't taste so bad after all. The head has reappeared in the window opposite, accompanied this time by Miles Davis—the only jazz JP had and the only jazz she knows. Languid and bluesy, the trumpet wails above a murmur of piano and bass, painting a smoky bar somewhere—New York perhaps, or Chicago. Incidental music to a film with no action. She still hasn't seen a face. The head sits completely still, as if in a trance, with the music packed around it. It has no routine. It appears at no set times and when she watches out for it, nothing happens. It's when she isn't looking that the head takes its place.

Antoine won't call, not today. He'll ring next week sometime, or drop by unannounced.

She perches on the edge of the table with her hands cupped around the tea and the song of the trumpet in her ears. She wonders when Simon first saw it coming. Whether he knew straight away that something was wrong or whether he ignored the signs.

Jude turned up at the house with no warning. She stood on the doorstep and held out a parcel.

'Peace offering,' she said. 'Disguised as a late wedding or early Christmas present—whichever you prefer.' She peered down the hallway.

'Don't worry. He's at work.'

'Oh Frankie, I'm sorry. I've behaved like a total shit.'

'You're here now, that's all that matters.' I threw my arms round her; she smelt of Covent Garden.

We went into the sitting room.

'Wow! It's a bit bloody pristine, eh? Looks like something out of a catalogue.'

'Hardly.'

'Bloody does. I suppose he makes you do the cleaning?'

'Don't start, Jude.'

'You're right. I haven't come here to have a go. Now how about a drink?'

'Tea? Coffee?'

'Not got anything stronger?'

'Don't think so, no.'

'What?'

'He doesn't drink. Don't…' I held up a hand to stem her horror.

'Good job I came prepared then.' She produced a bottle of vodka from her bag.

Three hours later we were sprawled on the floor, with the bottle all but empty and grins as wide as the sofa.

'He did *what*?' I said, giggling.

'I told you, he brought bits of the motor to bed! I mean, shit, I've shared my bed with some greasy nuts in my time, but…' She snorted with laughter. 'What's the worst thing JP does in bed? His most disgusting habit?'

'Not telling!'

'Go on. I'll make you!' She tickled me and I squealed and that's when JP walked in.

He didn't say anything. He just stood there.

Jude and I picked ourselves up. Struggling to keep a straight face, I pointed to the boxed pair of champagne glasses on the sofa. 'Wedding present.'

JP still said nothing.

'I'd better go.' Jude gave me a brief hug and saw herself out.

Trying to move with some degree of coordination, I picked up the glasses and the empty bottle. JP followed me through to the kitchen.

'What was all that about, Francesca?'

'Nothing. She came round. We had a few drinks, that's all.'

'A few?'

'Yes, we got tipsy. It isn't a crime.'

'I thought I'd made it clear: I don't want any alcohol in this house.'

'Well there isn't any now, is there? It's all gone!' I risked a smile, trying to drag JP into it. He refused to be dragged.

'You didn't say she was coming round.'

'I didn't know.'

'These things must be planned.'

'Why? What difference does it make? She's gone now.' I took the champagne glasses out of their box and held them up to the light. 'Nice glasses.'

'All that rollicking on the floor. Get a kick out of that, did you?'

'Don't be ridiculous. We were just messing about.'

'Don't ever say that, Francesca.'

'Say what?'

'That I'm being ridiculous. I deserve more respect than that.'

I swung round and glared at him. 'Respect? That works two ways, you know.'

Glowering, he grabbed a glass from my hand and hurled it across the kitchen. 'I'll show you respect!' he shouted, hurling the other glass after it.

'What the hell did you do that for? That was a wedding present!'

He left the room. The front door slammed and his car roared off down the road. I stood paralysed in the silence. Stood for a long time, then swept up the broken glass.

Night was falling and it had started to rain when I heard his keys in the door. I didn't move. I stayed in the armchair, with a book lying open in my lap.

He went upstairs to use the toilet. When the footsteps came back down again, I dug my teeth into my lower lip and gripped the book. He came over to where I was sitting.

'I'm sorry, Francesca. I shouldn't have done that.'

'Where have you been?'

'Driving. Thinking. I need to do that sometimes.'

'I didn't know where you'd gone.'

'I know.' He took my hand in his. 'I'm sorry about the glasses.'

'It's not the glasses, it's… I've not seen you like that before. And I don't know what you've got against Jude.'

'I've nothing against Jude. But you should have let me know she was here. I don't like coming home and finding someone in my house. You can understand that, can't you?'

I stared at the book. The same paragraph, unread.

'It must never happen again, Francesca.'

Two weeks passed. I wasn't that late: ten, maybe fifteen minutes, no more. He was sitting with two plates of food, untouched, on the table. He didn't look up when I came in. When I told him he should have started, or kept the food warm in the oven, he didn't react.

'This is our first Christmas together, Francesca,' he said then.

'I know.'

'So where have you been?'

'You know where I've been. I told you.'

'Tell me again.'

'The pub. They always go for a drink on Christmas Eve.'

'They?'

'People from work. You know.'

'I don't know.' His voice was tight. He still hadn't raised his head.

'Just people I work with.'

'Like who?'

'Like… Jess, Sally, Maureen. You don't know them.'

'What about Gordon?'

'And Gordon, yes. Everyone was there.'

'So why didn't you mention Gordon?'

'There are lots of people I haven't mentioned. Look I'm sorry, I lost track of the time. We were chatting.'

'You and Gordon?'

'Not just me and Gordon…'

He got up and stood at the sink with his back to me. 'You come home reeking of booze and tell me you've been out with some other man, while I've been making your supper, waiting here for you, and the meal was on the table at seven as it always is and *you weren't here!*' The draining board rattled as he slammed down his fist.

'I said I'm sorry.'

'Well sorry isn't good enough, Francesca!' He seized a handful of cutlery and threw it across the room. I was in the way and bits of the metal hit me, spiking my arms and legs. Spoons and forks clattered to the floor and it hurt where the prongs had stabbed, but something told me I mustn't cry, that it would only make things worse. Then he picked up my plate of cold food and I winced and covered my face as he smashed it against the wall and stormed out of the room.

I cleaned up the mess. Went upstairs and ran a bath. As I lay soaking in bubbles, I surveyed the damage. There were scratches but the skin wasn't broken. He'd only done it because he cared, because he loved me. And I'd been selfish, not getting home when I said I would. He was worried, you could understand that. He didn't mean it. He was angry because the food had gone cold.

When he walked into the bathroom, I sat up too quickly and water sloshed onto the floor. I looked at him warily with my arms held across my chest.

'I'm sorry,' he said. 'I shouldn't have reacted like that.'

'It's okay.'

'No it isn't. I didn't mean to hurt you. Let me see.'

Holding my arm gently, he checked all along it and kissed the red marks on my skin. Then he took a bar of soap and washed my back.

I'd dreamed of snow and log fires, but the next day there was neither. Only grey skies and the hum of central heating. I got up early and rang my parents. It was the first time I'd been away

138

from home for Christmas and guilt had been festering inside me. I wondered what they would do all day, the two of them. Wondered if they'd bother with a turkey and hoped they would. Imagined them shuffling round the house in slippers, trying to fill in the gaps. They'd think more about Craig than about me. The hole he'd left would always be bigger and blacker than mine: harder to avoid, easier to fall into.

When I put down the phone JP was standing beside me. He took my hand and clipped a gold-plated watch onto my wrist. It looked odd: I hadn't worn a watch for years. 'Happy Christmas, Francesca,' he said. 'No excuse for being late now.' There was no irony in his voice. And at that moment I felt like two people: the one he loved and the one he hated. It was as if we were both seeing double.

The leftovers are spread out on the table: cheese and *saucisson*, sardines and quiche, cold ratatouille and two half-drunk bottles of wine with corks stuck in their necks. Simon has made a bowl of salad and cut some bread.

'Right, let's stuff our faces and drown our sorrows.'

Between them they start to clear the table of food and drink. Because it's there. Because there's nothing else to do.

'Funny how leftovers taste so much better,' says Simon through a mouthful of quiche.

Frankie nods and helps herself to wine. The child's *maman papa* drawing is directly in her line of vision, behind Simon's head. She wonders how Monique will explain to the twins that there'll be no more *bisous* between Mum and Dad. What words she'll choose to help them understand.

'She'll want that, you know,' he says, following her gaze. 'And the painting. She's already taken the wedding album.'

Frankie turns to the opposite wall, where photos in clip frames show Simon in the mountains, his sun-beaten face set against a backdrop of wide skies and sparkling snow.

'The Alps?'

'Apart from the two on the left—they're the Lake District. There's nothing more exhilarating than being that high up, looking out across the peaks. It puts everything else into perspective. All life's little niggles and inconveniences.' He digs his thumbnail into a cork and picks bits off.

In the silence that follows Frankie wonders where Monique's leaving fits in with life's niggles and inconveniences. Where death fits in.

'How's work?' she says then, for something to say.

'Not bad. There's some bug going round, which I'm hoping not to catch.' He makes an ant hill of the cork crumbs. 'Did you hear about the chap who went to the doctor's with a fever and was told there was a bug going round?' She shakes her head. 'Well, we're crawling with bugs all the time, aren't we? Bugs in the gut and the eyelashes and all over the skin, so how come the doctor knows there's one going round? One little bug, spinning round and round? How would he know that?'

'Don't know. Doesn't he get dizzy?'

'The doctor?'

'The bug!'

'That must be how you catch it. When it gets dizzy and falls off!'

They're both laughing now. Simon opens a fresh bottle of wine and gets ice cream out of the freezer. Frankie roots around in the cupboards and finds chocolate sauce, bananas and raisins.

'Bloody stuff,' says Simon, stabbing at the ice cream with a knife. 'Should have taken it out sooner.'

'Let me try.' She scrapes slivers off the top with a spoon and drops them onto his plate.

'What do you call that? Ice cream shavings?'

'Don't you have a microwave?'

'Good thinking! Microwave!' He scoops up the tub with a flourish and slides across the room with it, dispersing the Lego as he goes. 'Now then…'—pressing buttons—'Instantly scoobable ize cream!' He ogles the microwave, anticipating the ping with small muttered 'pings' of his own. 'Oops! Fancy a milkshake?' He pours the ice cream into glasses, adds raisins and squirts on sauce. The plastic bottle farts and Frankie grips the table, weak with laughter.

Then Simon's face falls slack and the room is suddenly quiet.

'Would you believe it was me that put the Lego there? I wanted to make it look, you know…'

They both stare at the floor. The Lego is mostly bricks, but there are a couple of policemen there too, a spare torso, some sets of wheels and a broken window. A crime scene in fragments.

'So what's the story?' Simon says at last, looking up. 'You seem out of sorts yourself at the moment.'

'I'm confused, that's all.' She picks up a pair of wheels and spins them between her fingers. 'It's Antoine. I get the feeling you don't like him much, but we've been out a few times and we get on really well. The thing is…' The spinning wheels are annoying, but she can't stop. 'I don't know where I stand. He hasn't even given me his phone number.'

'You'd be better off without him, Frankie.'

'Why? What's the problem?'

'He's a dark horse, that one.' He peels a banana, lobs the skin into the sink.

'I told Monique,' she goes on. 'She's the only one who knows. She seemed pleased for me, but she said some weird things too.'

'Want some?' He leans across and slices banana into her glass. 'Like what?'

'Stuff about my face and her not wanting Antoine to scare me off. And you trying to protect me.'

'Has he shown you the studio?'

'Upstairs? Yes. But I'm still not sure what it's for.'

Simon sighs and leans his head in his hands. 'I should have told you earlier.'

'Told me what?'

'About the flat. The studio. What goes on up there. It's... complicated.'

'Try me.'

He sighs again. 'They run a business—that's what they call it. *Une entreprise.*'

'Who do?'

'Monique and Antoine. There's a website, which... I can't explain, I'll have to show you.'

They go through to his study. Frankie extracts a chair from under piles of papers and sits down, still fiddling with the wheels. As they wait for the computer to boot up, her mind jumps from one thought to another—thoughts of Antoine and Monique and the studio—but nothing quite connects. Simon logs onto the internet, types in instructions. She moves her chair closer. Graphics flick up on the screen and a gallery of pictures appears: all Magrittes, as far as she can tell. Simon clicks the mouse on one of them.

'This is what goes on in that flat,' he says, with quiet emphasis on every word. 'They call the site *Cinema Blue*. A play on a Magritte title, apparently.'

The picture expands to fill the screen. It shows a room with green walls, a grey door and a wooden floor. Beside the door is a vase of pink and white flowers on a small round table, draped with a cloth. To the right of the picture a woman stands naked with her arms up behind her head. She's tall, too tall for the room.

Below, on the left, there's a small figure with short black hair and a black suit.

As Frankie watches, the picture fades and is superimposed by another. A video this time of a room with similar décor, including the table in the corner. And a real woman standing there, naked, tall, her arms up behind her head and her red hair cut straight across in a fringe. Then a man Frankie vaguely recognises too appears from the bottom left-hand corner of the screen and walks towards the woman. They stand facing each other, his head level with her shoulder, and discordant electronic music plays as he takes off his jacket, his shirt, his shoes. Frankie's wondering how far... The trousers are removed, the underpants. What on earth...? She draws back from the screen, embarrassed to look with Simon sitting next to her. The angle of the camera changes, the lens zooms in and it's all there, nothing left to imagine as the man she met at the party turns the red-fringed woman round and bends her over. Frankie can't believe what she's seeing. She knows this sort of thing goes on all the time, but not in Flat Four. Not so close to where she lives. Not in the room where she and Antoine made love.

Simon shakes his head. 'This is the sort of smut they film, I'm afraid. They like to make out it's an art form, but all they really care about is money. It's lucrative, you see. There are enough sad bastards out there willing to pay.'

The last bit sounds like something Antoine would say.

'Seen enough?' He shuts down the computer and they sit in the cramped little study with the blank screen in front of them. Frankie's mind is blank as well, unable to function.

'They reconstruct different paintings,' Simon is saying, 'then add the porn on top. Monique says it's fine, that it's merely a business arrangement and no one's being exploited. I've never approved though, never liked it. It began as a sideline, but now it seems to have taken over. If the Paris art establishment got wind of it there'd be a right old scandal.'

'Is Monique that well known?' She homes in on the detail: the whole picture is too awful to look at.

'In certain circles, yes. As for Antoine, he believes he's a reincarnation of Magritte—or so Monique says. A load of nonsense about being born on the fifteenth of August and sharing Magritte's characteristics. Apart from the ability to paint, of course. For some reason, that's not relevant. It's completely insane.'

'He's joking, surely?'

'Who knows? He even says you're his Georgette.'

'His what?'

'Georgette. Magritte's wife, his creative muse. He's spent the last ten years looking for you. As has Monique, I suspect.'

'That really must be a joke.'

'You look a bit like her, apparently. Something in the bone structure, the eyes. That's why they were both so keen on you— your face fitted a lot of the paintings. You'd have been good for business.' He shakes his head again and sighs. 'At least you didn't get caught up in it, Frankie. You've no idea what the two of them get up to in that flat. You don't want to know, either. She shares him with all sorts of little tarts. Well they deserve each other. Let them get on with their sordid little affair, their sordid little business. It's the kids I worry about. What sort of mother is she when she carries on like that?'

'Their affair?'

'She denies it of course, says it's no one I know, but it's obvious, isn't it? Who else could it be? All those hours they spend together.'

Frankie chills inside. Her mind darkens. The last remaining threads of strength that have been holding her together snap. 'Monique and Antoine?'

'Yup, Antoine and Monique. Been at it for months. So now you know. I tried to warn you about that man, but what could I say? I didn't want to spell it out. But it doesn't matter any more, does it?'

Reality is spinning away from her, out of reach. Where does she fit into all this? Who is she? What is she? One of Antoine's little tarts? A substitute for Monique when she's unavailable and he can't find anyone else? The blood drains from her head and she slumps forwards. There are tyre marks on her arm where she's been pressing the wheels up and down.

'Are you okay?' Simon crouches beside her.

She sits up slowly. 'He made love to me in the flat. On one of the sets.'

A shadow passes over Simon's face. He stands up and turns away.

'Did he film us, Simon?'

'I don't know.'

She feels sick. Physically sick.

'Jesus, Frankie. I'm so sorry.' He's back at her side.

'Does Antoine... Does he appear on the screen?'

His gaze falters. 'Not often. He does the filming mostly, I think.'

It isn't quite the right answer.

The pillow is deep and soft. The sheets smell of fabric conditioner. When she opens her eyes she sees tigers, elephants and monkeys. A strip of jungle on a pale green background.

Shit. Please someone, tell her it's not true. Tell her it's all a bad dream and she's about to wake up.

She can hear him in the kitchen, washing dishes. There's a smell of coffee and toast. On the other side of the room is another single bed. The shutters are on the latch with sunlight edging in through the gap. Pushing away the thin duvet, she finds she's wearing a long white t-shirt that isn't hers. Her clothes are in a heap on the floor, next to a box of toys. She doesn't remember putting them there. She doesn't remember much at all after the images on the screen. Her thoughts feel like mangled strips of tape that she has to unravel in her mind. They were drinking, laughing, crying. Was she crying? She knew it was getting late but he begged her to stay. Just one more drink, he said. Oh my God. She puts a couple of fingers between her legs and feels for stickiness. Puts them to her nose and smells for sex. Surely he wouldn't have. Not Simon. He likes her, but not like that. Antoine, on the other hand… She hasn't a clue now what Antoine thinks.

There's a knock. She grabs the duvet. Simon opens the door and peers in. 'Morning, Frankie. Breakfast?'

She gets dressed quickly, uses the toilet and splashes cold water on her face. Dries her face and hands on a towel that smells the same as the duvet. Avoids looking in the mirror. There's only one toothbrush on the basin and the shelf is empty, all the perfume and make-up transferred to some other bathroom in some other part of Paris. Or sharing shelf space with Antoine's spicy aftershave.

'White, no sugar—am I right?' He's pouring coffee from a cafetière. The empty wine bottles have gone and the dishes have been left to drain by the sink. The Lego has gone too. 'There's toast,' he says. 'Three types of jam.'

'I can't. I'm late for work.'

The canned music is too loud. She craves silence. When Antoine was meant to ring, all she wanted was for the silence to shatter. That's the thing about silence: it depends what the alternative is.

Evenings with JP were defined by the clicking of his pen, which seemed to echo the twitching of his brain. I'd glance across at him sitting there, deep in a book or *The Times* crossword. He'd be twisting his signet ring round his little finger or biting his nails—I never knew how he found anything left to bite. He'd put on the *News at Ten* and even then he wouldn't speak. Then he'd disappear into the kitchen with his laptop and stay there well into the night. At first I thought it was me, that I'd done something wrong, but I soon learnt it was best not to ask. He simply needed space.

His CD collection was purely aesthetic—he seldom listened to any of it. So on Monday mornings, after he'd gone out, I played music at full volume to break up the air and put some life back into the house.

It wasn't always like this. There were times when he would hold forth at length, discussing the political climate in France or outlining the philosophies of Voltaire and Descartes. He seemed to know so much, to have an opinion about everything, and I listened, keen to learn. When I tried to add comments of my own though, he brushed them aside. *If it's not worth saying,* he'd insist, *don't say it.*

She watches herself transferring bulbs of fennel from one crate to another. Hears herself greeting customers and agreeing that there's rain in the air. The music is washing over her now, skimming the top of her head. Like the sound of the wind in the trees which she always knew was there, but which hid behind her thoughts sometimes. You hear what matters and what irritates, not the rest.

The smell creeps up on her without warning. The nudge of perfume. Years have passed but it still catches at her throat, keying in to jealousy and rage. Except that it isn't Stella's perfume at all, it's just scent that was worn by a stranger who happened to walk down King's Parade one lunchtime and which is worn now by a dumpy, middle-aged Parisian with an over-full trolley. Frankie turns her attention to the melons.

'Quiet today, isn't it?' Nathalie smooths down an eyebrow with a manicured nail. 'What did you get up to at the weekend?'

'Not much. You?'

'Nothing I can admit to in public! Actually, I've been sorting things out at home. I'm going to be away for a while.'

The woman with the perfume glares across from the cheese counter and Nathalie goes to serve her. Frankie finishes laying out the melons. She hopes Monsieur Villet won't be in today. Only one hour and twenty-six minutes to go.

The noise is deceptive at first, simply a voice that's louder than usual. But then the voice becomes more strident, and the woman at the cheese counter starts gesticulating and stabbing her finger at the glass. Poised and unflinching, Nathalie holds her ground. Frankie makes a start on the aubergines. The things Simon told her gnaw at her head, the images she saw on the screen. She'd been hoping they would fade in the daylight, fizzle out and leave her alone. But they haven't done any of those things. And something makes her want to tell Nathalie. She'll tell her because she doesn't really know her, and because Nathalie has no preconceptions about her. The words will slide over the French girl like water, slipping off before she's noticed they're there. There'll be nails to file, hair to push back into place, a smile to stick onto a face. Nathalie isn't interested enough in Frankie to care, and that's what Frankie wants: someone to listen but not to care.

The woman is still shouting. There's a call over the speakers for the manager. When he arrives he shifts from one foot to the other, hand in pocket, keys rattling, as the tirade continues. Then he ushers the woman and Nathalie down the soft drinks aisle and into his office.

Frankie finds herself back beside the biscuits, fingering a packet of chocolate-covered *petits-beurre*. It's too bulky to hide in a pocket, but there's no one about and if she's quick, if she crouches down... Sweating, slightly nauseous, she returns the packet to the shelf.

At midday Nathalie hangs up her uniform and leaves by the back door. Frankie follows.

'What was all that about earlier?'

Nathalie doesn't answer. A light drizzle is falling. They're standing next to the rubbish bins on a carpet of trodden lettuce leaves and greasy wrappers. The rancid smell is at odds with Nathalie's flawless face and nails.

'Are you going straight home?'

They order strong black espressos. Frankie sits with her back to the mirror. Unusually the men at the bar have already been and gone, leaving two yellow-stained tumblers on the counter.

'So?'

Nathalie tucks her hair behind her ears. 'That woman... She was accusing me of dishonesty, of fobbing her off with out-of-date cheese. And then along comes Monsieur Paulin implying it's my fault too—that's the worst part.'

She looks awkward on the chair, as if she's been cut the wrong shape for it. Frankie pictures the sofa at Monsieur Villet's and wonders whether Nathalie sits on the edge or sinks down into it. Whether she faces the old man as she reads. Whether what she reads is...

'You'd think they'd trust me after all this time.' Nathalie fiddles with the gold chain round her neck.

'Good thing you've got a holiday coming up.'

A weak smile. 'If you call a fortnight in hospital a holiday.'

'Hospital? I didn't realise.'

'It's not something I talk about much.'

'Anything serious?'

'You aren't squeamish, are you?' She leans down and rolls up a trouser leg. Frankie's stomach clenches. She looks away, and then forces herself to look back. The leg is a mass of scarring, a patchwork of bumps and hollows with the skin stretched tautly across like clingfilm. All greys and pinks and browns.

'That's my good leg,' Nathalie says, rolling the trousers down again.

'God, Nathalie.' A doll with badly scarred legs: it doesn't seem to fit somehow. 'What happened?'

'A fire. A couple of years back. I've had three operations so far. Skin grafts mostly.'

'And you're due another one?'

'The week after next. That's why…'

'What?'

'Never mind.'

'But you're always so cheerful.'

'It's easier for everyone that way.'

Tables glisten where the barman has wiped them. Voices chatter on the television. Frankie drinks her coffee and studies the glossy ice cream menu. She can't tell Nathalie about Antoine and the website. Not now.

Warm rain never feels as wet. Its softness on her face and arms is comforting. As she makes her way down the street, she's aware of the rain and she's aware of her legs. She's conscious of walking.

The flower seller is standing by her buckets with a hood pulled over her head. The flowers are catching the drizzle and no one's buying. As Frankie crosses the road, water seeps into her sandals and tiny bits of grit lodge themselves between her toes.

Worse things can happen.

As usual, the bookshop is empty: there's only her and the young man at the till, his head hidden behind a book. She doesn't get so much as a 'Madame' today.

She scans the labels on the ends of the shelves, where the tape still needs replacing: *Histoire, Archéologie, Cuisine, Animaux.* Round the corner: *Jardinage, Policiers, Poésie, Érotique*—a category that's never meant much to her before, apart from being slightly intriguing. And now? She doesn't know what it means now.

The Art label is at the top of the next section. This time there's an attempt at alphabetical order: Constable, Degas, Goya. Her eyes flit up and down the spines. Manet, Monet, Picasso. She goes back to the shelf above, pulls out a slim book on Magritte and flicks through the pages: a density of print with small colour photographs interspersed. Not brilliant, but it will do.

The Bois de Vincennes is quiet for the time of day: a few women pushing buggies and the odd lone male with time to kill. Frankie sits in the shelter of a tree with the book unopened in her lap. She can't see their faces: her brain keeps cutting out before the picture becomes clear, but he's kissing Monique in the same way he kissed her, he's touching her body, her dainty, petite body which is so much prettier than Frankie's, so much sexier. And he's telling her what he's done with Frankie, how naïve she is, how she's just a bit of fun on the side. They're laughing about her—at her—and she doesn't know which is worse: Antoine screwing Monique or Antoine screwing her.

What the hell has she done?

She sits for a while, trying not to think, watching a pigeon strut around his intended mate with neck puffed out. The female keeps wandering off, pretending he isn't there. He'll get his way in the end though. They always do.

She opens the book.

The illustrations are familiar: the apple that says it isn't an apple, the dove flying out of the sea, the bowler-hatted men raining down through the sky—or they could be floating upwards. She turns the pages slowly, hardly daring to look and yet impatient to see. The tall girl with the fringe is there, and a long-sleeved nightdress with breasts but no pubic hair. The title of the latter draws her eye: *En hommage à Mack Sennet*—Mack Sennet being, according to the text, a director of American slapstick comedies in the 1930s. An ironic choice for the door of Flat Four. Opposite the nightdress is a girl reading a book, mouth gaping and eyes wide with horror. Frankie pictures herself at Monsieur Villet's. She pictures Nathalie there too and shifts uncomfortably on the bench.

On the next page she sees the couch, chair and gramophone, with the brown suitcase in the centre. A woman lies naked, and seemingly dead, on the couch. Standing with his back to her is a man in a suit, staring calmly into the horn of the gramophone, whilst hiding in the wings are two men in bowler hats, one holding a sheet of netting, the other a club: the murderer's conscience, she reckons, waiting to ensnare him.

She wonders whether Antoine has a conscience.

There are more pages thick with type, followed by pictures of half day and half night, pipes and tubas, signs and symbols, detached limbs. She pauses on an innocuous-looking colonnade with a sign in front of it marked *Cinéma bleu*. And then she finds it: the boulder, the red curtains and the naked woman with the pink rose in her hand. The woman's eyes are blank and the hair is a little longer than hers, but the features are uncannily similar: the woman has her face.

She stares for a long time at the face, confused by its beauty, disturbed by its indifference. And then she studies the body. The thighs are too thick and the waist too long, but it has her breasts. Again there's no pubic hair—she's surprised Antoine didn't make her shave. *Les fleurs du mal/ Flowers of Evil*, it's called: some tenuous connection with Baudelaire? The text contains a quote from Magritte, describing the picture as an unexpected representation of a statue of flesh and blood, with the title intended to complement the image, not explain it. It's still a title that leaves her uneasy. An innocent painting transformed into something unsavoury. Surrealism redefined as a means of sexual gratification.

On the inside back cover are *Les amants*—the lovers with sheets over their heads. A sick joke on Antoine's part, she can see that now. If the sheets fell away they would take the skin with them, leaving raw flesh exposed, blood-drenched muscle twisting down from eye socket to jaw. Or the heads could be deformed and hideous, like lumps of clay some kid has poked with chubby fingers. Love is blind indeed.

She and Antoine are lovers by definition only. A classic case of the ingénue seduced by Gallic charm. Victim and aggressor. Prostitute and pimp. That's what it feels like. The trip to Paris, the meal, the cinema: all fantasy foreplay. Softening her up, luring her into his den, stripping down her defences along with her clothes so he could screw her in front of God knows who, God knows how many surfing perverts. Her image pasted on screens across the world to be gawped at by men—and women, she supposes—for whom that image stirs lust. Nice work if you can get it, that's what he'd say. No mention of payment. How much is her body worth?

You're not a natural, are you, when it comes to sex?

Monique is a natural, that's obvious. She doesn't need gentle handling or softening up. Whereas Frankie…

There's a man on the bench opposite, reading a paper. What did he do last night? Surf the net? Log onto the *Cinema Blue* porn site and pay good money to see the tall dark Adonis screwing the living statue? Get his kicks watching Antoine and her making love?

The man folds his paper, uncrosses his legs and sits in the open-crotched way men do, staring across in her direction. He can't possibly recognise her fully dressed, without the boulder and the lighting and the rose. He can't possibly guess it was her.

I know what you've been doing. You can't hide anything from me.

Maybe not. But revenge is still sweet, so they say.

The leaflet was clamped onto Simon's fridge, next to the children's artwork: an exhibition of new work by local artists, with Monique's name on the list and the name of the gallery. The name of the nearest métro station too.

The man on the door isn't keen to let her in. It's a private viewing, he says; if she doesn't have an invitation, she should come back tomorrow.

She can't wait that long. She lets her voice fall into a lazy English accent and tells him she's Monique's au pair, that there's something she has to tell her about the twins. The doorman steps reluctantly to one side, looking her up and down. She's woefully underdressed, but she's only the au pair after all.

The corridor leads into a large, high-ceilinged room crowded with sparkling glasses and noisy chatter. Sculptures mark out the space: a papier-mâché dog with its leg raised against a stepladder; metal structures shaped like lean, spiky trees; a fish tank filled with multi-coloured flashing lights. There are no unmade beds though and no sheep in formaldehyde. It's fairly tame as these things go.

Monique is with a group on the far side of the room, holding forth about one of her paintings: more blocks of colour and another meticulously placed black line. She's pointing out details, drawing shapes in the air with her hands, explaining the internal reality, no doubt, of that single black line. She and Antoine are made for each other.

Frankie stands on the edge of the script she's been rehearsing. The atmosphere will be intimidating, but she'll forget how out of place she looks. She'll make her way through the glitter of perfume and champagne, and as she draws closer, she'll recognise a face: the man from the website and from the party. He won't know who she is because he hardly looked at her that evening. And when she sees the young guy standing beside him, she'll smile to herself and keep walking, brushing past the tall girl with the fringe and the woman in the sari. Antoine may be there as well, or he may not. Probably not.

Monique will be the last to notice her. She'll detach herself from the group and draw Frankie to one side. 'What are you doing here? Is everything all right?'

'You tell me.'

'What's wrong? Is it Simon?' She'll look straight at her with her beautifully made-up eyes.

'No. It's you. Why didn't you tell me about your filthy little porn business?'

Monique's face will stiffen. She'll steer Frankie further away from the crowd. 'Don't talk so loudly, Frankie.'

'Simon told me. He told me everything.'

'And what did he tell you exactly?'

'That you've left him. That you and Antoine put surreal sex on the internet. That you wanted to drag me into it. It's disgusting, I don't know how you can do it.'

'Grow up, Frankie. People want it, we provide it. And anyway, I thought you knew about the business. You said you'd had fun in the studio.'

'I thought Antoine liked me, that's all.'

'He does like you.'

'No, he doesn't. It's you he likes. You've been at it for months—don't deny it.'

Monique will look uncomfortable and tell her to leave. But she won't leave. Not yet. Not until she's thrown the dog into the fish tank and climbed the stepladder with a chain of coloured lights around her neck. Not until everyone in the room knows precisely what the respected artist does in her spare time.

No one has noticed her. No one has offered her champagne. She's still standing by the door, looking in. Monique finishes her lecture and the group melts away. The man on the door barely acknowledges Frankie as she leaves.

PART THREE

Le double secret / The Double Secret

July has slipped into August and the exodus has started: Parisians heading south to the coast in their thousands, leaving behind shuttered apartments and scribbled *fermeture annuelle* signs on shop doors. Paris will soon be a city depleted, left to the heat and the tourists.

Light pokes into the room. Frankie sits on the table with her feet on the windowsill, staring out. There's no head in the window opposite, and no music. She's switched off the radio, bored with the traffic news: a relentless tale of *bouchons* and *embouteillages* interspersed with jingles and adverts.

She balances the laptop on her knee.

Hi Xavier. Sorry I've not been in touch for a while. Glad it went ok at the church. I've heard of people getting plastered at funerals, but I'm not strong on broken leg impressions which is why I didn't come. One reason anyway. Arty A is out of the picture by the way. You were right—far too cultural. Let me know when you get back to Paris. love Frankie.

There are new drawings in her sketchbook: a man standing on his head in a bucket; a silver-clad mime artist in robotic pose; the Centre Pompidou, with its external escalators encased in the transparent tubes of Antoine's entrails analogy. This last drawing was intended to be an impression, not a precise transcription, but the finished product still looks more like an inflatable dinghy than a building. The scene at Beaubourg reminded her of Edinburgh at Festival time: crowds gathered around street artists, necks straining and digital cameras held aloft. A familiarity that gave her the confidence to draw in public.

Now, looking out from the quiet of her room, she turns to a fresh page. It's a world of straight lines out there: rooftops, chimney stacks and aerials. She thinks of her father hunched over his desk, meticulously plotting each brick, each window, each drainpipe and internal beam. His architectural drawings were pinned-down maps of the imagination; her sketch will set the lines free again, open them up to interpretation.

She presses the pencil-end into her chin, forming a temporary dimple. The memory of her father at his desk is vivid, but she doesn't know if it's real. It's as if there's a row of cine films lined up in her head, and what she remembers are images from the screen, not the moments themselves. On the end of the row is a box labelled *Craig's Funeral.* She takes the spool out sometimes, but when she runs the film the tape is always blank.

There are other gaps too, large chunks of her adolescence that are missing, as if someone put the film in wrongly and it failed to record. What she has are mere snapshots, individual stabs of memory in the overall fog. She sifts through them like a wallet of photographs, catching glimpses of school—the posh one her parents sent her to at the age of eleven and of which remain images of scratched wooden desks, lacrosse games in the rain, being told off for chewing gum when she wasn't. There's the odd half of cider in a smoke-filled pub; clumsy kisses in the street from a boy she hardly knew; fish suppers at Kirsty's, fingers stained with vinegar and Kirsty's two brothers air-guitaring to *Top of the Pops.* Then come strained mealtimes with her parents and hours spent on her own, in her room, when she imagined her bed was a rock with sea all around it and waves crashing and no one able to reach her there.

160

A few of the memories are more detailed. Like one particular time at Kirsty's, after school, when she was twelve or thirteen.

'It'll be a laugh,' said Kirsty. With small scissors she cut a cornflakes packet into rectangles the size of playing cards while I wrote out the alphabet, one letter per card, in felt-tipped pen. We balanced a square of wood on a waste paper bin, put a glass upside down in the middle and arranged the letters in a circle around it. Sitting cross-legged on the floor, we practised gliding the glass across the varnished surface. Then Kirsty went to get one of her brothers, saying it would work better with three.

It's only a glass and a cornflakes packet, I thought as I sat there chewing my hair. My navy skirt was folded over at the waist and there were holes in my tights.

Kirsty returned with Stewart: the good-looking one who always ignored me. Sitting opposite, he snipped at tufts of carpet with the scissors. He had no shoes on and smelt of socks. I pulled at my skirt, trying to make it cover a little more of my legs. Meanwhile Kirsty drew the curtains and shone a lamp down onto the improvised table.

'Right then,' she said, joining us on the floor. 'We all have to think really hard about someone. Preferably someone famous, but anyone dead will do.'

I went hot around the neck and swallowed hard. Stewart stopped snipping. We each put a finger on the glass. There was the throbbing of a hi-fi in the background and voices on the landing, but in Kirsty's room there was silence.

I thought hard about Craig. Really hard. The glass began to move. My finger trembled as it glided from one letter to the next: W... H... E... My heart bumped against my ribs and hit the back of my throat. With her free hand, Kirsty noted down the letters.

'It says, 'Where's my spider?'' she said when the glass stopped moving.

'Must be Robert the Bruce,' said Stewart, deadpan. Then he burst out laughing and knocked the table over, sending the glass and the letters flying. It was all I could do not to cry.

The teenager has grown up. She doesn't drink cheap cider or mess around with upturned glasses any more. Instead she mixes with artists in Paris, drifts in and out of cafés and second-hand bookshops, has a face that draws interest and a creative talent that defines her. Film me now, Craig. Let the hand-held camera give an intimate portrayal. Branch out, add sound if you like, add colour. Make it look as if everything is normal.

'So this is you!' Jude casts her eyes around the room. 'Frankie in Paris! Sounds dead exotic, you know.' She props her rucksack against the wall and steps across to the window, trailing an odour of slightly stale clothes. 'It's so... *French*,' she says, leaning out. 'A world away from Covent Garden, eh? I can't believe you've ended up here.'

'Why shouldn't I have?'

'Dunno. It's a bit bohemian for you, isn't it? And I still don't get how the only person you know in Paris is your brother-in-law. Of all people!'

'But Xavier isn't—well, he's Xavier, and he's not the only person I know. Not any more.' She peers at Jude's ears: 'What are those? Industrial toolkits?'

'That's not all.' Jude pulls her t-shirt off one shoulder to reveal a prowling tiger staring out from behind her bra strap. She growls and claws the air. 'Had that done for someone a few months back—he had the same design on his chest. We shagged for a few weeks, then he buggered off with some bimbo with a lizard on her arse.' A wide grin softens her face. 'And look.' She flashes a ring in her navel. 'I've got others in places I can't possibly show you!'

'Whatever for?'

'Why ever not?'

'Don't they get in the way?'

'Not a bit, they're great conversation openers. At least I haven't gone for those tubes—you know, the ones with blood running through them?'

'No, I certainly *don't* know.'

'Both ends stick into a vein and the tube does a bypass. It's pretty cool if you can stomach it. But don't worry, I do draw the line.' She spikes up her hair with her fingers. 'I'm thinking of going red. What d'you reckon?'

'Red red, you mean?'

'Men prefer blondes, so they say. But I could do some research, publish my findings in a scientific journal. I can see the headlines: 'Reds Best in Bed', 'Scarlet Harlots', that kind of thing.'

Frankie smiles. The rapport she has with Jude surprises her sometimes.

Jude picks up a magazine and thumbs through it. A postcard falls out. She squints at the message as Frankie grabs the card from her.

'Who's Jacques?'

'No one. It's a restaurant.'

'Ah! A date with a mystery man, eh?'

'Just some guy. I've no intention of going.' She stuffs the card in her bag. 'So what about you? Any mystery dates I should know about?'

'Only this guy Claudio I'm meeting up with in Siena. There'll be no hanky-panky, mind—unless it turns out he's stinking rich, of course.'

'The things we do for money, eh?'

'The things we spend money on! I tell you, Frankie, this body of mine costs a fortune—piercings, tattoos, just as well I don't pay for the hair. And then there's the boob job...'

'You haven't?'

'Not yet. I'm saving up though. These poor devils could do with some help.' She plumps up her breasts, which look perfectly adequate to Frankie. 'I don't want it to be only the studs and the hair that stand out!'

She delves into her rucksack and extracts a crumpled Sainsbury's bag.

'Someone told me you can't get this stuff here. The cheese might be a bit iffy, what with the heat, but it seemed kind of essential. You've got wine, I presume?'

'If I'd known you were coming...'

'Wait here.' She grabs her purse and is gone.

The room is quiet but still full of Jude: her energy caught in the air and her rucksack against the wall, with her cord jacket draped over it and a *Hello* magazine poking out. 'I'll be at the Gare du Nord in an hour,' she'd said on the phone. 'You're joking,' Frankie said, more than once. But Jude wasn't joking.

It was a while since they'd seen each other. Not since that chilly morning in Cambridge when Frankie said she had to go home and for once Jude didn't question it. Just bundled Frankie and her bags into that old VW of hers and drove her to the station. They hugged on the platform, a long hug with tears in it, and Frankie hoped JP was nowhere nearby or he'd have read things into it as usual, things that weren't there. And that's what she wondered as she sat on the train, heading for the Gare du Nord: could they still be that close?

The train was late. She paced up and down, checking the arrivals' board and the clock, annoyed that she would have had time after all to get changed. Paris should have left its mark on her by now, she thought. She should look more worldly, more sophisticated. But she didn't feel it and was sure she didn't look it.

When the train pulled in she watched the carriages unload, scanning the faces, still not believing Jude would be there. But she was. Her smile was reassuring. They hugged, though not for long and without the tears this time.

'You've lost weight,' Jude said. 'And what happened to your hair?'

In the Sainsbury's bag Frankie finds a packet of digestive biscuits, a block of Cheddar and a small jar of Marmite. Resisting the temptation to open the biscuits straight away, she lies down on the bed and closes her eyes. There's something of Kirsty about Jude—a confidence that's taken for granted. A mood that draws you in. Sifting back through the snapshots of her adolescence, she sees herself slouched against a wall, with Kirsty saying her accent's gone posh and asking if all her classmates live in Morningside. In the next picture they're in a shop in Cockburn Street, trying on hooped earrings that look silly on her but suit Kirsty. Then there's her telling Kirsty she's been asked out by some boy when she hasn't. Those are the moments she remembers—times when Kirsty was in control of how she felt, just as Jude seems to be now.

'Bloody stairs! It's like climbing bloody Everest!' Jude plonks two bottles of red on the table and collapses on the bed. She peers over Frankie's shoulder with an elbow pressing into her back. 'What's that you're drawing?'

Frankie nods towards the rucksack.

'Not bad! It'll be worth a fortune one day, when you're famous.'

'Absolutely.'

'Does this mean we can't eat till you've finished?'

'Course not.' Frankie holds up the drawing. 'It looks kind of classy like this, don't you think? Half there and half not.'

She frees herself from Jude's elbow and gets up off the bed. It's the middle of the afternoon, but so what? She uncorks a bottle, pours wine into tumblers and puts two unmatching plates on the table. Then she remembers there's only one chair, moves the plates to the bed and sits down again next to Jude.

'Saw a cool guy on the landing,' says Jude.

'Blond and tanned, by any chance?'

'No—tall, dark and brooding.'

'Oh. Antoine.'

'What do you mean, 'Oh. Antoine'? He's fucking gorgeous!'

'Is he?'

'Don't tell me you haven't noticed?'

'He's not bad looking, I suppose, but…'

'Not your type, presumably. Too sultry.'

Frankie slits open the cheese wrapper with *le couteau qui coupe*. It smells okay and she's prepared to risk it. As she carves the block into slices, she wonders what her type is exactly.

Jude has opened the biscuits and unzipped the plastic collar on the Marmite. She holds the jar to Frankie's nose. Love it or hate it: Frankie loves it. Her mouth floods with saliva. She pokes a finger into the jar and licks off the salty gunge, then she smears some onto a biscuit with the knife, tops it with a slab of Cheddar and bites into it. The taste takes her straight back to Cambridge and Jude's narrow kitchen with the resident pile of dirty crockery in the sink. A madeleine for the twenty-first century.

I was in awe of Jude then. She was a couple of years younger than me, yet she had things sorted, knew what she liked and didn't like. It made me wonder sometimes what the point was of university, all that reading and grappling with ideas when Jude was already out there, earning her living, doing the hairdressing she enjoyed with only a handful of GCSEs to her name. Her adult life had begun whilst mine was on hold. When I left Covent Garden to move in with JP, I felt I was catching up with her, overtaking her even. That feeling soon waned. We spoke on the phone a few times and Jude came round with the glasses, but after that I found myself avoiding her without knowing why. Perhaps I envied her the freedom she still had, or feared what she would say about JP, the questions she would ask. Whichever, I started to feel even more left behind than before and seeing Jude would only have rubbed my nose in it.

They've eaten their way through most of the biscuits, all the cheese and a good deal of the Marmite. They're well into the second bottle of wine. Frankie has told Jude about her visit to Monsieur Villet. 'No wonder he's blind!' Jude said.

'Any real romance on the horizon then, Frankie?' she asks now.

'There might have been.'

'Blond and tanned?'

'No, not Simon, he's just a friend. There was someone else though.'

'Let me guess—a hot-blooded Gallic male spotted you amongst the cabbages and whisked you off for a dirty weekend. Except you turned him down, of course.'

'If only I had.'

'Not the gorgeous Antoine?'

'He was bad news, Jude. Not right for me at all.'

'Well who'd have thought it, eh? Married?'

'No, just… not right.'

'More enticing than safe old Simon though. You should go for it, Frankie, get stuck back in with body-to-die-for Antoine. This is Paris, after all, city of lust and debauchery.' She reaches for the wine bottle, tops up both glasses. 'Mind you, the riskiest thing you've ever done was eating my lasagne—and marrying that twerp.'

'People change.'

'Nah, they don't. Leopards and spots and all that.'

Frankie stares into her glass. The wine is rough: more vinegar than grape. Jude must have gone for the cheapest.

'What's with the masking tape?'

'Don't know yet.'

Jude gets up off the bed and fishes a black marker pen out of her rucksack. Frankie isn't sure if she wants her to, but she starts drawing anyway: a face with spiky hair, wild eyes and an off-centre mouth. Rings and studs in the ears, way out of proportion.

'Your turn. Draw the first thing that comes into your head.'

Frankie begins with a tail, adds a body, head, whiskers and legs. One foot held high with claws splayed. A snarl of teeth. Stripes all over.

They stand back to assess their efforts. Jude's self-portrait has spirit; Frankie's tiger is adequate apart from the legs, which look like they're made of Plasticine. Not bad for a hairdresser and a porn star.

'Guess what,' says Jude, swinging herself up onto the table. 'Claudio's got this cousin who works in a nightclub off the rue St-Denis. We should go—unless it's too trendy for you, that is.'

The pen top clicks as Frankie snaps it on and off.

Women skulk like wildcats in doorways: shiny black leather, legs wrapped in fish-net, expressions as defiant as their clothes. She and Jude walk arm in arm: security in numbers, even if the number's only two. They walk briskly, trying not to stare, but even so the skulking women flash them scornful looks, mouths pouting around cigarettes and nail varnish glinting. At least these women will get a glimpse of who's paying. Not like Frankie, bounced off a satellite somewhere and spied on by anonymous eyes. That's the worst case scenario anyway.

The entrance is framed in indigo light. Two black-suited bouncers stand on guard: stocky, with broad shoulders and no necks. Custom-built rectangles with heads. They wear their faces like masks and their hands are weighted with gold. Jude gets Frankie to explain about Claudio—'You're the linguist'—and Frankie stumbles over the words, feeling a prat for trying it on. But the second face drops its mask and breaks into a grin. '*Ciao!*' he says, thumping them both on the back. He asks for news of

Claudio in heavily-accented French and they have a three-way conversation in two languages with some sign language thrown in too. Then, with the mask back in place, Rectangle Number Two escorts them past the grim-faced cashier and points them along a murky passageway.

'That's the first time the Mafia's done me a favour!' Jude whispers loudly as they make their way down the stairs. Orange light seeps from each carpeted step and the walls are studded with shining stars. It gets darker as they go down. Music throbs below and a pungent smell of sweating bodies rises with the heat.

On the dance floor disembodied limbs jerk in the pulsating orange lights. The surrounding darkness is intense, making it impossible to tell how big the room is. The rhythm of the music shudders up through the floor. Frankie has seen places like this in films and on TV, but she's never been in one before. She's grateful for the darkness.

'I'll get the drinks,' Jude shouts into her ear before disappearing into the din, her body flickering on and off like a faulty light bulb.

Frankie is sweating. The thumping beat of the music fills her chest. She doesn't know what she's breathing, but it's hard to believe it's air. The effect is hypnotic: the senses sated, with no room left for thought. The limbs on the dance floor twist and twitch as the rhythm intensifies.

'Bloody rip-off.' Jude hands her a warm glass. 'There was this guy at the bar though. He may come over.'

He does. Jude passes Frankie her drink as the man snakes an arm round her waist.

Frankie retreats into a corner. The lighting is swirling now in waves of indigo and yellow. Jude dances like water, her body fluid and rippling, her arms raised above her head. The man has his eyes on her breasts and all the movement is in his hips, thrusting forwards in time with the beat, edging closer until their bodies are almost touching. There's something beautiful about it, the way she's dancing, the way he's responding.

Someone taps Frankie on the shoulder. With a flick of the head he asks her to dance. She's not as skilled as Jude and it's not her kind of music, but the man she's with doesn't seem to notice. He gyrates in a world of his own, spinning round, eyes closed. After two or three tracks that merge into each other, Frankie curls out of his orbit.

There's peculiar, tinted lighting in the Ladies and the walls, like the stairs, are studded with stars. Frankie uses the chrome toilet and washes her hands at a sink that looks more like something you'd serve salad in. Her face is grey in the mirror. She blames the lighting and applies lipstick—a deeper shade of grey. Jude's face appears next to hers.

'How's it going?' says the face.

'Pretty cosmic. I've been dancing with a spaced-out planet.'

Jude raises an eyebrow. Her eyes are glazed and Frankie wonders how much she's had to drink. What else she's had.

'That guy looked keen,' she says.

'Told him I had a sexually-transmitted disease.'

'Why?'

'Saving myself for Claudio, aren't I? Italian cock, not French.'

'No hanky-panky, you said.'

'Yeah well, depends what's on offer. Cock-a-doodle-doo, cock-a-doodle-don't!'

No change there then: she's still coarse when drunk. Something scratchy like hessian comes to mind—not that she was exactly silk to start with. Frankie burps and tastes Marmite.

'Waste of fucking breath though,' says Jude. 'He didn't speak a word of English.'

They head back to the dance floor. The moves come more easily to Frankie now, with the music taking root inside her and blotting out all concept of time. There's no way of knowing if it's day or night. All that matters is being here.

Jude has gone back inside to use the toilet. Frankie waits for her on the pavement, safe within the range of the bouncers. There's been a twitch of a wink from Rectangle Number Two, nothing more. The music has left a muffle over her ears, a hot fog around her head, and her body is drenched in sweat. She feels like a dish that's come out of the oven and refuses to cool down.

She hadn't noticed the young couple going past, but when the shouting starts, she notices. The woman is leaning into her partner, spitting insults, and although he glares back at her, his body is bent, as if cracked in the middle. The woman keeps shouting, swearing, turning round and appealing to an invisible audience on the other side of the street. When the young man turns and walks away, saying nothing, the woman follows, her words clawing at his back. And that's when the man spins round and slams his fist into her stomach. Her body crumples. The action freezes for a moment with no sound, no movement, and then the woman begins to wail. Poker-faced, Jude's Mafia friend strolls across and offers her a handkerchief.

Frankie's fists are clenched. Her head is spinning. She staggers down the side of the nightclub, clings to the shadow of the alleyway and gasps for breath as a surge of red-tinged vomit splatters on the ground by her feet.

I left work shortly after six. It was chilly out and dark. I wound a scarf round my neck and pulled on a hat—the one he'd said he liked, in the teashop, some two years before.

My bike was locked to the railings, in the usual place. As I drew closer I saw something in the basket. A bunch of pale yellow carnations and a note, which I read under the streetlamp: *To darling Francesca, Happy First Anniversary. With all my love, JP.*

I looked around: there was no one. Wondering how long the flowers had been there, I bent down to unlock the bike.

His hands round my waist made me jump.

'God, what a fright! What are you doing here?'

'Meeting the woman I love after work. You don't have a problem with that, do you?'

We hugged on the pavement, in the pool of artificial light, and I felt rescued somehow. Gathered up and transported to a warm, safe place.

'Like the flowers?' he said.

'They're lovely. I haven't got anything for you—only a card.'

'I don't need presents. I've got you.'

He took charge of the bike with one hand and put his other arm round my shoulder, and we walked home like that, snuggled closely together, our breath misting the air.

The house was in darkness. He took the flowers and made me wait in the hall. Then he summoned me into the sitting room.

Candles shimmered in the hearth. There was soft music playing. Cushions were scattered on the floor around a low table that hadn't been there before. The table was laid with a white cloth, white serviettes and straight, frosted glasses. The carnations shone out of a vase in the centre.

'Sit down,' he said, pouring sparkling apple juice into the glasses. 'Happy anniversary, Francesca.'

I raised the glass to my lips and didn't care that it wasn't champagne. What mattered was the effort he'd gone to. The things he did for me.

He came back from the kitchen with two plates of poached asparagus: tender fingers of green, fanning out.

'A little something I made earlier. The mayonnaise is homemade, of course.'

Of course.

After that there were mussels cooked in cream with parsley and garlic; fresh crusty bread with a selection of cheeses; chocolate mousse made to a recipe of Colette's.

'Why eat out?' he said.

When we'd finished eating we sat on the floor in the candlelight, and he pulled me towards him and held my face as he kissed me, and then he undid my blouse and slipped in his hand and we made love right there on the carpet, next to the bookcase, just like the first time.

I went up to the bathroom and checked my face in the mirror. My skin had a glow that I put down to the sex. As I sat on the bidet, splashing warm water between my legs, the phone rang downstairs.

'What are you doing?'

I looked round with a jolt. I hadn't heard him come up. 'Nothing. Just washing. Who was that on the phone?'

'Why?'

'Just wondered.'

'Why are you washing?'

'No reason. Who was it?'

He left me to it.

The sitting room was bright and stark, lit only by the overhead light. Smoke drifted from the snuffed-out candles and there was no music. The plates had been cleared away, leaving the table square and white and empty.

JP was doing the dishes.

'You should have left everything as it was,' I said to his back. 'It was nice. I liked it.'

'Did you?'

'Yes. Is something wrong?'

'The washing up won't do itself, you know.'

'I'd have done it.'

'Would you? You were too busy washing yourself.'

'What's that supposed to mean?'

He didn't answer. Returning to the sitting room, I switched off the main light, put on a lamp and began sifting through the CDs.

'What the hell was he phoning for?' He was standing in front of me, water dripping off his hands. He had that look on his face, the one I dreaded.

'Who?'

'Gordon. That chap of yours.'

'He's not that chap of mine. What did he want?'

'You tell me.'

'Well what did he say?'

'He wanted to know if you were here.'

'So why didn't you let me speak to him?'

'It's our wedding anniversary, Francesca.'

'So?'

'What did he want?'

'I've no idea. Something to do with work, probably. If you'd let me speak to him…'

'You were busy. Washing yourself. Getting rid of our sex.'

'That's not what I was doing. Oh come on, JP, don't be like this.' I stood up and touched his hand. 'Tonight's been wonderful. Don't spoil it.'

He took hold of my arm, drew me towards him and kissed me. 'I love you, Francesca,' he whispered. 'You've no idea how much I love you.'

I melted into his words as he held me tightly, tighter. I felt my arm twist behind my back, he was twisting my arm, it hurt and I told him to stop, but he went on twisting and it hurt even more and by now I was crying out and gasping. He flung me to the floor.

'Don't you dare make a fool of me, Francesca.'

I held my arm and tried to hold onto my tears as well. JP glared down at me, anger stretched across his face. When he knelt beside me, I flinched.

'Hey,' he said, his voice suddenly calm. 'I'm not going to hurt you. You know I'd never mean to hurt you.'

'Why did you do that then? What's your problem?'

'I'm not the one with the problem, Francesca, it's you. You undermine me all the time and you don't even know you're doing it. What do you expect if you treat me like that?' He coaxed my head against his shoulder and held it there.

Jude stuffs clothes into her rucksack and glances round the room.

'If I've forgotten anything, you can send it on care of the Mafia.' She squeezes out a smile. 'You okay?'

'The booze,' says Frankie, raising her head off the pillow. 'It does things.'

Jude looks at her, about to speak. But she's clearly hung over too and she has a train to catch. It's a lucky escape, or not, depending which way you look at it. Frankie can only look at it upside down this morning. Back to front. All over the place.

'I'll send a postcard from Siena,' Jude says, stumbling out through the door with the rucksack.

Her voice lingers after she's gone, the smell of her clothes, but the room feels empty. Perhaps Frankie should have asked her to stay. The one person she can talk to, though for some reason she never does.

She drags herself out of bed. The clothes she's wearing are crumpled with sleep and she has that brittle, dried-out feeling, the stale taste in the mouth, the furred tongue. That's it. No more wine. No more alcohol of any kind. Ever.

On the floor by the window there are clippings of reddish-brown hair and it comes back to her in fragments. They went dancing. There was a fight on the pavement and she was sick, and she felt sick again in the taxi and almost had to ask the driver to stop. But somehow she kept it down and then the cool air helped when he dropped them off at the end of the street and they walked.

God knows what time it was. She was knackered, completely out of it, jittery after the business on the pavement, but Jude had come all this way and she was leaving in the morning. They finished the biscuits and ate Marmite neat from the jar, with the piano playing again in the rooftops: oddly comforting after the din of the nightclub. Producing a pair of scissors from her rucksack, Jude offered to cut her hair. It seemed like a daft idea, but Frankie was in no state to resist. 'Stone, paper, scissors,' she said, holding out a fist. Jude presented a flattened hand. Not as pissed as she seemed then.

Frankie sat on the chair, facing the window. 'Just the ends,' she said. 'Nothing drastic.' Jude's hands felt warm on her scalp. A sour smell of sweat shot out from her armpits, but Frankie didn't mind it too much. She closed her eyes and drifted, light as gossamer, hardly there at all. The scissors clicked around her head, little sparks in the air. She heard Jude say she'd liked her hair long, the way it was before, so she explained that when she left Cambridge, having it cut had been symbolic—reinventing herself, as they say. But she'd always regretted it. 'No regrets about leaving JP though?' Jude said.

The first mention of his name and Frankie wished she hadn't. It was like a skin growing back over her, one she'd been struggling to shed. She told Jude he was dead now, end of story. The scissors stopped clicking. 'Dead?' Jude said. 'How?'

That's when the tears escaped from her eyes. Jude assumed she was crying for JP but she wasn't, she was crying for herself and it was also something to do with the fingers in her hair. But then the fingers wandered down her neck, slipped in under her collar and across the tops of her shoulders. Frankie heard JP gloating, saying he'd been right about Jude all along, and she pulled herself away.

They had no option but to share the bed. Jude got changed quickly and lay on her side, with her face to the wall. Frankie crawled in fully clothed, with her back to Jude, and tried to switch off the lights in her head. All the bright corners where memories blaze and shout. The raw, shiny bits which hurt too much. Sleep was the only way out.

She doesn't want to go to work, but her body goes there anyway, dragging her with it. Her muscles are stiff, from dancing or from sharing the bed, she's not sure which. Her head throbs and she's turned in on herself. She doesn't want contact with anyone. She can't be bothered to sort through the vegetables or restock the crates. The nectarines are mixed up with the peaches and that's how they'll stay.

A different girl is serving on the cheese counter. She doesn't have Nathalie's flair: the pyramids of Crottins are slightly adrift and there's a smear on the glass that she's missed. Her face is rubbery and pockmarked like a lump of Gruyère. There's no smile to cheer Frankie up, no banter to keep her going.

Nathalie will be in hospital now. She'll be lying in a hospital bed, swathed in hospital noises and smells, surrounded by white. White sheets and white walls. White-uniformed nurses with white-toothed smiles. White plastic cups on white plastic tables with white plastic straws...

'A pound of plums please, Mademoiselle—*des jaunes*, if you have them. And some tomatoes.'

Tensely Frankie weighs the plums and shoves a few ripe tomatoes in a bag. One of the tomatoes misses and falls on the floor, red flesh splattering in globules across the tiles and green seeds spurting out like exploded frog spawn. 'Damn it,' she mutters, stepping clear of the mess. As she does so, an image of the couple in the street comes back to her: the man's fist, the woman's tears. A sense of something in her own past, half remembered…

'Are you well, Mademoiselle?' His gaze falls below her eyes.

'I'm fine.'

Monsieur Villet shakes his head and shuffles away, following the diagram that must be etched on the inside of his head. It's high time they changed the layout of the aisles.

The four hours lump together like clay; somehow she stumbles through. On the way home she stops off at the café. The men at the bar turn their heads with barely perceptible nods of recognition. Frankie sits in her usual place, with her back to the mirror, and orders a hot chocolate—the new alcohol, she tells herself without conviction. She drinks the chocolate slowly, trying not to scald her tongue this time. The barman is polishing the counter. There's a film on the TV: spits of gunfire in some Far West saloon. When the action hots up the barman gawps at the screen, cloth in hand, wiping suspended. The scene reminds her of wet Sunday afternoons in Edinburgh, when she and Craig lay on the sitting room floor with their noses six inches from the telly and a packet of chocolate éclairs between them. But that little girl isn't her any more: she's a character in an old movie, a piece of clothing that no longer fits. How often does that happen? How many different people are we in one lifetime?

She thinks of the early cine films of her father's: no colour, just shades of grey, the images punctured by twitching scars and dots. In one, a small girl—the girl Frankie used to be—rushes up to the camera and peers into it, her face too close and out of focus. The camera draws back. The girl dips a plastic wand into the tube she's holding, brings the wand to her mouth and blows. Bubbles float in front of her like rings of breath. Her hair is tied back, with errant wisps softening the outline of her face, and she's wearing a patterned dress and flipflops. As the bubbles dissolve, she clambers onto a nearby rock and sits there, watching the waves.

The scene cuts to the open sea and to Craig in an open boat. He's hidden in oilskins, with only his head poking out. Beside him an old man with a pipe hauls in a net on which fish are trapped, tails flicking. Craig stretches across to help, but with the movement of the sea the picture is indistinct. When the camera zooms in he holds up a fish, its eye shining like glass, scales glinting. He drops it in the crate with the others and reaches out to take the camera. There's a flurry of sky and water. The next shot shows her father, smiling back into the lens. On the horizon behind him is a ship. The horizon is squint. They used to tease Craig about that: the ship that sailed uphill.

Frankie counts out change for the hot chocolate. By the time she leaves the café her head feels less brittle, her step lighter. She buys herself a bunch of pink carnations.

There are noises from inside, thuds and bangs. She wonders what he's doing. Who he's doing it with.

The door opens suddenly. Bangles chink and there's a waft of perfume as Monique comes out onto the landing, dragging a large canvas behind her.

'Looking for Antoine?'

Frankie blushes. 'I thought I heard something, that's all.'

'He'll be here later if you want him.' She looks Frankie up and down, her eyes resting on her feet, her unpainted toenails. Frankie transfers the carnations to the crook of her other arm. This is the woman Simon fell in love with, the one Antoine has been screwing. The one who's disappearing down the stairs now with the canvas.

She should have said something, damn it.

Halfway up the stairs to her room, she stops. There are more thuds from inside the flat. Despite what Monique has just said, her stomach lurches. She wants to see him and she doesn't. Wants to scream at him and doesn't. She sits down in the shadow of the wall, with the flowers in her lap, and waits.

It's Monique she sees first, going back into the flat. All goes quiet. Frankie knows exactly what they're doing. She sees their bodies pitching and writhing on the couch, his hands in her hair, his mouth on hers. Is the camera running? Are they filming their affair for prying eyes and maximum profit?

The door opens again and Monique comes out with another canvas, followed not by Antoine, but by the woman in the sari. Turquoise today, not pink. Resting the canvas against her thigh, Monique gently removes something from the woman's hair—a piece of fluff, a splinter of wood? They kiss tenderly on the lips before setting off down the stairs.

The room is still defined by Jude. She's left behind a sense of something slightly out of kilter, and her face on the wall, and an empty jar of Marmite that really ought to be thrown away. Frankie cuts the stems of the carnations and puts them in water. Opens the window. Sweeps up the commas of hair and brushes biscuit crumbs off the sheets. She has a new scenario in her head now, one that's easier to look at: the two women on the couch, their bodies tangled in lengths of turquoise silk, limbs sticking out in all directions like the legs of a drunken octopus smothered in seaweed.

Smiling, she perches on the edge of the bed and unscrews a pot of nail varnish—the one Monique gave her once when she was down doing her washing. The varnish smells strong, like fruit-flavoured creosote. One by one the nails of her left foot become stained a deep purplish-red. Very Monique. Frankie holds out the foot, swinging it back and forth through the air to dry it.

Whatever is she doing? Magenta toenails aren't her style. She screws the top back onto the varnish.

When she was small she used to sneak into her parents' bedroom and experiment with her mother's make-up. With painted lips and eyelids she felt like a princess. She feels more like a call girl now—or does she? How much does she really know about Antoine? Was it misplaced jealousy that turned Simon against him? She needs to find out the truth from the horse's mouth.

Strange to think of Antoine as a horse.

She rummages in her bag and pulls out the card: *Le double secret/ The Double Secret.* A picture of a woman with a section of her face torn away, revealing brown sinew dotted with spheres that look like jingle bells. An image as enigmatic as the writer of the message.

Fucking gorgeous. Perhaps he is.

They're at a table by the window. Antoine sweeps his hair out of his eyes and pours wine into her glass. She doesn't meet his gaze. A tear of wax slips down the candle in front of her. She's going to be careful: three glasses, no more. Her insides are shaking. She doesn't know what the hell she's doing here.

'*Le bœuf?*' says the waitress, one hip angled upwards and steam rising in front of her breasts.

Antoine raises a finger and the waitress puts the food on the table. His eyes are on her cleavage as she wipes a smear of sauce from the edge of his plate. And on her back as she leaves. *Beau cul*, he's thinking. Nice arse. Frankie can see it written on his face.

'What have you been up to then?' he says.

'This and that. I had a friend staying.'

'Oh?'

'From Cambridge. She's a hairdresser.' What did she say that for? He'll be wondering how big her tits are.

She toys with the risotto on her plate. Takes a deep breath.

'Simon told me about the studio. What goes on.'

Antoine frowns. 'It's nothing to do with Simon.'

'He wanted to warn me.'

'I thought Monique had explained.'

'Well she didn't. You should have done that.' She looks straight at him now.

'Look Frankie, I never promised you anything. What you see is what you get.'

'Is it?'

He spears a chunk of beef with his fork. Frankie grips the stem of her glass. Her head is already light from the wine.

'Did you film us?' she says, her stomach taut with nerves.

'I intended to, yes. But when it came to it… That's why we moved out of the light.' She's searching his eyes, trying to see what's real. 'You'll have to take my word for it.'

'And why should I do that?'

'Come on, Frankie,' he teases. 'You enjoyed it. Don't pretend you didn't.'

She extracts a prawn from the rice with her fingers.

'And what about you and Monique? Are you having an affair?'

'Me and Monique? Is that a joke?'

'Simon told me.'

'Did he? Good old Simon.'

'So you *are* having an affair?'

'Look, Monique's not really into men, you know.'

'The woman in the sari?'

'Tasha, yes, they've been at it for a while now. So there's no way Monique and I… And anyway, what if I *was* seeing her? Would it matter?'

She wonders how to play it. 'Not really. It's not as if we're an item or anything.'

He grins. 'I was worried, you know. I thought maybe…'

'What, that I'd fallen in love with you? Is that what you thought?'

He shrugs and tears at a hunk of bread. 'It was just a bit of fun, *hein*? And we can have some more fun if you like. It pays well, you know. You just ignore the camera, concentrate on what you're doing, like before.'

'You said you didn't film me.'

'I didn't. But maybe next time.' He spears another chunk of beef.

Frankie helps herself to wine and prods at the risotto. She doesn't know the person sitting opposite. He's simply a man eating stew in a restaurant. Yet when she thinks of what they did. Of how he's seen her body, felt her body, been inside her body. And now they're sitting here, fully clothed, and he's asking her to do it for money. To do it for sad old gits who can't get their kicks any other way.

'You should have told me what you had in mind. You should have said.'

'Would it have made a difference?'

'Of course it would have made a difference!'

'We wouldn't have fucked, is that what you mean?'

She winces when he says it. When he says that word. Feels a shudder of lust too.

'How can you do that stuff? Film those things?'

'Monique said you didn't mind.'

'Well she's wrong, I do mind.'

'Look, it's only a job. We don't make people do it. It's their choice.'

'And me?'

'You need time to get used to the idea, that's all. And the sex…' His gaze wanders off again as the waitress slinks by.

'Trying me out, were you?' The anger is flooding back. 'Seeing if I'd be good for business?'

'It was Monique's idea. She noticed your face. A perfect match, she said.'

'Us or my face?'

He pushes a mushroom onto his fork with a piece of bread, his hair flopping down over his eyes. The wine is between them on the table. As she reaches for the salt, Frankie nudges the bottle with the back of her hand. It topples over. Antoine's glass goes flying and red wine gushes over the tablecloth, spilling into his lap. He jumps up, cursing in French, as the bottle crashes to the floor. She's never seen him move so fast! The restaurant falls quiet and all eyes look in their direction.

'Sorry,' she says, deadpan. 'I don't know how that happened.'

Antoine sits down, dabbing his trousers with his napkin. The waitress brings a mop and a clean tablecloth, transfers their food and crockery to a tray and deals with the spilt wine. This time Antoine ignores the cleavage.

'Surely you'd rather work with art than vegetables,' he says when the waitress has finished.

'You call that art?'

'Define art.'

Frankie takes a large gulp of wine and a small mouthful of risotto. Reflections float in the window behind Antoine's head: wraith-like torsos and fluttering candles superimposed on the drab street outside. She wonders if that would qualify as art in Antoine's book and wants to ask if he really thinks he's Magritte, but the question seems so ridiculous it sticks in her throat.

He's explaining about the pictures, how he and Monique decide on the sets. 'It has to look good, you know—and so do the girls.' He wipes his plate. The waitress reappears and asks if everything's all right with the food. She asks Antoine, not Frankie. He orders more wine.

'You look great in those photos, by the way.'

'In the cemetery?'

'Mmm—very sexy.' His eyes linger on her face and she doesn't want to blush, but she can't help it.

'Can I see them?'

'Sure. Why not come to the studio next week, pose for a few more stills, see how it goes?' The waitress returns with a bottle, her breasts dancing as she wrestles with the corkscrew. 'Think of it as developing an art form with your body. Creating a living sketchbook, if you like.'

Frankie pushes what's left of the risotto to the side of her plate. Antoine's foot touches hers under the table and neither of them takes their foot away.

'What do you do with the photos?'

'Nothing. They're for personal use.' He looks across at her. A dark, intense look. Challenging, enticing.

Frankie almost smiles. Stops just in time and pours herself a fourth glass of wine.

The church bells fill a vacuum in her head and she realises she's awake. Nine o'clock. Shit. She sits up, pushes back the bedclothes, rubs life into her face. She should have been at work an hour ago. Too late now. A slice of her life has melted away unnoticed. Two hours lost without trace, swallowed up in the dark nothingness of sleep.

She has a feeling she's been dreaming about Craig. The detail teases, like a taste she can't place, almost slipping away before she can grasp hold of it. There was a mermaid on the beach, a back-to-front mermaid with a woman's body and a fish's head, like one of the images on the frieze. And she thought it was him, so she tried to change the body into a man's, but it didn't work and in a way she was glad, because that meant it wasn't him after all and she could walk away and leave it lying there. Not her problem. Nothing to do with her.

And in the dream she was naked. No, not naked, but there was something not right. Her clothes didn't cover her properly. When she pulled them up to hide her breasts, her pubic hair was exposed. And when she tugged them down, they no longer covered her breasts. People were looking, staring. Crowds of people, suddenly, on the beach. All staring.

She gets up and goes through to the toilet, where she squats and holds her breath. Her stomach feels bloated: her period must be due. The excretion of her innards that will bring with it a mixture of relief and dismay. Always has done.

There was blood on my knickers and I didn't know why. My mother said it was normal, gave me a thick pad to stick inside my pants. I went to my room and sat clasping my stomach, because it hurt, and I didn't understand the point of the illness or why it should happen every month. Kirsty laughed when I told her. 'It's so you can have babies,' she said. 'Did no one tell you?' I was too young to think of things like that. But bleeding changed me. I stopped doing without thinking and started thinking without doing. When I got back from school I'd spend hours in my room, staring at the trees through the window, searching for something I never quite found.

The phone will be ringing in their house. If they're there, they can hear it. She hopes it will be her mother who answers.

'Hello.'

'Hi Dad, it's me. How's things?'

'We're fine. You?'

'Not bad. I'm having a quiet time, you know. A fruit- and veg-free day.' She's doodling on the back of a magazine: a pattern of loops and circles.

'Your mother's out. Tesco's.'

'Oh. Okay. I can still talk to you though, can't I?'

'If you like.'

'So what are you up to then?'

'I was in the garage.'

'Another bread bin?'

'I don't do bread bins any more.' That flatness in his voice. A tone as empty of colour as the world he inhabits.

'Something else then—more creative, less bread bin-like?'

'Shelving.'

'Oh. Any particular kind?'

'Just shelving.'

'Right.'

There's a pause.

'What's the weather like in Edinburgh?'

'A bit chilly for August.'

'It's stifling here—really airless, you know, in the city. We could do with a good storm to clear the air.'

Another pause. The doodle is densely shaded now, a swirling mass with snake-like prongs curling out.

'Right, well I'd better be going. Give my love to Mum.'

It was the same when I told him about the wedding: all his thoughts were in the silence. Worse than that, he didn't let me speak to my mother. She was out, he said, but I knew that wasn't true: I could hear a tap running in the background. My father wouldn't waste water like that. 'You'll have to meet him,' I said; 'I'll bring him to see you.' It never happened, of course. JP decided it always rained in Scotland and that a return visit wasn't required.

She bends over the basin and runs both taps at full strength, slapping her face with the hot-cold water. As the mirror furs with steam, the ghost of the five-pointed star creeps into view, still there, where she traced it. Like the aeroplanes Craig used to draw on the back window of the car when there was condensation and which stayed there, engrained, reappearing at odd times when sunlight hit the glass at a certain angle.

She wipes away the steam and stares into the mirror. The more she stares, the less she sees. It doesn't look like a face, it's just a random splodge in front of her. She could carry on staring forever.

That's what you did to me Craig, when you died. The mirror you'd held up to me became a sheet of darkness that reflected nothing back. I couldn't see myself any more.

There are footsteps on the stairs. She waits on the landing with her towel draped over her shoulder.

'Morning, Frankie.'

She's glad it's only Simon. She hasn't seen him for a while. It's strange how that happens, how you can live in the same building as someone and not see them for ages.

'I was thinking of you,' he says from three steps down. 'Wondering how you were.'

'So so. I overslept.'

'Me too. I phoned in sick.'

She sinks down onto the top step with her nightshirt pulled in around her knees. Simon slides his back down the wall and ends up sitting too. A rod of sunlight from her room cuts through the air between them, dust dancing in its path.

'I've knocked on your door a couple of times,' she says.

'I've been staying at work late, eating out. Anything to avoid that empty flat.'

'And I thought it was me you were avoiding!'

'I wouldn't avoid you.' The words float on the silence with a hint of an echo. Frankie fiddles with a thread in her nightshirt.

'Monique hasn't come back then?'

'No. She'll have been in Flat Four though, working on that beloved frieze of theirs.'

Frankie nods. 'I...' She pauses. 'I went to her exhibition.'

'Whatever for?' He looks up at her and there's a child in his face, the boy he was and still is, with time layered on top. He reminds her of a classmate at primary school, a cheeky lad who was always in trouble but never seemed to care. Simon cares though, that's the difference.

'There were things I wanted to get clear. But I chickened out.'

'*He* was there, I suppose.'

'Don't think so.' She rotates her foot inside the shaft of sunlight, warming her toes. 'I have seen him though. We went for a meal the other evening.'

'How come?'

'I wanted to get his side of the story.'

'And?'

'He says he didn't film me.'

'You don't believe that, do you?'

'Why shouldn't I?'

'Well he's hardly going to own up to it, is he, least of all to you?' He licks a finger and rubs dirt off his shoe. 'There's one way to find out for certain, of course.'

'No, I couldn't. I'd rather just take his word for it.'

'You're not still...?'

'Course not. Like you said, I'm better off without him.'

She stretches out both legs. The sun wraps itself around her shins in bangles of light and she feels childlike too.

'I've been worried, you know,' says Simon, 'showing you the website and everything. It was wrong of me.'

'No, I'm glad you showed me. It's better to know.'

'It's just, there are some things you don't dare touch in case they break.' His head is lowered. He's running his finger back and forth along the wood of the stair, following the grain.

Downstairs a door opens and closes, followed by whining and muttering. Simon looks up and catches her eye. '*Allez mes petits,*' he says, pulling his face into a taut, purse-lipped impression. 'Time for walkies.'

'Shh,' says Frankie, grinning.

'Walkies with mummy. A little crap here, a little crap there.'

'Simon!'

'She can't hear, silly. And even if she could, she wouldn't understand.' He purses his lips again and plumps out his chest. The main door closes and the stairwell falls silent.

'Any idea who's moved in opposite me?' says Frankie, lowering her voice.

'No, we're… I'm only a tenant here, like everyone else. No one tells me anything.' He scratches at a stain on his t-shirt. 'You can still bring your washing down, you know, if you need to. The machine hardly gets used these days.'

'Thanks. I've got that book for you too. *Regain.*'

Simon nods and goes back to his caressing of the stair. 'Were the boys there?'

'It wasn't that kind of thing. You have seen them, haven't you?'

'She's dropped them off a couple of times, but it's not the same. It feels like rent-a-kid or something. Like I should be paying an hourly rate for the privilege, damn it.' He leans back into the wall and they sit like that for a while.

'I asked in the bookshop,' he says then, his voice brightening. 'The chap said he might have some work.'

'Isn't he closed for August?'

'Must be one of the few shops that isn't. It's only mugs like us who work right through.'

'You should get away for a bit, Simon. Do something you really want for a change.'

'That's just it—I don't know what I want right now.' He glances up at her. 'Do you know your eyes keep changing colour? They're deep blue today. The colour of irises.'

'My mother's favourite flowers.' The bangles of light glow and fade on her shins. She sees the grey stone Edinburgh semi with its neat garden and tall bay windows. The curve of her mother's waist as she sat at the piano and the way her father smiled on the film. A special smile, reserved for Craig.

'Do you have brothers and sisters?' says Simon, reading her thoughts.

She hesitates. 'I had a brother. He died.'

The words hover in the air: cold words, like snowflakes. Simon says nothing as they drift to the ground and melt away. And she remembers how she told JP about Craig, wanting him to know. Wanting to share that part of her with him. Maybe she hoped he'd have wise words to comfort her, that he'd take away some of the pain. He listened until she'd finished, then he said: *I don't want to hear any more about that. It's the present that matters, not the past.* That's all he said.

Simon stifles a yawn. 'Sorry. Not been sleeping.'

'Join the club.'

'I didn't really sleep in. Truth is, I couldn't face work. Couldn't really face being at home either, but…' He looks at her, then looks away, as if he doesn't want her to catch him looking. 'I'm no good on my own, Frankie.'

'Perhaps she'll come back. You never know.'

'Leave her lover for me, you mean?'

'It happens. Monique might get bored with her in the end.'

'With *her*?'

Damn it. Now what?

'Did you say *her*?' His eyes have narrowed.

Admit or deny? No time to decide. 'Look, I wasn't going to tell you, but you know the woman in the sari, the one at the party? I saw her with Monique, and you can tell, can't you, when people are more than just friends? Antoine says they've been together for a while.'

Simon stands up. 'You're telling me my wife has left me for another woman?'

'Well at least you can stop blaming your friend Antoine!'

'A woman? She's left me for a *woman*?' He slaps the wall. Slumps back down onto the stairs with his head in his hands.

'Oh Simon, I'm sorry, I shouldn't have told you.' She shuffles down to where he is and puts an arm round his shoulders. Laying her head next to his, she holds him.

She stands at the sink and swallows a couple of aspirin to ward off stomach cramps. Watches the shifting patterns of the water as she rinses the glass. Perhaps she only imagined he wanted to kiss her. Perhaps he imagined it too. 'Pop down later,' he said, 'if you're bored. There's a film on Canal Plus at nine.' That's how they've left it.

There's a noise. She opens her door and looks out. A pair of shoes has been left on the landing: red, with three-inch heels and pointed toes. The new lodger must be tall then. Tall with red hair and a fringe.

She picks up the book on Magritte. The images are unsettling: things as they are, but not as they seem; false mirrors held up to reality. There's an apple filling a room. Flames bursting from a tuba. A crowd of identical, bowler-hatted men staring in at a window. A woman's face with breasts replacing the eyes, a navel for a nose and a triangle of pubic hair for a mouth. *Le Viol*, that one's called; *The Rape*. Frankie turns quickly to the next page and finds a woman's naked body sheathed in netting, its arms and head concealed in a metal cylinder. Quotes from Magritte explain that he wanted to make thoughts visible, reveal the mystery of familiar objects, make them 'scream aloud'. As she reads on, she discovers that he worked in advertising; he liked silent movies; he was a first-rate photographer; he collected postcards and played games with words.

Antoine has done his research all right. He's worked hard at being reincarnated. No doubt he saw his mother's body being pulled from a river with her nightdress covering her head. One legend replacing another.

Music trickles out from the radio: a wheeze of voice on a crackle of drums and guitar. She should get new batteries, not keep squeezing the sound out of nothing. A headache whispers behind her eyes. Closing the book she pictures herself on the stairs with Simon, her arm round his shoulders and their faces close. The kiss still doesn't work.

The laptop purrs on her lap. She types in a search. A few more clicks of the mouse and the gallery of pictures appears on the screen. The scene with the tall girl, the one Simon showed her, can be viewed free as a sample, the others have to be paid for. With heart pattering, she scrolls down past obscured faces, naked bodies in mirrors, a woman with skin marked like wood. There's the woman with the book and the gaping mouth, the lovers with the sheets over their heads and others she hasn't seen before. She reaches the end of the page. Scrolls back up and checks again: no boulder, no red curtains, no red couch. Her heart stops pattering. He didn't film her.

The head has reappeared in the window. Music blasts into the air: an upbeat jazz number with chattering saxophone and thrumming bass. With her toes squashed into the points of the red shoes—just as well she's only borrowing them—Frankie stands, arms outstretched, her feet tilted at an alarming angle on the stick-like heels. Cautiously she starts to dance, head swaying, feet shuffling and twisting on the square of wooden floor. It's like bopping in a cardboard box. Well they always said she was self-contained.

Still dancing, she takes a last sniff of the empty Marmite jar and crams it into the bin. The bin reeks in the heat and needs emptying, but she's alone and that's up to her. She can leave it over-full and foul-smelling if she likes. She smears a smudge of Marmite from her finger onto the wall. With a beak drawn on in pencil it becomes a bird in flight.

He's Magritte, the great painter, and she's his Georgette. She likes the idea. She knows she shouldn't, but she does.

I'm in a house that's strange and yet familiar. The room is white and there are French windows leading out onto a balcony, with steps leading down—it's one floor up, I think. I sit at the top of the steps in my pyjamas, shivering. There's water flowing below, as if the house is on stilts with a river running underneath it. You're down there, Craig, in the water, poking about in the sludge, and I don't know how you can bear to do that—it's damp, it's night, it's cold. 'Stay where you are!' you call up. 'There's a lot of pollution.' I worry about what will happen if you bring the dirt in on your clothes and contaminate the inside of the house. Then suddenly they're there. Flies, I think they are at first, buzzing round my head. I swat them away and look down. You're engulfed by insects too, a thousand frenzied beasts, flashes of red and yellow. 'It's locusts! Locusts!' you shout out, arms flailing, and then I can't see you any more, there's nothing of you left. Only a swarm of screeching locusts beating their wings above the filthy scum on the water. I don't even know what locusts look like.

I try to scream. My voice is hoarse with trying to scream. 'Mum! Dad! Help me! I need help!' I don't want to leave you but I have to. In the corridor there's light and the sound of a radio. I rush into what could be a kitchen. 'He's dead!' I wail. 'The locusts got him!'

My parents continue with their breakfast, sip their tea. 'These things happen,' says my mother, showing no emotion. I can't believe the no emotion. I run back to the room and look for the windows, the steps, try to reach you, but all I find is solid wall...

The noise startles her. The knocking on the door. She pulls herself out of bed, creased and groggy.

'Who is it?'

No one answers. She opens the door. He's wearing a crumpled black shirt that reflects how she feels.

'Sorry, I was snoozing.'

'In the middle of the day?' The glint in his eyes cuts through her drowsiness. She moves back into the room, but he stays on the landing. 'Come down when you're ready.'

He's left the door ajar. It's dark inside, like the first time, and the smell is the same. Her heart rate quickens as she remembers what happened, what he did. When she thinks of what he does.

There are three coffins now, positioned in the centre of the room and lit by spotlights. Two of them stand upright, the third is bent in the middle and is sitting—if a coffin can sit—on a stool.

'Recognise it?' says Antoine from the dimly lit edge of the room.

She looks at him blankly.

'Le balcon. Magritte's version of a Manet. A posed portrait, with coffins replacing the figures.'

He adjusts the lighting, moving the spots so that one side of each coffin is in shadow. She looks for a camera, a lens, but the lights kill off the space behind them. On the floor in front of her, in a pool of sawdust, lies a large sheet of wood with a square cut out of the centre. Stepping round it, she wanders over to the frieze and reaches up to feel the paper.

'Wouldn't touch that if I were you—there's two years' work there.'

'Yours?'

'Mine and Monique's. A labour of love, you could say. Deconstructing the traditional to make something more provocative.' He appears at her side with a candle. 'Magritte's *Enchanted Realm* fresco reworked. A retrospectively postmodern interpretation.'

'Right...'

The candlelight shivers on the painted and photographic images, plays across the mountains, leaf-birds and mermaids before settling on an impressionistic view of Paris out of which looms a giant figure: a man in top hat and tails, with a rose in his hand and pale eyes staring out from behind a narrow mask.

'Our latest addition,' says Antoine, 'The enigmatic hero, based on an old movie character. One of Magritte's many passions.'

The pale eyes follow Frankie as she moves back into the light.

'Did you bring the photos?'

'Not this time, no.'

Nerves jostle in her stomach. She doesn't know what he's going to do or how far she'll let him go. 'And you're not filming today?'

'I thought we'd agreed—this is just a bit of fun.'

'Like with the other girls, you mean?'

'That's business. You're different.' He blows out the candle and comes over to where she's standing. With a thumbnail he slits open a packet of gum, unwraps a tongue and curls it into his mouth. 'Want some?'

She shakes her head. 'Why am I different?'

'You're harder bloody work, that's why.' There's a flirtatious edge to his voice. He touches her cheek, her hair, kisses her softly on the forehead and then on the lips. Her insides stir with a force that's stronger than her. His mouth tastes of spearmint and reminds her... But she doesn't want to remember.

'You're going to take a few photos then, that's all?'

'Sure.'

He pushes a bundle of material into her arms: a long white dress with a high neck, long sleeves and flounces. Victorian in style and scented with lavender.

'Try it on.' His eyes have that look, that coaxing glint of a smile that makes her want to please him. Stepping clear of the spotlights, she strips down to her underwear.

'Take everything off.'

'What?'

'Come on, Frankie, don't go prudish on me.'

She considers throwing the dress back in his face and retrieving her clothes from the floor. But the way he's looking at her…

The material feels rough against her skin. Antoine stands her in front of a long mirror and starts on the buttons that run up her back, taking his time, easing them into their holes.

'It doesn't fit that well,' she says, pulling spare material out to the side.

'It's fine.' He gathers up her hair, tying it into a bun.

'What are you doing?'

He pins something that looks like a doily onto the front of her head. 'There. You look perfect. A living artwork.'

'What's all this for, Antoine?'

'Shh.' Standing behind her he runs his hands down the front of the dress, round each breast and back up to her face. 'I want you,' he says, his eyes locking onto hers in the mirror. Her stomach flips, her breathing sharpens. This isn't what was meant to happen—or is it? Isn't this exactly what she wanted?

He disappears into the unlit part of the room. She can hear him moving about and there's that noise again, a humming in the background. She tenses. Her clothes are there, on the floor, just a few steps away. But then he's with her, wearing a dark suit now, white shirt, black tie. His hair is greased back and he's drawn on a moustache. Nerves make her laugh.

'Like it?' he says. 'Smart's the new scruffy.' He leans down and kisses her, his hands caressing her body through the dress. 'You aren't claustrophobic, are you?'

'Why?'

He steers her into the light, across to one of the standing coffins. The hinged lid opens like a door. 'See what it's like being dead.'

She assumes he's joking, but his face says he isn't. 'Why would I want to do that?'

'Because I want you to. Go on, try it. Just for a few seconds.'

'There's no way I'm going in there. No way.'

'Then there's no way I'm going inside *you!*' His smile is seduction mixed with threat. She casts a sideways glance at the coffin. Peers into the shadow at the back of the room where the humming noise is coming from.

'Just a few stills, you said.'

'You're too cautious, Frankie, that's your problem. You should just, you know, go for it. Let your hair down for a change.'

'You only live once, you mean?' She looks at him, but Magritte the Second fails to react.

'Perhaps you don't want to make love with me?' His hands glide down her back and rest on her buttocks. She feels a fizzing deep inside, in her gut, her bones. Her whole body dissolving.

Hardly believing what she's doing, she bends a little, shortens her neck to fit the space.

'There's no lock on this thing, is there?'

Antoine tuts and the door closes, leaving only a thread of light down the side. The coffin smells of wood and resin. Frankie closes her eyes and tries to steady her breathing.

There's creaking and scraping, as if he's shutting himself into the other coffin, the taller one standing behind hers. This is crazy. She has no idea what he's up to. She's sweating and there's pressure on her chest that feels like fear, like panic. That could almost feel like lust.

Then the door of the coffin opens and there's light, though less than before and she doesn't know how he had time to do that. He's standing in front of her, and he's undoing his trousers, and when she stumbles out he grabs her and yanks her round and pulls at the buttons of her dress, ripping it open, saying he wants her, he wants her, he wants...

'*Il y a quelqu'un?*' A voice hits the air. A voice that could be male or female. 'Hello?'

'Stop!' Frankie pushes Antoine away. 'There's someone there!'

'Doesn't matter,' he says, breathing heavily and hoicking up the skirt of the dress from behind.

'Of course it bloody matters!' She twists out of his grasp.

'*Merde!*' He pulls up his trousers. She clasps the dress to her chest. The owner of the voice has come into the room but remains hidden in the shadow.

'Why have you stopped? That looked great.'

'You're early, Helga,' Antoine says tersely.

'Is that a problem?' The person moves into the light, red shoes clacking on the floor. 'So this is the new recruit, is it? You could have waited for me.'

'We were practising, that's all.'

'Why's the camera rolling then? Is Monique here?'

Antoine doesn't answer. Pouting, the tall girl with the fringe retreats into the shadow and there are voices. Two voices. The air round Frankie's head goes cold. She grabs her clothes and rushes out of the room, with the dress flapping open on her back.

It's the middle of the night. The light is ticking and her footsteps are loud on the stairs. Her heartbeat is loud as well.

She flings the dress on the floor, in front of the door marked *M. Sennet*. The skirt is ripped to shreds, the bodice peppered with holes. The buttons clatter like coins as she chucks them across the landing. To the side of the door the wall is blank and white. She dips the brush into the tin of watery black paint. The light keeps ticking. Paint drips onto the floor as she stretches up, moving the brush in wide sweeps across the wall, reloading it between each stroke. When she's finished, black paint trickles down the wall like blood. The light stops ticking and goes out.

got back to paris this evening and now it's 3 am frankie, i can't sleep and if i don't tell someone i'll go out of my mind. i don't mean to scare you, but there's something weird going on. it's like there's someone in the room, some kind of presence. i can't explain it but i know it's there. it's freaking me out.

    xavier

Frankie goes to the window and stares out at the rooftops. The sky is bruised with clouds, but there's little chance of rain. A finger of ice runs up her back. When she turns round there's nothing there.

He was in the garden when I got home. He hadn't heard me come in. I watched him through the kitchen window, pacing, checking his watch, pulling the odd weed out of the flowerbed. I wasn't even late—it was only ten to six. As I drank water from a cup, my mind locked onto its usual fantasies: a fire in his office, a fatal accident on the road, grains of a bitter white powder dissolving in his coffee...

I took a deep breath and went outside.

He stopped pacing. 'How was Jude?' he said.

'She's fine.'

He stooped for another weed. 'I thought we'd have fish for supper. With potatoes and spinach.'

'Sounds nice.'

'The buddleia's looking good, isn't it?'

'Yes.' The purple flowers were spilling onto the path. A butterfly landed, wings quivering.

'It's our fifth wedding anniversary this autumn, Francesca. We should book a hotel.'

'If you like.'

The butterfly moved to a different flower.

'You're not saying much,' he said.

'Aren't I?'

'Used up all your conversation on your friend, have you?'

'No, of course not.'

'So what did you talk about?'

'This and that. Nothing really.'

'Nothing? Two hours talking about nothing?'

'Leave it, JP.'

I went back into the house. He followed.

'I don't understand,' he said as I loaded the washing machine. 'How can you talk about nothing for two whole hours?'

'Well of course we didn't talk about nothing, but I can't remember all the details. We just talked.' I shook powder into the powder compartment.

'Cosy was it, just you and her?'

'In her kitchen, that's right.'

'Mmm. Very cosy.'

'I went for coffee with Jude and we talked. What's wrong with that?'

'There's no need to over-react.'

'It's not me that's over-reacting, it's you. You just won't let things be, will you?' I poured in fabric conditioner. Crouched down and squinted at the dial.

'Tell me what you talked about.'

'Why?'

'Why not? You know I don't like it when you hide things from me, Francesca.'

I cranked the dial round to forty degrees and the machine started to fill. I was trembling inside. I stood up and swung round to face him.

'We talked about you and what you do to me—happy now?' The words hung in the air, as if it was someone else who'd said them.

JP's expression was wild and unblinking. He stepped towards me. He was breathing hard and his fists were tight. He pushed me against the washing machine.

'You had no right to talk to her,' he said into my face. 'What goes on in this house is our business, not hers.'

'What about Stella then? I bet she knows all about us.'

His face darkened. 'I haven't seen Stella for years. You know that.'

'Do I?'

'You have to learn to trust me, Francesca. And I have to be able to trust you. You've no right telling Jude our business.'

He leaned into me. The pressure on my back intensified, the edge of the machine digging in.

'All right,' I gasped. 'I didn't tell her.'

'You said you did.'

'Well I didn't, I swear I didn't.'

'So you're lying to me now, are you?'

'I was—I don't know why—but I'm not lying now.'

The weight against me eased. He stepped away, flexing his fingers. I straightened up and rubbed at the pain in my back.

'I'm sorry,' he said. 'I didn't mean to hurt you. You know how much I love you.'

'Well you've a funny way of showing it.'

'I know. But you wind me up sometimes. You have to stop doing that.'

'We've been through all this.'

'I need you to try a little harder, Francesca, that's all. Make more effort.'

'I *do* make an effort, you know I do, but it doesn't work, does it?'

'Yes it does. It is working. I didn't hit you just now, did I? I didn't do it.'

'But you shouldn't have even *thought* of doing it.'

The machine stopped filling and the drum began to turn. JP filled a pan with water and placed potatoes on the worktop, in a row. Got the sharp little knife out of the drawer.

'I wasn't going to do it, you know.' His tone had changed and he was standing taller now. 'What made you think I'd hit you, Francesca? Mmm? You see, you're the one with the problem, not me.'

He turned away and started peeling the potatoes. I dug my nails into my palms. Why not a heart attack? I thought. No mess, no guilt.

It took me three more years to leave him after that.

This is Paris, but it could be anywhere. Slabs of grey spat on by dabs of colour. Flashing lights and revving engines. People walking.

She's walking too. At least her legs are moving, but she doesn't know where they're going, her legs and her. They're just going. There are tiny flecks of water in the air. Hard ground beneath her feet. Exhaust fumes in her nose.

And in the street there are shops. Things to buy. Things you can take home in exchange for bits of paper and metal. Some of the shops are closed but that doesn't matter, she'll find one that's open. Choose one with a door that looks easy to get through—as good a reason as any. She'll buy something, anything, because that's how it works, it's what people do.

The shop is laden with clothes—bits of material draped on curls of coloured plastic. The sale rail has tops marked with red labels. On the end nearest to her there's a plain black t-shirt. She won't go straight for it, she'll start at the far end and sift through all the other tops first, homing in. That way, when she reaches the black one, it will stand out as being so much better than the others.

Some are too small, too big. There are high necks and low necks. A vagueness of beige and white drowned out by shouts of crimson and yellow. One of the crimson blouses is pretty, with the right size of collar and beads round the cuffs. It's unusual. Fun. There's no point in trying it on though…

I couldn't decide what to wear—all my clothes were too tight, clinging to my hips and making my stomach look rounded. When he came upstairs the bed was strewn with outfits. *For God's sake Francesca, there must be something here you can wear.* He picked a black dress up off the bed. *What's wrong with this?* It's too tight. *And whose fault is that, Francesca?* I don't know. *Why is it too tight, do you think?* I bought the wrong size, that's all. *I don't think so, Francesca. You need to be careful, keep an eye on your figure or you'll soon be past your sell-by date.* I sort of laughed, he didn't. He was observing me the way a doctor does when making a diagnosis. As if he was looking for the solution to a problem.

And the problem was me. I was the problem. I needed to watch my weight, keep myself trim or he wouldn't like me any more. He didn't like women with too much fat on, he'd told me that.

The red dress was my favourite, I said, I could wear that one. *Bright colours are vulgar,* he said. *Stick to black.* So black it was. He stood behind me and tugged at the zip. I pulled in my stomach, but the dress still clung. He studied my reflection in the mirror. *You were pretty when I first met you*, he said. Yes I was, I thought, but I'm not pretty now. That's why black is better, I suppose. It helps me merge into the background. After all, let's face it, I'm not worth colouring in.

The curtain of the cubicle won't stay in place, it gapes open at the side so she changes quickly, hoping no one sees. Of course she rushes too much and gets in a tangle, pulling the t-shirt on back to front, and she's sweating because it's hot in the cubicle, with no air. Once the top's on properly she gives her shoulders a brush, just in case—that's the trouble with black. In the mirror she sees her mother staring out: the heaviness of the eyelids, the turn of the mouth, something deep in the eyes. Her own skin is young and firm, but she's wearing her mother's expression. She frowns and looks away.

The top fits well. It's a size twelve—that would have pleased him—and the black looks fresh in comparison to the faded cotton at her feet. She'll get it. She may as well.

On her way to the cash desk her gaze is drawn back to the sale rail. She stops. Her stomach quivers and she feels queasy...

The sky has lightened by the time she leaves the shop. The air has dried. She takes a peek inside the bag.

Bright colours are vulgar...

She likes bright colours. There's nothing wrong with them.

Stick to black.

A flash of red speeds past on roller blades. Orange trainers slap the pavement.

Stick to black.

She walks faster, breathing hard.

Stick to...

She drops the crimson blouse in a bin by the side of the road.

More shops and a person reflected in a window. A person walking like she's walking, but going the other way. The person is slim with short, wispy hair. Her face is pretty. It can't be her.

The person goes into a chemist's, lured by the shiny floor, the gold-edged shelves, the scent of citrus spiked with antiseptic. A salesgirl glides towards her, flat-shoed, flat-chested, streamlined in her smooth white, cool white uniform.

'Madame?'

'I'm just looking.'

'Of course, Madame.'

You can look, but don't touch. That's what the salesgirl is saying.

Pale lotions in tall bottles, slim boxes sealed with cellophane, white bowls filled with silky soaps and soft white pads of cotton wool. All neatly placed, like precious jewels on display. She should be sick to come in here. She should have an illness, need a cure, let the salesgirl soothe away her pain with a tube or a bottle in a stiff white paper bag. The kind of bag that says the contents are worth paying for.

In Boots, it was different. In Boots you could touch and spray and squeeze. You could read the labels for as long as you liked, no one troubled you. The blurb on the tube said it would make you radiate with natural beauty. Oh, how you longed to radiate! It was expensive, but it might just do the trick, it might just make him love you properly again, like he used to. You were on your own in the aisle. The eye of the camera was on your back, it didn't see what you did. No one saw. You felt a buzz, a frisson of excitement as you left the shop with radiance in your pocket and money in your purse. Easy. Not difficult. The one thing you were good at.

He didn't notice. He didn't comment when you went downstairs with radiance smeared across your face. So you shoved the tube in the drawer with the others, the other promises of glamour and glow, the potions and pills, the glitter and gold. Things that fitted neatly in the pocket without showing. You told yourself you wouldn't do it any more, that you weren't that sort of person. Each time was the last. One last thrill.

Were they nightmares or dreams, the visions you had at night of being locked in a police cell where he couldn't reach you, couldn't find you?

You opened the drawer again, pulled back the towel and took a biscuit from the tin. You knew it would make you fat, but once you'd had the thought you had to eat it, and another, and another, and just one more until the scales that measured sweetness tipped inside you. Chocolate digestives were the best. You'd tried plain ones, but it wasn't the same. The guilt was less but so was the pleasure, and you needed all the pleasure you could get.

He never looked in the drawer. He didn't know what you kept there. You tried to ration yourself to one small packet a day, but that wasn't always enough. When your mind was empty, you couldn't cope with emptiness in your body as well, it added up to too much emptiness. And there came a point when it didn't matter any more. If you were going to be ugly, you may as well be ugly. I mean, ugly's ugly. Fat's fat. When you're ugly and fat, you need a treat now and then to cheer yourself up. Something that tells the world you don't give a damn about how you look, it's the person inside that matters.

And it was true, you didn't give a damn when you were eating. You just hated yourself afterwards.

Outside the chemist's a man is drawing in chalk on the pavement. A horizontal Mona Lisa spread across four paving stones, copied from an A5 print. A face to walk all over. Half a smile to spit on.

The artist glances up. She tries to avoid his gaze but she can't, not straight away. Their eyes connect for an instant, witnessed by the almost-smiling lady...

He thought I flirted. With men in the street, with men in shops. *I saw that man look at you*, he'd say; *I saw the way you looked at him.* And I'd think: How can I possibly flirt when I'm this fat, this ugly?

There was a party at work, someone's birthday. I persuaded him to come. That way, I reckoned, he couldn't accuse me of anything because he'd be there and he'd see for himself. He's lovely, they said afterwards. So charming, so polite. Lucky you, landing someone like that. And I could see the questions in their eyes, the why has she let herself go, the why does she always wear black, the why doesn't she smile any more. *You should keep your mouth shut when you smile.* Perhaps I had bad breath. Perhaps my teeth were rotting with all those biscuits.

It could be the middle of a day, but she can't be sure. She doesn't feel that she's in the middle of anything. She's out of shot, miscast, with the wrong script and an out-of-sync soundtrack. It's not her that's moving, it's the pavement. The buildings and the lampposts and the cars. Go down. Hide away. Burrow deep. Up here everything's too big, there's too much space, vast oceans of emptiness above her. She's scared of falling off. If she fell off, she'd float forever like a midge in a cloud.

The métro platform is blotched with chewing gum. Dregs of newspaper are stuck to the rails. There's that smell, footsteps clattering on concrete, adverts for furniture and bottled water. She sees people, but there's no room for them inside her head. Her brain is out of focus. Everything is fragmented and blurred.

A train stops. Doors clunk open and bodies tumble out. Other bodies take their place. With a lazy drone, the doors seal the gaps and the train slides away. Footsteps fade into the end of the platform and for a moment she's alone. There's only the smell and a ghost of a breeze that nudges the paper on the track.

Somewhere, in a corridor, a busker is playing. She hears without listening, the tune first, then the words. The music traps her in its net and she's back in that chilly rented room with the lumpy bed. Back with JP, his glasses in a case and his clothes folded neatly on a chair. *Ne me quitte pas.* Don't leave me. Words that were his in the end, not hers.

A couple of youths saunter onto the platform, kicking a beer can. The clink-clanking of thin metal is intrusive: she can't make out what shape her thoughts are against such a busy backdrop. The can jumps onto the rails and rolls into the dirt. More footsteps clatter. A gush of warm air from the tunnel says another train is on its way and the music fades to a whisper, barely audible. She inches forwards, her toes testing the edge of the platform. She has to time it right. Too soon and the train will be able to stop. Too late and the chance will be missed altogether.

The train rattles and squeaks, its hum rising in pitch and peaking to a scream as it whooshes through the tight throat of the tunnel. There's no air inside the carriage. Frankie clings to the handrail, feet apart and elbows out, staking territory. It doesn't work for long. Soon she's squashed up against the door, a man's chin level with her eyes. If she had jumped in time, she wouldn't have felt the elbow in her ribs or seen the stubble sprouting in the pores. Wouldn't have smelt the garlic or the sweat.

Next stop Reuilly-Diderot: tiled walls, plastic seats and rows of heads lined up on the platform, countless sets of eyes staring blankly with mouths and noses to match. All identical, and yet... She looks away, scared of what she might see. Scared he might be there, his face in the crowd...

I'd packed the bags and the suitcase and folded down the lid of the box. As I walked out through the door, just before I pulled it shut, he appeared in the hallway. *You'll never get away from me,* he said. *Even when I'm dead, I'll always haunt you.* That's the last thing he said to me. The thing I've been trying so hard to forget.

*

The dogs are barking behind Madame la Concièrge's closed door. A voice drifts down the stairwell: 'I told you, she's back in hospital. You'll have to cover for her.'

Another voice, female, responds. What she says is unclear. Antoine's voice again: 'Look, there's no other option—the new girl's a dead loss.' Then footsteps, coming down. He's carrying a bin liner of rubbish. A dead loss wrapped in plastic. Magritte must have done a painting, it must be hanging in a gallery somewhere. *The Disconsolate Bystander*, it's called, or *The Missing Curtain*— something like that.

He stands to one side to let her past.

The floor is patterned—a dappled effect like sunlight on water. She hasn't noticed it before. A hint of spice hangs in the air where Antoine's been.

'Frankie?' The voice comes from behind her head. If she doesn't look, she won't have to answer.

The spice is replaced by turpentine. He's made a start on the words, but you can still make them out: NICE FACE, SHAME ABOUT THE PRICK. Faint shadows smudged across the wall, the letters crude and badly formed. There's a tin of white paint by the door and a brush. All this she takes in at a glance; she doesn't stop.

The floor changes to wood. The steps are worn. There are fresh parts at the edges which feet have seldom touched. She waits on the top landing, hoping the tall girl isn't watching through the keyhole. Below, footsteps tap down the stairs and disappear. The light goes out.

Is that what she does then, the pretty doll with mangled legs? Was that the plan: try the new girl out on Monsieur Villet, line her up as a stand-in while the cheese girl was in hospital? It didn't work though, did it? They didn't reckon on her being a dead loss.

Her room smells musty. The tiger snarls on the wall. With the pen Jude left behind, Frankie draws a road twisting into the distance and off the edge of the picture. 'Follow the mellow thick road,' she mumbles, glaring at the tiger.

More Miles Davis plays out across the rooftops. The sun has dropped out of sight and the head is pasted in its frame, a grey shadow in the half-light of evening. She wants to know who it is, what he does the rest of the day, why he sits there with his back to the window. If he turned round, what would she see? The pinched face of a drunkard with glasses and thinning hair?

Ex-husband, ex-lover, ex-everything: that's what she calls him in her head. Because that's what she wants him to be. Extracted. Extinguished. Expelled from her life. When he was alive, at least she knew where he was, she knew when he could see her and when he couldn't. But now that he's dead...

Watch me paint then, JP. Watch me blot out the face and the tiger. Watch me dip the brush into the tin of black paint and glide it across the wall, working down from the top, filling in the space until there's nothing of the picture left.

The paint has to dry now. Mustn't spoil the effect by peeling the tape off too soon. Mustn't make any mistakes. Not with him watching.

The trumpet calls out, a lone voice looping through the air. Behind it the bells strike nine.

Let the paint dry.

She lies down on the bed with her face to the wall. There's a stain on the wallpaper that looks like a scream. She can't take her eyes off the scream.

Even when I'm dead...

The phone rings. She stiffens. Tells herself there's no one here to answer it.

When the ringing stops, the music stops too and the room is quiet. He's lying next to her, breathing softly, so softly she can barely hear him, and she doesn't dare move in case she wakes him. A light sleeper. One dream short of an insomniac—that's what he says. Her heart is thudding. It's the only thing that moves in the room. The only sound.

In a moment he'll choke a little, fumble for breath. He'll turn onto his side and she'll cling to her half of the quilt, keeping covered. If she wanted, she could reach out and touch him, feel the heat from his back. But she doesn't.

He may get up of course, slip out of the room. She'll hear the click of the light on the stairs, his dull footfalls going down, the song of teaspoon on china. In the morning, when he asks, she'll say she slept right through.

She gathers the sheet around her, closes her eyes and floats somewhere inside her head, just above the deep pool of sleep. Doesn't see herself falling into it.

It's morning. The bedclothes trap her heat, smearing dampness behind her knees, under her arms and round the back of her neck. With her head muffled by bedding she's aware of her smell, the smell of her body mixed with the stale sleep in the sheets. She doesn't want to move. She doesn't want to open her eyes. She wants to stay where she was a moment ago: safe, protected, far away. You think you've got rid of the bad bits, cut out the bruises, but it's never that simple: the rot extends beneath the surface, festers unseen in the flesh.

The ringing is harsh and insistent. She waits for it to stop. When it does, she peels back the covers and crawls out of bed. The shutters are open and the room looks exactly as it did before. She wonders why that should surprise her.

The bundle of letters is encircled by an elastic band. The band's worn out, the rotting rubber clinging to the paper. She picks it off and fingers through the envelopes until she finds it: a sheet of lined paper, folded twice.

It's the first time in years that she's felt able to look. She can hear his voice in the writing, the way he spoke: *Dear Frankie, Sorry about the Doll, I didn't mean to chuck it in the Sea but it'll dry you know if you give it time, from Craig.* On the line below the name is a row of five kisses.

You were fixing the wings on your balsawood plane. I watched and felt something slot into place in my head. A sense of pure calm, like glass gliding on skin.

'What's it like, being thirteen?' I said.

'You'll find out soon enough.'

'Not for ages.'

The plane was ready. You threw it and it crashed in the tall grass.

'Ages comes quickly,' you said, scooping up the plane and straightening the wings. 'It's not as long as you think. It's like, you imagine the future and then the future becomes the present, and you look back and think, I knew this moment would come, I imagined it and now it's here.'

'I don't get it.'

You stood there, with the plane in your hand. 'You'll understand when you're older.'

'And what about dying? What happens then?'

'Well death must be like that too—here before you know it.'

You threw the plane again. It landed next to Clementine, who was drying on the wall. 'Stone, paper, scissors,' you said, spinning round. We both held out scissors. Then you stood on the wall, tossing a pebble from one hand to the other.

'Are you scared of death?' you said.

'Don't know. Depends what it feels like.'

'It can't feel like anything, can it, if you're dead? It must be the same as before you're born.'

The words sank into me. I thought of how you were alive for nearly seven whole years before I knew anything at all. Where was I all that time? How was it possible not to exist?

'Except that when you die,' you went on, 'you kind of go on living too, in people's heads, when they think about you.'

'It's not the same at all then.'

'The same but different.' You were losing me now. 'Of course, if no one thinks about you, not ever, then that's that, you're completely dead.'

'So where do you go when you die?'

'Dunno,' you said, lobbing the pebble into the dunes. 'If I die first, I'll let you know.'

You've never let me know.

Dear Craig,

You died on a Tuesday—that's all I was aware of at the age of eight. But one morning the following summer, Mum put a bunch of irises in a Tesco bag and said, "Right then, I'm off to the Dean." Dad hardly raised his eyes from his *Scotsman*. When Mum had gone I looked up Dean in the Bartholomew Streetfinder and found *Dean Cem K17*. It was marked in green on the map and was patterned with small white crosses.

After lunch I said I was going shopping with Kirsty. It took two buses and a walk to get there. I searched the alleys until I found the blue irises in a jar. The headstone was a slab of grey marble with your name on it, the date of your birth and the date of your death. "In loving memory", it said, "of our son who was lost at sea". There was sunlight but the marble was cold to the touch, and it was hard to believe you were down there, in the soil, like buried treasure. I stayed with you for ages, not angry any more, just sad. Wondering if you could hear me through all that earth. When I got home I found your jumper in a drawer and hid my face in it.

That was twenty years ago today.

With all my love, always,

Frankie.

She types his name into the address box and clicks on *Send*. A moment later *Mail delivery failed* appears on the screen. But the message is still out there, somewhere.

The phone rings again. This time it will be her mother, back from Tesco, the cold things transferred to the fridge and the rest waiting in bags on the table. Or back from the cemetery with an empty plastic bag.

'Hello?' That voice. She freezes with the phone to her ear.

'Frankie? It's me.'

She relaxes. 'Xavier. Hi.'

'I've been trying to get hold of you.'

'Have you?' Her own voice sounds unfamiliar, detached from the rest of her.

'Look, I'm sorry about that e-mail—I don't know what happened, I totally lost it in the middle of the night.'

'You don't think…?'

'What?'

'It wasn't some kind of ghost?'

'Course not! It all felt a bit surreal, to be honest.'

'*Ceci n'est pas un fantôme.*'

'Sorry?'

'Nothing.'

'Oh, I get you—Magritte and his famous pipe!'

'Don't.'

'Don't what?'

A pause.

'I was thinking we could meet up later,' he says. 'Go for a pizza or something?'

'There's someone I want to visit in hospital.'

'No problem. I'll take you.'

The grey Citroën screeches round the corner and draws up in front of her.

'Sorry,' he says, leaning across to open the door. 'Roadworks on the *périf*.'

She straps herself in. The carnations look sad in their brown paper bag, but she hasn't had time to buy fresh ones. Her hair is unbrushed and there's no make-up on her face. Getting out of bed took all her time.

'No more lover boy then?' says Xavier.

'That's right.'

'Ah well. Plenty more fish in the sea, as they say. What d'you fancy—haddock or cod?'

She looks away. The bottom of the bag is going soggy in her lap.

'That was tactless of me. Sorry.'

'No, it's not that.' She stares out at the street. 'Will they have a vase?'

'At the hospital? Bound to.'

'What if it's the wrong size?'

'What?'

'Nothing.'

'Are you okay?'

'Mmm.'

He doesn't push it. His fingers drum on the steering wheel as he waits for the lights to change.

'How was the coast?' she says, forcing the words out.

'Not bad. It was good to spend some time on my own.'

She grips her seatbelt as he puts his foot down. Her head hurts and nothing is in focus. She hopes Xavier will keep talking so that she doesn't have to.

He does, with descriptions of coastal delicacies, things he's heard on the news, tales from work. She nods now and then, taking nothing in. The streets of Paris flit across her vision and she can't take that in either. She's asleep with her eyes open.

Revolving doors steer them into an air-conditioned foyer with padded seats and a polished floor. She'd thought it would be all right, but it isn't. Her mouth is dry, her stomach churns. Xavier holds the carnations as she rushes to the toilets.

In the cubicle she holds her breath against the stench produced by her own body. The odour of irrational fear. All that filth inside her. Pulling sheet after sheet of paper out of the holder, she wonders what she would have done if there had been no paper left. She avoids eye contact with the woman waiting next in the queue and washes her hands quickly, not bothering to dry them.

They're directed to a ward on the third floor. She grips the stems of the carnations as Xavier leads the way. It's all corridors and lifts, with signs pointing to departments with convoluted names. The smell is a cocktail of chemicals that would make anyone feel sick.

The ward itself is quiet and mercifully lacking in odour: a bland box performing a function. Nathalie is in the bed nearest to the door. Frankie doesn't know what she's going to say to her— they're out of context here and her mind feels dull. The hope that they may have something in common after all, experiences to share, seems suddenly foolish.

'*Tiens!* I wasn't expecting visitors.' Nathalie eases herself into a sitting position. Her face is pale, less defined without make-up but still pretty. The nightdress slipping off her shoulder reveals perfect skin, smooth as unblemished fruit.

'This is Xavier,' says Frankie, 'an old friend of mine.' She lays the flowers on the bed and Xavier pulls up a couple of chairs. 'How are you feeling?'

'A bit sore, but that's no surprise.'

'It went to plan then—the operation?'

'More or less.'

'That's good.' She can't bring herself to ask for details.

'You look tired,' says Nathalie.

'I'm fine.'

A fan at the side of the bed blows out cool air and there's a tall jar marked with waterlines from previous rotting flower stems. Frankie fills the jar at the sink. Her face in the mirror is drawn and sallow. Reflected in the background, Xavier and Nathalie are bent over a book of *mots fléchés*.

The carnations look stunted in the jar; she hopes they won't turn brown overnight. She puts them on Nathalie's bedside table and sits down. The old lady in the next bed along is lying very still, as if she can only move her eyes. She's surrounded by cards and flowers, magazines and fruit. Nathalie has nothing. Only the carnations.

Nathalie hands the puzzle book to Xavier and sips water from a plastic cup. Bars of sunlight cut through the blinds and pulse across the bed sheet. A slow, irregular heartbeat.

'Has your father been in to see you?' says Frankie.

'No, he can't leave the house. A neighbour's doing his shopping, but that doesn't stop me worrying.' Her face falls still. She scratches her neck with a manicured nail and Frankie wonders whether she does the nails herself, in her father's house, sitting beside him with the television on and a photograph of her mother on the mantelpiece. Whether that's what she does when she isn't selling cheese or posing for the camera.

Xavier is stuck on a clue. He taps the pen on the bedstead: a dull ringing of plastic on metal.

'*Allez*,' says Nathalie. 'You're the one with all the answers.'

He lobs her a grin. A nurse brings a fresh jug of water and checks the notes at the foot of the bed.

'How's work?' Nathalie asks Frankie.

'Same as ever. Only not the same, of course, without you. Your replacement's hardly a laugh a minute. Doubt if she'd know a Roquefort if it hit her on the nose.'

Nathalie laughs, then winces.

'You okay?'

'A bit tender. I want to get back to work as soon as possible though—provided my legs are up to it.'

'It depends how much you're asked to do, I suppose.'

'Well the regulars will expect service as usual, that's for sure.'

Frankie wonders exactly what's being talked about. Her mind flits uneasily from one depraved scenario to another. As in some crazy dream she sees a spotlight, a burning tuba and a naked body trapped in mesh. A gaping mouth and scalding legs.

A woman arrives at the next bed, a nurse's uniform showing under her jacket. '*Ça va, maman?*' Maman doesn't answer. The woman talks of a long shift, of incontinence and sickness. Geriatric ward, no doubt. She wrings out a cloth in a bowl of water and wipes her mother's forehead. Calm and efficient, not quite off duty yet. The old lady still doesn't move.

Nathalie and Xavier are wrestling with another clue. Further down the ward pictures flicker on a TV screen and in the nurses' room a phone is ringing. Frankie swallows hard. Holds a hand to the side of her head, under her hair, and feels along the ridge of the scar.

There were bleeps and low voices, wheezing and coughing, the thin rattle of music on headphones. A phone rang somewhere and the air stung with disinfectant. When I opened my eyes I saw white sheets, and brown and green squares on a curtain. A machine by my side whirred into action, inflating and deflating a band on my arm. I was pinned down, unable to move. There was a stain on the sheet, starched in, the remnant of someone else's malfunction, someone else's bodily fluid.

I wanted to ask what had happened, why I was there, but I didn't know if my voice worked any more. I tried to think. Tried to pull my thoughts into a line inside my head.

A mask. There'd been a mask on my face. Voices pressing in, hands lifting, the sound of an engine and a siren that was loud and yet seemed far away. A ceiling had rushed past my eyes and there'd been strips of light with papers flying, and more voices, and pain. Pain in my head as I lay there, drifting back and forth to some other place, some other part of myself that had allowed this to happen.

The following morning I lay very still, afraid to move. They'd warned me it would hurt when the painkillers wore off. I might be tearful, I would probably feel sick. Breakfast would be a cup of tea sipped through a straw. If I could face it.

That's what they said: 'If you can face it.' I wanted to smile. But you can't smile when your head is gripped in a vice of bandages. When the skin beneath is stretched so tight, you're sure the slightest movement will crack it.

A white plastic cup sat poised on the white plastic table. A white plastic straw was crooked over the edge of the cup. I couldn't face it.

The flowers he brought were lilies, creamy white. Their sickly-sweet smell scratched at the back of my throat. When I asked him what had happened he said he'd found me there, out cold on the kitchen floor with my t-shirt soaked in blood. I must have fallen, he said, and cracked my head on the edge of the sink. Then he talked about what we'd do when I was better—take a holiday somewhere warm, perhaps, or spend a few days by the sea. I could choose, he said, taking my hand in his; it was up to me.

One of the nurses told me later that I'd be home by the end of the week. I should have been relieved, but I wasn't. And that was when it struck me: I felt safe in hospital, safer than I'd done for years. My fear of staying with him was now greater than my fear of leaving. I knew what I had to do.

Xavier has gone for a breath of air. The old lady's daughter has left too and the old lady has closed her eyes. Nathalie is flicking through the book of *mots fléchés*.

'You any good at these?'

'Not in French, no.'

'What about Xavier, then?'

'Quite the expert, by the looks of it.'

'I meant, are you going out with him?'

'No, of course not! He's just someone I've known for years.'

Nathalie looks unconvinced. She starts on a fresh puzzle, her brow furrowed in concentration.

How long does it take to get a breath of air?

'Nathalie…' She lowers her voice. 'Do you know Antoine and Monique?' Nathalie looks up with a slight raising of the eyebrows. 'You see, I overheard something.'

'It never does to eavesdrop.'

'You do know them then?'

Nathalie's gaze on her remains steady, uncommitted, as if poised between one expression and another. But then the nurse comes back to adjust the blinds and she looks away.

'I've always meant to apologise for that business with Monsieur Villet,' she says when the nurse has gone. 'It was hardly fair.'

'That was their idea too, was it? Some kind of test?'

The pretty smile. 'Life is full of tests. It's how you choose to react that matters.'

Xavier reappears, wafting tobacco. Nathalie sinks down into the bed and Frankie sets about rearranging the carnations in the jar.

They're back in the car. Just them now, no flowers.

'Nice girl,' says Xavier. 'Which days does she work?'

'Don't know. It varies.' She doesn't know why she said that— she knows fine which days.

'I was worried about you earlier,' he goes on.

'Why?'

'You seemed, I don't know… The last few weeks must have been difficult.' He brakes abruptly at a red light. 'And you were rambling on about vases and stuff.'

'Was I? It's just, I need a proper vase. I've only got this silly jug thing.'

'You could always buy yourself one, you know. Splash out a bit.'

'Sounds risky.'

'Some risks are worth taking.' He leans into the glove compartment for a CD, his arm brushing her knee. 'Like having nail varnish on one foot and not the other.'

She smiles. 'I've got kind of used to that.'

The lights jump to green and he hits the accelerator.

'Is this the only music you've got?'

'What's wrong with it?'

'We listened to it ad nauseam on the way south, that's all.'

'Once more won't hurt then!' He turns up the volume.

'So it went okay in the church?'

'As well as could be expected. Strange business though.'

He falls quiet and although she tries not to, Frankie sees the coffin being lowered into the ground, with Xavier and his parents and people she doesn't know, dressed in black, huddled around the grave. That was her husband once. She loved him once. How deep is the hole they've put him in?

'There's a lawyer sorting out his estate,' says Xavier.

'I was wondering about that. About what'll happen to his house and everything.'

'Look, I hate to have to tell you this Frankie, but...'

'But what?'

'Well, the thing is... He's left everything to Stella.'

'*What?*' She looks at him. His face is contorted and his eyes... 'Xavier! You bugger!' She punches him in the ribs.

They turn off the main road and into one of his infamous shortcuts. Nursing his ribs, Xavier sings along with the disc: *Faut pas oublier, oublier...*

'Is she always that cheerful?' he says then.

'Nathalie? On the surface, yes.'

'Will you visit her again?'

'Don't know. I may do.'

There's a queue of traffic ahead. They slow down.

'You two seemed to get on well,' she says.

The traffic slows to a halt. Xavier yanks on the steering wheel, but there isn't enough room to turn. The driver behind blasts his horn.

'*Merde alors!*'

'Still swearing at motorists?'

'Too right! And I bet you're still scared of my driving.'

'Not at this speed.'

He laughs. His thumb cracks as he bends it back on itself. There's a second crack as he bends the other one.

'Don't do that!'

'Sorry.' He puts the thumbs away.

A new song starts on the disc: *Je t'aime depuis toujours...* Xavier clears his throat and turns down the sound.

'You know what I remember about the first time we met?' he says.

'What?'

'Your not knowing what to do with the olive stones.'

'You left them on the table when we went out. You didn't even clear them away.'

'So *that's* why you were so uptight all evening?'

'I wasn't uptight!'

'You clung to your seatbelt and kept looking to JP for approval. But then we went for that meal and with a few drinks inside you, you loosened up.'

'JP thought I was flirting with you.'

'You mean you'd never flirt with me?' There's mock hurt in his voice.

'You were my brother-in-law then. Almost.'

'And now?'

'You're my ex-brother-in-law, I suppose.'

'And that rules out flirting, does it?'

The traffic remains at a standstill. There's some sort of danger in the air, which Frankie doesn't know what to do with. She stares at the number plate of the car in front.

'We should stop meeting like this,' says Xavier, lighting a cigarette. 'We always seem to be stuck in the car.'

What if she doesn't mind being stuck?

'How's Béatrice?' she says, challenging her own reluctance to mention her.

Xavier's tone changes. 'Staying with friends. I'm meant to be joining her, but… We'll see.'

'Doesn't that bother you?'

'What?'

'Her going away without you.'

'Not really. I went away too, remember.' He taps the spent match on the steering wheel in a rhythm that bears no relation to the music. 'She's not my type, by the way,' he adds.

'Béatrice?'

'Nathalie.'

Frankie looks straight ahead and says nothing.

A gap appears in the on-coming traffic. Circling the wheel with one hand, Xavier pulls out, does a U-turn, cuts through a light that has just changed to red and swings the car round the corner. He navigates his way around Paris like a ball in a pinball machine: only the quickest route will do.

They speed round another corner and into a street that looks familiar. The seatbelt digs into Frankie's chest as he slams on the brakes. *'Putain!'* The road ahead is blocked as well. Xavier gets out and throws his cigarette in the gutter. She can see it through the open door: smouldering wisps of grey.

'Accident,' he says, getting back into the car.

Frankie peers down the street. A crowd has gathered by the side of the road and she can tell from how they're standing that there's a casualty. Someone lying on the ground.

She turns to Xavier. 'Do you think… Do you think I killed him?'

'Who?'

'JP.'

'What on earth are you talking about?'

'If I hadn't left him, none of this would have happened. He'd still be alive.'

'How do you work that one out?'

'I made him start drinking.'

'Hardly!'

'But he never touched a drop before I left him.'

The traffic creeps forwards and the body comes into view, lying on its back, with a yellow hat stained with blood and grubby trainers. Frankie catches her breath, puts a hand to her face.

'He could have gone back on the booze any time,' says Xavier, pulling on the handbrake again. 'That wasn't your fault.' He turns to her. 'What's wrong?'

'The man who's been knocked down—I know him.'

'How come?'

'He shops at the supermarket. Gives me the creeps, to be honest.'

The young man from the bookshop is there, in shirt sleeves, blowing into Monsieur Villet's mouth and pumping on his chest. Someone arrives with a blanket. A short distance beyond, there's a motorbike on its side with a man in leathers crouched next to it, his helmet in his lap and his face starkly white. Cars crawl past on the other side, drivers rubber-necking, while the man from the bookshop keeps blowing and pumping.

'What were you saying?' says Frankie.

'The booze. He could have gone back on it at any time.'

'What do you mean, *back* on the booze?'

'Well they never fully recover, do they, they just learn to control their addiction.'

'Who do?'

'People like JP.' He looks at her. 'Don't tell me you didn't know.'
She tries to take in what he's saying. First Stella, now this.

'It was years ago,' he goes on. 'Long before he met you. He was in a bad way for a while, did some damn stupid things. But he got help in the end and managed to wean himself off the stuff. That's why he was so wary of it—one drink and he'd have been back where he started. I'm sorry, I assumed…'

A police car draws up and two policemen get out. They assess the casualty, talk into their radios and take down details from the ashen motorcyclist. There's a siren in the distance and everyone looks down the road. The bookshop man is sweating. He wipes his forehead on his shoulder and continues pumping on the chest. The old man's face remains immobile, like plastic.

Xavier's words career round Frankie's head.

'Sometimes I feel I didn't know him at all,' she says.

'You can never know another person completely. There are even parts of ourselves we don't know.'

He crushes an empty cigarette packet in his palm and throws it onto the back seat. When the music stops he ejects the CD and slots it back inside its case. Brushes her knee again as he leans across to the glove compartment.

At last: a blue flashing light and *SAMU* on the side. More like a car than an ambulance. The paramedics take their time. They walk back and forth from the ambulance. They crouch by the body. They don't talk to anyone. Eventually they replace the blanket with one from the ambulance, lift the body onto a stretcher and slide it into the back of the vehicle. The man from the bookshop stays seated on the pavement with his head in his hands. No one pays him any attention.

The ambulance is still blocking the road, blue light flashing, but there's no more to see and the crowd is dispersing.

'It can't have been easy,' says Xavier quietly.

'There are things…'

'I know.' They both keep their eyes on the road.

226

At her door there are flowers: a bunch of deep blue irises. She puts them in the jug that's still too small, not knowing what to feel. Thinking she ought to feel something.

A thud against the window makes her jump. She looks up and sees nothing, but it can't be nothing. Easing the window open, she leans out. Below, on the flat part of the roof, there's a mess of black feathers askew, legs and beak jutting out. The beak opens and closes, making no sound, a last stutter of life, and then the bird goes still. It's left a smear of feather on the glass.

She grabs the cards from the back of the door—the ship, the lovers, the girl with the bird, the torn face—and rips them into pieces, as small as she can make them. She throws the pieces out of the window. They fall through the air and settle like confetti on the roof, around the dead bird. A wedding and a funeral.

Blobs of Blu-tack cling to the door. She prises them off, kneads them together and presses the lump under the lip of the table. You mustn't chew gum. She wasn't. It wasn't her. She's done nothing wrong.

On the table is a *pain de seigle*, a tin of tuna and a large beefsteak tomato. Frankie opens the tin and gouges the fish out onto a plate. Washes the tomato and cuts a slice of bread with *le couteau qui coupe*. Flakes the tuna with the knife as she stands there, staring at the square of black paint on the wall. A formless void that she drains into as the daylight fades behind her and her eyes lose their grip...

An elderly couple sit on the steps below the Sacré-Cœur, heads down and faces hidden. The steps are made of the sea, with grey waves rising and crashing within the solid structure. The woman holds up a photograph: a picture of a mother and a child. But she doesn't really need the picture. The image is in her head, moulded on. She has to look past it to see the rest of the world.

Beside her the man pours dense liquid from a bottle. The liquid spreads down the steps like a slick of oil on water. The words aren't there any more. He's stopped using words to describe how he's feeling.

The image changes. An old man is perched on a cloud with a computer screen in front of him. Objects float around him in the sky: a white stick, a courgette, a tin of cat food, a silver bookmark. A few clicks of the mouse and she's there on the screen: the girl with the rose in her hand. The old man knows how each item of clothing slips off her and falls to the floor. He knows every curve of her body, every shadow on her skin. He knows how she moves, how she lies down on the couch, how her body shudders when she comes. Rewind. When she comes. Rewind. When she comes.

It's a shame she didn't read to him again. She was pretty and he could have had fun, pretending he couldn't see. The blond girl was more reliable though.

Now there's a woman in an empty room. She's naked and her face is indistinct. She's struggling. She's trying very hard to be her, but she keeps slipping out of herself and what's left is a pale shadow, an outline that needs filling in. A man walks up to her: short and wiry, fully dressed, eyes hidden behind a narrow mask. The woman doesn't move. He used to dig his teeth into her, bite bits off. The tasty bits, the best bits. He chewed them well and swallowed them. Ugly things grew in their place. Things she couldn't bear to look at.

The man wipes a cloth across her face, smudging it some more, rubbing out what's left of her features. There are lines on the skin, like cracks in porcelain. The woman's head is breaking up. There's nothing keeping it together. It crumbles and falls in lumps to the floor, then the man brings a foot down onto the rubble and with a shoe that's too big for the foot, he grinds the rubble into dust. In his hand, the man has a stone. In her hand, the woman has a knife...

The tuna is like mince now, with the tomato sitting pristine beside it. Frankie is sweating. She holds the sharp blade of the knife to the tomato, pressing hard enough to make a dent, not hard enough to break the skin. One thrust would be enough. One quick movement and it would pierce through, lacerate the outer covering and release its crimson contents, leaving only skin behind, deflated and shrivelled like a spent balloon.

There's still a murmur of light and ghost-like images that shift and flutter on the wall. A drone of voices drifts up from below. Frankie's heart thuds in her ears. With her hand clenched round the knife, she makes her way down the stairs and into the flat where fucking gorgeous is: Mr Cool fucking gorgeous girls.

Subdued lighting hugs the shoulders of figures in suits and bowler hats, all identical: the same masks, the same blank expressions, milling like guests at a party. In the centre of the room the sheet of wood, painted a muddy brown, has been raised to form a backdrop of interior wall with skirting board and a window that opens inwards. Through the window back-lighting imitates moonlight. The red velvet couch sits in front of it, with the brown leather suitcase, the hat and coat on the chair and the gramophone on the table. Facing the set are the sari woman, draped in yellow, and the man from the party. Antoine and Monique are checking the camera.

Frankie stands, unnoticed, in the doorway. To her right, lit by a candle, the props table is laid out with spare bowler hats and masks: oblongs of cardboard with slits for eyes and male features painted on. Dark suits hang on a clothes rail with white shirts and grey ties. Behind the table and running the length of the wall is the frieze on its rod. A labour of love. Two years' work.

The stage is flooded now with stark white light, which casts dark shadows across the floor.

'Right everyone,' says Monique, clapping her hands. 'Take your places.'

The masked figures line up behind the open window in serried ranks, silent and immobile, like an army of tailors' dummies. Another masked figure, the only one without a hat, stands centre-stage with his back to the window, staring into the horn of the gramophone. Frankie hangs back in the shadow, knife in hand, as Antoine and the man from the party, wearing suits and hats and masks of their own, take up position on either side of the set. The man holds a club, Antoine a length of netting. *The Threatened Assassin* combined with the one of the empty-faced men at the window—Frankie can't remember what that one's called.

'Okay, this is our first live composite,' Monique announces, 'so it's crucial we get it right. We'll try a run-through.'

No one moves. Then Antoine walks up to the window and leans out. He throws the netting over a figure in the second row and hauls it in like a fish, dragging it through the window and flinging it down onto the couch. The figure's hat falls off, its mask slips as it writhes, trying to break free, but the man from the party is there with his club. He raises it and swings it down to within a centimetre of the figure's head. Swings it down again. And again. The figure twitches and stops moving. The bare-headed man stays where he is, staring into the gramophone, while Antoine discards the netting and unties the captive's shoelaces, removes the shoes...

You'll never get away from me.

Frankie's pulse is racing, her palms are hot. She averts her eyes as he moves on to the trousers, the G-string...

You're not a natural are you, when it comes to sex? You should see a doctor, get yourself checked out. You should be pregnant by now.

He kept a note. Knew where I was in my cycle and when it was best to try. Knew when my period was due and watched for the

230

signs. If I was more than a few hours late, he was hopeful. *It's the least you can do for me, Francesca.*

I woke in the night. When I got out of bed I felt blood trickling down the inside of my legs. I put a hand there to catch the drips, to stop it from soiling the carpet. Hobbled through to the bathroom and locked the door. Tried to be quiet as I opened the cupboard and eased a tampon out of the box.

The door handle turned. *What are you doing? Why have you locked the door?* I fumbled with the tampon, wiping away smears of blood. *Let me in, Francesca.* I pulled the flush and washed my hands. He was banging on the door now. The longer I left it, the worse it would be.

'I was feeling queasy,' I said, 'I don't know why I locked the door.' He pushed me against the wall, shoved his hand up between my legs, grabbed the string. *What the hell's wrong with you?* he shouted, waving the bloody tampon in my face. *All these years of trying, and still nothing!*

It could have been blood that stained the sheets. Blood or tears, I'm not sure...

'The angle's wrong,' says Monique, with the sari woman standing next to her. 'We can't see what you're doing. And someone in the back row moved their head. We'll stop there, take a short break.'

Antoine and the man from the party step off the set. The figure on the couch—the tall girl with the fringe—pulls on her trousers, the bare-headed man wipes dust from the horn of the gramophone and the masked onlookers at the window fall out of line. Frankie stays where she is, in the shadow, her eyes fixed on the red velvet of the couch...

When he found the pills, it was worse. I should have hidden them better, but I'd always kept them there, in the zip-up pocket of my bag. I never thought he'd look. And now he was standing in the hall with my bag at his feet and the slim pack of pills in his hand.

I know what you've been doing; you can't hide anything from me. I felt transparent, like he could see straight through me. Like there was nothing there to see through. He dragged me up against the wall. Yes I know it was stupid, I should have told him, I shouldn't have deceived him like that... He threw me to the floor and kicked. Kicked my back, my legs, my back. Kicked some more.

Sorry didn't seem to be the hardest word, it was the easiest. We both said it, and when we'd said it enough times there was nothing else to say. Just sorry.

He flushed the pills down the toilet, one by one, saying that's what I'd been doing to our babies. I swore not to take them again. Promised on the life of our unborn child. Hid the next lot inside a boot I never wore.

'Okay,' says a voice in the room. 'Let's try again.'

Let's try again.
He pulled me by the hair, my beautiful long hair, cascading down. The hair my mother used to plait and I loved it, loved the feel of her hands in my hair. He grasped it like a rein to get me where he wanted me. My scalp screamed in pain. I thought the hair would rip right out at the roots, but it didn't, it was strong. Stronger than me. I couldn't stop him from trying. Again, again, again...

The figures slip back into line.
'Final run-through. Action!'
Antoine nets the girl, drags her over the windowsill and onto the couch where she's clubbed unconscious and he starts to remove her clothes...

There were bruises, not that bad, just livid marks on the skin in places no one else could see. Everyone gets bruises now and then. And it wasn't really him, it was someone else who lost control.

232

'You should get help,' I said, but that made him angry too because it wasn't him who had a problem, it was me. When you hear that so many times. When you're told it's your fault, your fault, your fault. Well there must be some truth. And he forgave me, said he knew I didn't mean it and that he loved me, always how much he loved me. And when you see a grown man cry...

The voice is an echo, far away: 'Good, stop there. You all know what happens next—we don't need to practise that. Is there anything anyone wants to say at this stage?'

I don't want his child. I don't want any bit of him growing inside me. I'm scared of what we'd create together, him and me. Scared I couldn't love it. That's what she wants to say.

'Take your places again then everyone. This time's for real—no second chances.'

The camera is running and Antoine is back at the window, peering out. Frankie's head is gripped with tension. There's energy inside her that has nowhere to go. Energy trapped in a tight twist of panic in her brain. She moves silently, unseen. Steps across to the table with the knife in her hand and he's there in the frieze above her, in the candlelight: the pale-eyed man with the mask and the rose, bearing down in his top hat and tails.

Even when I'm dead...

He was quiet when we got home. Too quiet. Even his footsteps were silent, as if he was holding everything in. I drank at the sink, turned away, but I could feel him in my back, feel his anger spiking into me. The words were released slowly, his voice brittle with restraint. *You're a slut, Francesca. Begging a stranger for sex with your eyes, pleading for it, wanting to fornicate with another man.* He breathed in sharply. *You're no better than a whore, a perverted ugly whore, and you know what happens to ugly whores like you...* There were plates on the draining board with the sharp little knife lying beside them. I gripped the edge of the sink and when he grabbed me from behind and spun me round, the knife was in my hand. I aimed for his stomach, his chest, any part of him, but he was too strong, too quick, he grabbed my wrist and wrestled for the knife and then his fist came at my face, huge in my eyes with the hard glint of the ring as I twisted my head away. The pain was black at first, then purple, then white dots floating and warm liquid in my mouth, red when I spat, red on my hands, red everywhere before everything went blank…

Heart pounding she leans across the table, stabs the knife into the masked man's chest and swipes it down, slicing through the paint. With her other hand she holds the candle to the frieze. The flame dances, catches. Spreads like ink on blotting paper, devouring the cleaved body, the doves, the rocks. The leaf-birds and the mermaids, the night-lit buildings and the floating apple. An acrid smell of burning hits the air as flakes of charred paper curl and fall.

'The frieze!' someone cries. There's confusion on the set, figures stumbling out of line. Frankie slips out of the room.

Five colours wrapped in shiny paper. She doesn't remember where she got them—in her mind she's always had them. She opens the little box and tips out the crayons. They smell of then, that time. Oil and plastic. Dreams.

You drew a blue nose on my face, Craig, and a huge red mouth, and fat yellow diamonds round my eyes. You told me not to scrunch up my face because you couldn't draw on it like that. It tickled though and it was hard not to scrunch. 'Bright colours suit you,' you said. I remember that now. I didn't want to wash the clown away, but Mum wouldn't let me go to bed until I had; the wax would mark the sheets, she said. The clown's smile left a smear of red on the white enamel of the basin.

A pale face looks out from the mirror. Frankie takes the blue crayon—touching what was last touched by you—and presses it onto her skin, dragging it across. Then the green, the red, the yellow. Not a clown this time, just stripes, in a multi-coloured tiger effect that even Jude would be proud of. With the side of a finger she smudges the edges, filling in the gaps. On her forehead she draws a white star. A five-pointed star.

It was the last day we spent on the beach before you died. You'd flown your kite and we'd searched for crabs in rock pools. The sea was cold, even though the sun was on it, and my feet were numb from paddling. I lay down on the sand, gazing outwards. The clouds kept changing shape and I couldn't work out how many of them there were, couldn't tell where one ended and the next began. It was the same with the stars, you said: there were too many to count, and anyway, most of them were already dead. I didn't understand. Dead things don't shine, I thought.

That's when you showed me. You found a stick and drew a star in the sand. A five-pointed star made with five strokes of the stick. I tried to copy. I couldn't do it at first and I snapped the stick in half and hurled it into the waves. You made me try again. By the end of the day the beach was covered in stars. I drew a moon as well, and I wanted to stay there all evening and watch the stars being rubbed out by the tide, see them take their places in the darkening sky. You had to drag me home, crying.

She stands for a moment, caught between what she's just done and what she's going to do next. The room smells of washing powder and damp cotton, from clothes drying on a makeshift line. Using the shower tray wasn't easy, but when she'd stood at Simon's door with her bundle of dirty washing, something had stopped her from knocking.

It's late. The shutters of the window opposite are closed and there's no noise from outside, no music. The voice in her head has been quiet all day as well. Her eyes rest on the irises in their jug. Bending down she sees the vibrant blue petals set against the black square of wall: a colour photograph in an old-fashioned album.

Her window is open. She climbs out and scrambles down onto the roof. The dead bird is still there, stiff and spiky, with the flakes of card confetti scattered around it. She kicks the bird out of the way and lies down where it's flat and where a slice of light falls from the window. Cool air fills her lungs. She runs her fingers down her face, feels its contours, its texture, its sticky colour. Above her, in a jagged frame of rooftops, the sky is tinged with orange and pricked with starlight.

'Frankie?'

She keeps her eyes on the sky. Feels she should get up, but doesn't. Lying down is where she wants to be.

'Both doors were open and your light was on.'

He lands heavily on the roof, his shoes scuffing the gravel. A faint smell of tobacco plays in the air as he lies down beside her. They don't touch, but her skin tightens with goose pimples.

'Like the face,' he says. She smiles. She'll paint the rest of her toenails too: pink this time, not magenta.

'What are you doing out here?'

'Thinking.'

'And is it a good place to think?'

'As good as any.'

They lie there, side by side. She rolls a crumb of grit between thumb and finger. There's noise where she thought there was silence. The background hum of the city, like a buzzing in the ears. True silence is a myth.

'I brought you this,' Xavier says then. 'Hope it's big enough. You can just fill it with water and stare into it if you like.'

The vase is large and curved, its clear glass catching light from the window. She holds it up. Dangling inside is a card shaped like a fish. The card turns slowly on its thread and swings into the light. The words are written at a slant: *This is not a fish. And I am not in love with you.*

She turns her gaze back to the sky. Her breathing is shallow and tiny beads of sweat are breaking through the mask of colour on her face.

Sue Rullière was born in Edinburgh and now lives in East Lothian. Two of her short stories have been read on BBC Radio 4; others have appeared in collections, including NW15 (British Council/ Granta) and Shorts 4 (Polygon). *Cinema Blue* is her first novel.

France has been a consistent influence on Sue's work. As a student she spent a year in Bourg-en-Bresse and also worked in Paris for a while. She has taught French for many years and makes regular visits to the country which inspires her.

Lightning Source UK Ltd.
Milton Keynes UK
UKOW051728211111

182437UK00001B/202/P